FAULKNER AND THE MODERN FABLE

Kiyoko M. Tôyama

International Scholars Publications
Lanham · New York · Oxford

International Scholars Publications
4720 Boston Way
Lanham, Maryland 20706

12 Hid's Copse Rd.
Cumnor Hill, Oxford OX2 9JJ

Library of Congress Cataloging-in-Publication Data

Toyama, Kiyoko.
Faulkner and the modern fable / Kiyoko M. Tôyama.
p.   cm
Includes bibliographical references and index.
1. Faulkner, William, 1897-1962—Criticism and interpretation.
2. Faulkner, William, 1897-1962—Ethics. 3. Fables, American—
History and criticism. 4. Ethics in literature. I. Title.
PS3511.A86 Z9785 2001   813'.52—dc21   2001016997 CIP

ISBN 1-57309-417-X (cloth : alk. paper)

Table of Contents

Foreword

A Personal Approach to Literature

by Peter Milward

"Where am I from? Where am I now? And where am I going?" How, it may be asked, can a critical study of the writings of William Faulkner begin in such an uncritical vein, with such personal questions? Or rather, it may also be asked, how can such a study not begin in such a manner? It all depends, I would answer, on the approach one takes to literature, and to literary criticism considered as a valid form of literature.

The composition of literature is, needless to say, a deeply personal affair - even or especially when the author himself is committed, as was T. S. Eliot, to an impersonal theory of literary or poetic composition. Take *The Waste Land* for instance. It was composed only a few years after the poet's profession of what he calls "this impersonal theory of poetry" (in his 1919 essay on "Tradition and the individual Talent"), and yet the more we have come to know of the young Eliot and his tragic relationship with Vivienne Haigh-Wood, the more we have come to learn how very personal this poem was to him and how unsuccessful was this attempt of his at what he calls in the same essay "a continual self-sacrifice, a continual extinction of personality."

Or take any of Shakespeare's *Hamlet* for instance. What, we may wonder, has Shakespeare the creator to do with his creature Hamlet? Some critics may see in Hamlet a projection of Shakespeare, while others on the same evidence may prefer to emphasize the not inconsiderable differences between creator and creature. Yet, turning back to T. S. Eliot, this time as critic, in his other celebrated essay on *Hamlet* (also dated 1919) we find him coining the memorable term "objective correlative," referring to the apparent lack of correlation between the objective circumstances of the drama and Hamlet's subjective response to it. Perhaps what is wanting in the drama of *Hamlet* has to be supplied from the personal background of the dramatist at the time of composition - as we may well conjecture from a comparison between the prince's soliloquy "To be, or not to be" and the poet's sonnet 66, "Tir'd with all these, for restful death I cry."

Literature then, we may conclude, even when it seems most impersonal, as in the poems of Eliot or the plays of Shakespeare, may well be most personal; when we read it, even or especially without realizing the extent of its hidden personality - when we read it, putting ourselves wholly into it - when we read it in the spirit of "Heart speaks to heart" - then we surely get most out of it.

Here precisely is the beginning of literary criticism: when we read a work of literature not for the sake of criticizing it, or of weighing its merits against its defects in a judicial balance, or of using it as evidence for some literary or political or psychological ideology, but simply for the sake of enjoyment. We do not, at least we should not, read the plays of Shakespeare or the poems of Eliot for the restricted purpose of writing an academic thesis about them in the hope of gaining the empty shadow of a name in the academic world. What would the dramatist or the poet think of us if he knew what we were doing with, or to what ignominious use we were putting, his inspired literary efforts? On the other hand, how happy he would be if he knew what intense enjoyment we were deriving from those efforts and how deeply we were imbibing the precious liquid he had distilled in them?

So let it be with the novels of William Faulkner. If Kiyoko Tôyama has read them with deep personal enjoyment, and if they now prompt her to make deep personal reflections on her own life with answers or hints of an answer to such basic questions as "Where am I from?" and "Where am I now?" and "Where am I going?", who can legitimately blame her, least of all the novelist himself? Faulkner himself, if only he could have had some perception of her response from his

Mississippi grave, would surely have leapt for joy, if not risen from the dead, to know that someone among all the multitude of Faulknerian scholars had reacted to his writings and their inner meaning with such personal enjoyment and appreciation.

In this connection I am reminded of a Browning scholar who once approached the poet while he was still alive with a question on the precise meaning of a word he had used in one of his poems. "As for that word," replied the poet, "I have quite forgotten what I meant by it. You'd better ask the Browning Society." What is important in every literary work is not the jots and tittles of words as the spirit in which they are written; and it is when this spirit inspires the spirit of the reader, that heart speaks to heart, the heart of the author to the heart of the reader.

After all, concerning the difference between science and literature - where literature may be taken to include literary criticism, though literary scholarship may be seen as a branch of historical science: "Science has to do with things, literature with thoughts; science is universal, literature is personal; science uses words merely as symbols, but literature uses language in its full compass" (Newman, *Idea of a University*). Such is the approach to literature I find in this very personal approach by Kiyoko Tôyama to the writings of William Faulkner and I cannot but praise her for her courage in offering it now in print, considering both her academic position at Tokyo Woman's Christian University (Tokyo Jyoshi Daigaku) in Japan and her decision to have it published in America. For both here in Japan and there in America there is a strong current of academic prejudice against such an approach, if not in literature, at least in literary criticism. And that is why, I venture to say, so much of the criticism produced in either country has become in recent years so unreadable, so tedious, so meaningless, and the sooner it is shown up for what it is, undermined by such works as this, the better for us all and not least for the poor authors who have to endure it all.

Tokyo, June 21 2000

Preface

Where am I from? Where am I now? And where am I going?

Desire under the Elms, in Japanese translation, led me to spend three undergraduate years reading Eugene O'Neill, word by word, always with a dictionary at hand. He offered me his "religious faith in life," a faith I had long sought in vain in the literature of my homeland. When he abruptly let his Christian God solve all questions of how to live, though, I could not but feel betrayed. Still, after several years, when I had myself made the existential choice of life over death, I found Catholicism to be the only metaphysics for me to live by.

While I was studying in Madison, still attached to O'Neill, *"The Sound and the Fury"* by William Faulkner appeared on a reading list provided by Professor Keith L. Cohen. The novel offered me more substantial affirmation of life, and *Faulkner at Nagano* moved me to tears when I read it in a dimly lit carrel of the University of Wisconsin Library. Faulkner first appeared on the Japanese literary scene in 1955. In 1974 he loomed on my personal horizon as a writer whose "duty and privilege" it was to help humans "endure and prevail." I was sure that Faulkner wrote for me, a stranger from a remote Asian country.

Near the end of my fifth year in the United States, my earlier decision to cut myself free from the roots of my Japaneseness began to waver. The search for my true roots led me to find myself nothing other than Japanese, however much anguish that identity brought me. Where should I live? What should I do with my life? Is my life worth the effort of being lived at all? These questions, the answers to which are self-evident for most people, have continued to demand of me deeper and deeper responses. It has been the pain of this uncertainty in my existence that has moved me to re-examine the literature of my homeland alongside the works of William Faulkner.

This re-reading of Japanese literature has been closely linked to my search for where I ought to be, both physically and metaphysically. While reading Faulkner as the central writer of my studies, my tension relaxed instantly when I turned again to the works of Yukio Mishima, a writer to whom I had, I thought, bid farewell. I found myself reading Faulkner with my head and Mishima with my body. Mishima was still within me. Brought up in a land where no clean-cut distinction is drawn between aesthetics and ethics, Mishima was too intellectually and spiritually honest not to agonize over the clash within him between Eastern aesthetics and Western intellectuality. Then, too, there was Shusaku Endo, who also recorded his struggle to adapt the ice-cold monotheism of Catholicism to the warm-blooded pantheism of his heritage.

Also I discovered the ancient songs of the *Kojiki*, "*The Chronicle of Ancient Things*," and the *Manyoshu*, "*The Collection of Ten Thousand Leaves*." Re-read in America, they resounded with an affirmation of life, long lost in the more tenuously aesthetic literary works of our day. The pain I had as I transplanted those songs word by word into the soil of the New World prompted me, unconsciously at the time, both to go back to Japan and to major in American literature.

My reading of Faulkner in a desperate search for affirmation has led me, quite unexpectedly, to a teaching position in Tokyo Woman's Christian University (Tokyo Jyoshi Daigaku). Ever since 1982 not a single year has passed without my asking my students to read Faulkner, which I have found rewarding both physically and metaphysically. Indeed, Faulkner has helped me quite literally to make a living. He keeps telling me, as he tried to tell us all, how to cope with the human condition, we who are born between words and deeds, each in our arbitrarily assigned time and space. At least to me, he is more a poet of human, universal fables centering around the theme of words and deeds than merely a chronicler of the American South, a modernist, or for that matter a post-modernist.

Saul Bellow and Carlos Fuentes, more than any other North American writers, have succeeded Faulkner in offering their own human, universal fables. From quite another place and heritage, Bellow struggles for affirmation through probing into the problems of words and deeds; Fuentes, by painting on a Mexican canvas, presents us all with the difficulty that confronts us as we attempt to establish our identity in the modern world.

In time, I came to recognize within myself, after a lifelong effort to negate him, the figure of my own father, Sadataka Nozaki (1903-1965). A grandson of a man who raised himself to a baronage in the turmoil of the Meiji Restoration, my father, after finishing the Peers School, was expected to take up a military career like all the men in his family. Instead, he went to Germany to study drama. After his return, he was for a while involved in the new theater movement in Japan. One of those Taisho liberals who were at eternal war with themselves, he did not provide his children with a tranquil home life. Unable to act as a paternal authority, he had no recourse but to treat us as individuals, responsible for choosing our own paths. In my eyes, he was less a father than a man who searched his way, constantly and clumsily, through the tangled web of conflicting cultures. Now, across the distance of time and space, he has gradually transformed himself into that rare-to-find kind of father, one who by his example pointed the way to asking oneself "why?" and then, with all one's strength, striving to put into words a possible answer.

I used two papers out of *Ikyou de Yomu Nihon no Bungaku*, eight out of *Faulkner to Gendai no Guwa*, published in 1994 and 1995 respectively; all completely revised, not the translation. I have found liberation and joy in expressing myself in English, but the endless process of proofreading (though I know it is necessary) has wearied me. My challenging struggle with the English language and the personal computer would have been even more nerve-racking without the support generously given me by a great number of people.

Dr. Lee C. Colegrove has helped me since 1977, first as my actual teacher at Waseda University and after 1982 as both a tutor and a colleague at Tokyo Woman's Christian University. Also greatly helpful has been Dr. Richard Spear, colleague at Tokyo Woman's Christian University as well. I owe my deepest gratitude to Professor Kenzaburo Ohashi for his encouragement and fine review backboned by his love and understanding of Faulkner and, let me say, present writer. Dr. Robert West encouraged me to publish in the land of Faulkner. I pay a tribute to Anne Pellowski and her family, the gold mine I struck right after landing on the shores of the United States in 1972. Anne and her family helped me to find my way through America, though they had lost an adored brother on Okinawa during the war. I have to add that Anne, a distinguished scholar and a writer in the field of children's literature who has published 18 books, helped me on my way through preparation of my work for publication. Finally my appreciation to Ichiro and Leo Tôyama who put up with a wife and mother and supported her during her writing travail.

Only now have I come to understand this clumsily sought enterprise of mine, my urge to scribble on every wall, "Kilroy was here." Where am I going? I'm off to work on Faulkner's neglected trilogy, *The Hamlet*, *The Town*, and *The Mansion*, a fable that echoes with Faulkner's compassionate cry, "Poor sons of bitches, poor mankind."

Kiyoko M.Tôyama
遠山清子

Acknowledgement

Thanks to:

Professor Keith L. Cohen, The University of Wisconsin
The University of Wisconsin Library

Professor Robert W. Hamblin, Director of the Center for Faulkner Studies, at Southeast Missouri State University
Amy E. C. Linnemann

Professor Noel Polk, The University of Southern Mississippi

Professor Joseph R. Urgo, Bryant College

Professor Charles A. Peek, Director of the Prairie Institute at the University of Nebraska at Kearney

Professor Donald M. Kartiganer, The University of Mississippi
The University of Mississippi Library

Professor Marsha A. Freeman, Humphrey Institute of Public Affairs, University of Minnesota

Referencers,
Tokyo Woman's Christian University Library

Waseda University Library

Koichi Shioya, Robagoya-Juku
Daisuke Takada
Tatsuhide Mizoe

1. *Silence* by Shusaku Endo
A Japanese Christianity

> The Japanese till this day have never had
> the concept of God; and they never will.
>
> Shusaku Endo, *Silence*

According to the *Kojiki*, the ancient chronicle of Japan, early Japan was surrounded by gods: divine gods, lowly gods, strong gods, weak gods, good gods and bad gods. Everything awe-inspiring—a human being, a beast, a mountain, a river, a tree—became a god. People lived with gods who had no power to make moral judgements. In this beautiful land, blessed with a mild climate, their lives fused into nature rather than confronted it. If evils like guilt existed, people believed those evils could be blown off as "morning wind and evening wind puff away the morning mist and the evening mist" in the words of *Shinto Prayer of Purification*. The act of purification was believed to clear away guilt and all other environmental and spiritual pollution. Thus, "There is no such thing as guilt under heaven" (*Shinto Prayer of Purification*).

The ancient Japanese believed nothing could threaten the basis of their world. They could not think of a transcendental world, for such a concept would be based on the negation of this world, and they believed that this world was good. *Takamagahara*, the equivalent of heaven, was not beyond this world, but a projection of this world, the land of *Yamato*, which the ancient Japanese actually occupied. People lived in harmony with nature, the gods, and other living things. Also, in the ancient agricultural society where people planted and harvested rice and shared the same water source, harmony and cooperation, not individual independence, were the most important virtues. Therefore, in Japanese mythology, the most hated crime was that of breaking the harmony. Immersed in homogeneity of feeling, they did not, as did the West, seek a transcending principle or an absolute, which binds individuals.

In the minds of the ancient Japanese who lived in harmony with nature, what was unwholesome was the act of polluting their natural environment. The word *tsumi*, the equivalent of guilt, meant not only the unwholesome conduct of men, but also illness, harm, everything that pollutes the natural state or condition. Purification, the ritual of cleansing, contributed much to developing Japanese aesthetics. There was no distinction between aesthetic judgement and moral judgement in the minds of the ancient Japanese. While moral judgement is socially oriented and presupposes an objective principle, aesthetic value is based upon subjective feeling. One judges something to be pure or beautiful intuitively and subjectively. In the West the objective perspective evolved as man thought of himself as an individual confronting nature, God, and other men. In Japan, where people fused into nature and into their gods, objective thinking, which makes a clear distinction between self and others, did not have the ground to grow. Thus, the value judgements of the ancient Japanese were aesthetic and subjective.

Although the optimistic view that this world is good and beautiful has gradually been lost in the course of history, the ancient aesthetic value took deep roots in the Japanese mode of thought; Japanese ethics have always been extremely aesthetic. In dealing with the process of the Japanese domestication of alien cultures and systems of thought, I may even offer the hypothesis that Japanese aesthetic concepts assimilated and transformed elements of Buddhism, Zen, and Confucianism. When the Japanese confront such a religion as Christianity, which makes a clear distinction between ethics and aesthetics, they can only respond with feeling. They cannot entertain the notion of a clear distinction between God and humans. This type of thought pattern can be traced back to the ancient Japanese. This paper will later examine *Silence* written by

Shusaku Endo, a contemporary Japanese Catholic writer, focusing upon his acceptance of Christianity.

First, let us examine how the Japanese have assimilated foreign cultures, such as Buddhism, Zen, and Confucianism. When Buddhism first came to Japan as a composite of religion, art, and philosophy, the Japanese attitude of acceptance was intuitive and subjective. People accepted the phase of Buddhism which best suited their temperament. Since the beauty of the Buddhist statues strongly impressed them, they accepted Buddhism through the creation of their own Buddhist arts. As a purely religious philosophy, little content is found in the Buddhism of this era (seventh and eighth centuries). Under the patronage of the emperors, who at this time were uniting the nation, Buddhism produced gorgeous, ornate cultural treasures. These early Buddhist works of art evoke in us, agnostics or not, a dear sentiment of being in the homeland. The historian Saburo Ienaga says that he cannot deny that Japanese people have a poor record of logical thinking, while they excel in creating works of art.

He adds that, in the Kamakura period (twelfth and thirteenth centuries), new religions offered ways of thinking which could compete with the philosophical ideas of China and the West. In the turbulent society of that day people sought religions which could give them spiritual support. In the Kamakura Era, the consciousness of *mujoh,* the uncertainty of this world, led the people to aspire to The Pure Land, the Buddhist equivalent of heaven. When detestation of the impurity of this world made them aspire to The Pure Land, the people put the value of purity above every value. The pure world was also an ethically good world, and this goodness was judged by an aesthetic standard, not by an ethical standard. The reason Pure Land Buddhism flourished more in Japan than in China can be explained by saying that it appealed to the Japanese mode of thinking. While Pure Land Buddhism spread among the commoners, Zen gave spiritual support to warriors.

Zen, a profound religion in the Kamakura Era, did not lead to any significant change in the religious thinking of the Japanese people as a whole. In fact, ironically, the flourishing of Zen culture effected the transformation of a religious culture into a secularized culture. Zen gave an impetus to the growth of various forms of art in the Muromachi Era (fourteenth and fifteenth centuries). These arts were nourished by the Zen aesthetics of simple beauty and stylization. For example, the stages and actions of the Noh plays were made extremely stylistic and symbolic. The tea ceremony, a stylized way of making and drinking tea, originated at this time; the tea ceremony is characterized by an intense attention to any single movement. In painting, the artists tried to express an object from spiritual angles in both line and composition by using only black and white. Gardens, which originally were an artistic expression of the pantheistic philosophy of Buddhism, were deprived of their religious character and transformed into pure art. Aspects of temple structures were copied in the building of secular residences. The art of flower arrangement developed similarly; flowers which were originally offered to the statues of Buddha came to adorn secular houses. These arts are now intrinsic in Japanese daily life, though in modified and fragmented forms.

In 1549 Francis Xavier first brought Christianity to Japan. Later, at their height, Japanese Catholics were said to number four hundred thousand out of about twenty million.[1] This period of Japanese history particularly welcomed the new religious faith. The relevant political and economical factors may be summarized as follows: *Shogun* Nobunaga, the new ruler of Japan, hated Buddhism, especially that of the Pure Land Buddhism Sect, which opposed him. Thus, he took a favorable attitude toward the missionaries. Also, feudal lords welcomed missionaries because they provided an opportunity to trade with Portugal. Yet these factors do not fully explain the rapid infiltration of Christianity. It is during this era, after the persecution of believers started in 1587, that Shusaku Endo sets his novel *Silence*. After the death of Nobunaga, society came to be stabilized under a feudalistic system with new rulers. The new rulers, seeing the strong union of missionaries and believers, began to think that the spread of the Christian faith would threaten the basis of the feudal system then being formed.

Endo explains in *Silence* what made Christian faith spread among peasants so readily:

> I tell you the truth—for a long, long time these farmers have worked like horses and cattle; and like horses and cattle they have died. The reason our religion has penetrated this territory like water flowing into dry earth is that it has given to this group of people a human warmth they never previously knew. For the first time they have met men who treated them like human beings. It was the human kindness and charity of the fathers that touched

their hearts.[2]

Christianity appealed to the hearts of the peasants. Since they thirsted for tenderness, they tended to honor Mary more than Christ himself. They remained true to their faith until death because they had to work "like horses and cattle" in this world, but they believed there were no such things as heavy taxes and forced labor in the paradise the missionaries preached of. Also, the beauty of martyrdom fascinated them. Through experiencing the heroism of martyrdom, they could cast away their fetters and choose their own cause for the first time.

When the persecution started, people were forced to trample on *fumie*, the image of Christ, to prove they were not *Kirishitan* or Christians. Yet these tortures only made them more proud and upright; the number of Christians even increased. After this, the rulers adopted more cunning methods to compel them to apostatize. The rulers invented numerous tortures which made the Christians writhe in an extremely ugly way, depriving them of any space for heroism to enter. For example, in *"anatsurushi"* they were hung upside down in a hole stacked with excrement, with a hole drilled behind one ear to let the blood out so that they would not die too quickly. This method is said to have been invented by a recanting Christian who well knew the psychology of Japanese Christians.

Many proved their faith in their martyrdom. Yet it is doubtful whether the faith to which they were true until death was that of authentic Christianity. Endo has Christovao Ferreira, a Portuguese Jesuit who recanted his faith after twenty years of missionary work in Japan, say in *Silence*:

> 'No! In the minds of the Japanese the Christian God was completely changed.' . . . 'The Japanese imagine a beautiful, exalted man—and this they call God. They call by the name of God something which has the same kind of existence as man. But that is not the Church's God.' (239, 241)

Almost all Japanese historians agree that the Christianity of this period was erased out of the history of Japan without affecting any apparent change in the Japanese psyche.[3]

In the Edo Era (seventeenth - nineteenth centuries) the rulers used Confucianism to stabilize the feudal system. *Bushido*, the way of the warrior, became the morality of the *samurai*. Loyalty to one's lord until death is the central moral of *bushido*. The most famous *bushido* manual, *The Hagakure*, shows the profound influence of Confucianism. The book also preaches the beautification of daily life by always being prepared to die for a cause, for one's lord. Its most famous sentence is "*Bushido* consists in dying—that is the conclusion I have reached." One's life is given shape by being prepared to die a beautiful death. As Yukio Mishima, a contemporary writer who killed himself acting upon this theory, says, "ethics and beauty are one and the same" in *bushido*.

After Japan opened itself to the West in 1868, early Japanese Protestants largely consisted of sons of the former *samurai* class. Christian faith was now interpreted as loyalty to Christ, one's lord. Kanzo Uchimura, a prominent early Protestant in Japan, says:

> A man who discards *bushido* or slights it, cannot be a good disciple of Christ. What God particularly seeks among the Japanese people is that person who, having become a spiritual *samurai,* holds Christ in his heart as lord of life. (Spae, 99)

Another early Protestant, Inazo Nitobe, explains:

> We are too matter-of-fact in our everyday life to become zealots; but should persecutions arise, martyrdom would be hailed in heroism rather than in faith, and death courted as an honorable exit from this life rather than as an entrance to the next. (Spae, 155)

These Protestants could die for Christ as *samurai* should, not for their faith but for the beauty of moral consistency. Their Christian faith thus conformed to traditional aesthetics. The concept of the trinity still seemed absent from their faith.

Endo, a contemporary Catholic (1923-1998), examines his own Japanese Christianity through writing his novel *Silence*. The word "silence" signifies the silence of God and also the silence of the Church regarding the recanting *Kirisitans*—those Christians in seventeenth-century Japan who were forced to renounce their faith. Numerous records of martyrs are left but very little has been written about the apostates or the recants. Perhaps missionaries and the Church have tried to ignore or hide the existences of the apostates, who were dark spots on the Church records. To probe into the depth of his own problem, Endo recreates the life of one of these apostates. He tries to locate and affirm his own Christian faith by recreating this apostate and allowing him to talk about his life. By shedding light on this person, whose very existence the Church refuses to recognize, he tries to transform the Christian faith so as to make it acceptable to the Japanese mind. This transformation ultimately entails changing the Christian concept of God.

Endo was brought up by a Catholic mother and was baptized at the age of eleven. As he grew up, he became conscious of the fact that he was being raised in a foreign, Western religion, Christianity, without his mature consent. He says that he tried to abandon the faith many times, but he could not. His literary career is the record of his struggle as a Japanese Catholic. In his early essay "God and gods," he says: "The more we know about Catholicism, the more we have to listen to the murmur of our blood, which is nurtured in the world of the gods" (trans. mine). Also, he has to confess: "to enter the system of God, we feel sorrow as if we were losing the dear blood within us" (trans. mine).

His literary works reveal his effort to recognize the distance between his Christianity and his Japaneseness. Christovao Ferreira (Chuan Sawano), the Portuguese apostate priest, says in *Silence*: "It's not because of any prohibition nor because of persecution that Christianity has perished. There's something in this country that completely stifles the growth of Christianity" (243-44). This "something" is the Japanese conception of God, which comes out of a pantheistic eclecticism and which does not accept the concept of one, absolute God. Endo's intrinsic pantheistic blood rebelled against the monotheistic theory of Christianity. It can be said that in *Silence* Endo, who had consciously fought to purify himself of his Japanese blood, at last resigns himself to his Japanese eclecticism. Nevertheless, this resignation does not mean any rejection of Christianity. Endo accepts Christianity, but only after an agonizing effort to transform it so as to accommodate his Japanese heritage.

Sebastian Rodrigues, a fictitious Portuguese Jesuit, is the hero of *Silence*. He volunteered to come to Japan because he wanted to learn about his former teacher, Christovao Ferreira, who ceased to write to the Church after 1633. Endo equips Rodrigues with essentially Japanese-like characteristics: an emotive approach to Christ and God, a weakness in the face of beauty, and a warm sentimentality. Endo makes this character struggle with his role as Jesuit missionary and drives him to the extremity of either denying his faith or letting others be killed because of him. By enclosing an essentially Japanese character in a Portuguese name, Endo depicts the way in which Japanese blood and Christian faith clash in one person.

For Rodrigues, Christ is a person who embodies every human beauty. He is a beautiful, exalted man. And this Christ he calls God: "I am always fascinated by the face of Christ just like a man fascinated by the face of his beloved" (47). He can endure hardships through identifying with Christ, and the sense of suffering always shared with Christ softly eases "his mind and heart more than . . . sweet water." Since he perceives Christ as if he were a person physically near and approachable, Rodrigues is deeply hurt by the silence of God when he witnesses the miserable and painful martyrdom of peasants:

> What do I want to say? I myself do not quite understand. Only that today, when for the glory of God Mokichi and Ichizo moaned, suffered and died, I cannot bear the monotonous sound of the dark sea gnawing at the shore. Behind the depressing silence of this sea, the silence of God . . . the feeling that while men raise their voices in anguish God remains with folded arms, silent. (105)

He begins to question whether God exists. If God does not exist, his life and the martyrdom of others become absurd. With this doubt within him, Rodrigues is forced to choose between martyrdom and apostasy. Rodrigues' belief in God was always based on the assumption that God would behave in accordance with man's idea of what constitutes a proper response. Thus, his resentment of God's silence is different from that seen in Western literature. He wants to have a direct response from God as if God were a person. Endo, of course, knows God does not answer directly, but he depicts in Rodrigues a Japanese person who, because he emotively talks to God without having the abstract concept of an absolute being, expects a direct answer.

At the same time that Rodrigues suffers from the silence of God, he is deeply troubled by the lack of beauty in the martyrdom of the peasants. He had long entertained the image of a splendid martyrdom: but "the martyrdom of these peasants, enacted before his very eyes—how wretched it was, miserable like the huts they lived in, like the rags in which they were clothed" (196). As he is susceptible to the beauty of heroic conduct, he is keenly conscious during the inquisition that he is being watched by the peasants. This consciousness keeps him upright, and he is satisfied with himself when he thinks he has managed not to show an ugly, cowardly attitude. Similarly, the reason he cannot forgive Kichijiro, a traitor, is that Kichijiro has no beauty, not even in his wickedness:

> Could it be possible that Christ loved and searched after this dirtiest of men? In evil there remained that strength and beauty of evil; but this Kichijiro was not even worthy to be called evil. He was thin and dirty like the tattered rags he wore. (188-89)

Rodrigues thinks it is easy to die if the act of martyrdom is achieved in heroic beauty. For him, aesthetic judgement comes often before moral judgement.

Rodrigues is, then, sensitive to beauty and tenderness in other persons. He is easily moved by the tenderness of others, while he himself is full of tender kindness and sentiment. He has to make numerous compromises to avoid hurting others. He cannot help shouting, "Trample it!" when the peasants are going to be tested by trampling the image of Christ carved on a plaque, even as he realizes that, as a priest, he should not be saying this. Also, he cannot put a cruel end to the peasants' happy dream of their paradise when they talk about a place where they will not suffer from heavy taxes, forced labor, starvation, and illness. He has no strength to let others suffer because of him, even while he should instruct them to maintain their faith at any cost and when he should teach them about the real concept of heaven. He is affable and cannot bear solitude. It is the temptation of meeting another human being after a long day's wandering in the mountains that makes him fall into the hands of Kichijiro, a traitor, who sells him to the officials.

Rodrigues is made to recant at the end because of the situation he has been forced into. With all these Japanese characteristics, he is driven to the choice between martyrdom and apostasy. He is told that some peasants, whose groaning he can hear, will be killed if he does not trample the *fumie*, the sacred image. His resistance begins to crumble when Ferreira points out that Rodrigues thinks more of himself than of the peasants. Rodrigues sees in himself an egoist who wants to die out of vanity: "For a moment Ferreira remained silent; then he suddenly broke out in a strong voice: 'Certainly Christ would have apostatized for them'" (268).

Rodrigues then performs "the most painful act of love that has ever been performed." In the very act of trampling the image of Christ, he hears the Christ on the plaque, "rubbed flat by many feet," speak to him. Thus God's silence is broken. The Christ who breaks the silence is not that Christ whose image Rodrigues had always embraced in his heart, that is, the beautiful exalted man. Now it is the Christ whose face is "concave, worn down with the constant treading," who speaks to him:

> 'Trample! Your foot suffers in pain; it must suffer like all the feet that have stepped on this plaque. But that pain alone is enough. I understand your pain and your suffering. It is for that reason that I am here.' (297)

Feeling love and forgiveness in this Christ, Rodrigues affirms his faith. Rodrigues affirms his internal faith in the very act of breaking an essential teaching: "Everyone who acknowledges me before others I will acknowledge before my heavenly Father. But whoever denies me before others, I will deny before my heavenly Father" (Matthew: 10, 32-33).

When Rodrigues feels the love and pity of Christ, he can, for the first time, come to terms with the nagging question he has long embraced: Why did Christ say to Judas "What you are going to do, do quickly"? Judas is a tool, a puppet to achieve the glory of Christ's life and his death on the cross. Why does Christ, if he is a man of love, let Judas fall into eternal sin? As long as Rodrigues cannot solve that problem, he cannot forgive Kichijiro, who treads the *fumie* whenever he is threatened by the officials. He also informs on the villagers and sells Rodrigues, but yet he persistently follows Rodrigues, asking for the sacrament of confession. Kichijiro has the logic of the weak:

> 'But I have my cause to plead! One who has trod on the sacred image has his say too. Do you think I trampled on it willingly? My feet ached with the pain. God asks me to imitate the strong, even though he made me weak. Isn't this unreasonable?' (186)

When Rodrigues feels Christ's forgiveness, he acknowledges that there is no difference between Kichijiro and himself. Rodrigues' Christ says of Judas: "I did not say that. Just as I told you to step on the plaque, so I told Judas to do what he was going to do. For Judas was in anguish as you are now"(297). Once he has recanted, Rodrigues is given a Japanese name and a Japanese wife; in other words, he endlessly slips now from Church doctrine. Yet *Silence* ends with a reaffirmation of his faith:

> He [Rodrigues] loved him [Christ] now in a different way from
> before. Everything that had taken place until now had been
> necessary to bring him to this love. 'Even now I am the last priest
> in this land. But Our Lord was not silent. Even if he had been silent,
> my life until this day would have spoken of him.' (298)

Rodrigues can reaffirm his faith in the act of denying the concept of God as the
Word incarnated. Since Rodrigues deprives God of his logical ground, he has to
find another way to prove the existence of God. He has no other way than to let
his life prove it. Rodrigues' apostasy becomes the acquisition of a firm internal
faith by the very fact that it is a complete apostasy.

Endo says: "This is the statement of my faith. I, of course, acknowledge
theological criticisms, but I can do nothing about it" (Postscript to the first
edition of *Chinmoku* published in 1966, trans. mine). He continues:

> This problem of the reconciliation of my Catholicism with my
> Japanese blood . . . has taught me one thing: that is, that the
> Japanese must absorb Christianity without the support of a
> Christian tradition or history or legacy or sensibility. Even this
> attempt is the occasion of much resistance and anguish and pain,
> still it is impossible to counter by closing one's eyes to the
> difficulties. No doubt this is the peculiar cross that God has given
> to the Japanese. (*Thought*, winter 1967)

In *Silence* Endo denies logic as a basis for the affirmation of love. His idea that
the more one suffers, just like Job in the Old Testament, the more one is entitled
to God's love, goes beyond logic. Here, this quality of God's love has to be
transformed into a Buddhist, all-embracing love.

The Western concept of God has an absolute quality which surpasses
humanism since humanism has only relativistic premises and values. In order to
act in accordance with the absolute principle of God, one often has to kill his
Japaneseness, his spontaneous humanistic feeling, which always functions
through a relativistic mode of thinking. Thus, he who is a foreigner to Western
Christians becomes a foreigner to his own people. Endo tries to Easternize

Christianity by denying universal logic and by, at the same time, affirming the love of God. Whether this is "true" Catholicism or not, Endo has reached this conclusion after a long, painful struggle as a Japanese Catholic. In "Translator's Preface" to *Silence,* William Johnston wrote:

> Anyone familiar with modern theology in the West will quickly see that Mr. Endo's thesis is more universal than many of his Japanese readers have suspected. For if Hellenistic Christianity does not fit Japan, neither does it (in the opinion of many) suit the modern West; if the notion of God has to be rethought for Japan (as this novel constantly stresses), so has it to be rethought for the modern West; if the ear of Japan is eager to catch a new strain in the vast symphony, the ear of the West is no less attentive— searching for new chords that will correspond to its awakening sensibilities. All in all, the ideas of Mr. Endo are acutely topical and universal.

Japan has assimilated Buddhism, Zen, and Confucianism, and now Christianity is engaged in a desperate search for assimilation. When the Japanese accept a foreign culture, they modulate it for the Japanese mentality. Ferreira, another of Endo's spokesmen, says:

> 'This country is a swamp . . . . This country is a more terrible swamp than you can imagine. Whenever you plant a sapling in this swamp the roots begin to rot; the leaves grow yellow and wither. And we have planted the sapling of Christianity in this swamp.' (237)

Yet, is it not true that every country carries "something . . . that . . . stifles the growth of Christianity"? (243-44). Endo has reached the place where he can say:

> But after all it seems to me that Catholicism is not a solo, but a symphony . . . . If I have trust in Catholicism, it is because I find in it much more possibility than in any other religion for presenting the full symphony of humanity. (*Thought*, Winter 1967)

Perhaps the only possible standard of judgement a Japanese person can form is the intuitive judgement of whether an act or an object in question is prompted by love, whether or not it gives life.

2.   The Death and Dying of Yukio Mishima
A Prolegomenon

"He always wanted to exist but never could."
By Chiyuki Hiraoka, Mishima's younger brother

Everyone is destined to be born at one specific time and into some specific space. One has no choice, it would seem, but to accept the reality of one's being time-bound and space-bound as long as one physically exists. Mishima, born Japanese, accepted his being space-bound, but he willfully denied his being time-bound, his always having to live in the progressive tense and thus never achieving that stylistic perfection with which he was obsessed. Denying being time-bound, the condition of every man, Mishima struggled with the all-absorbing nihilism that was not only his own view of life, but also a significant aspect of his culture.

This kind of struggle with one's culture is not unique to Mishima. William Faulkner, for instance, had a similar struggle with *his* culture. The difference is that Faulkner, through accepting the fact of his being not only space-bound but also time-bound, was able to leap over the boundaries of the specific culture he was born into. Faulkner saw cosmos and human destiny in his "little postage stamp of native soil"; by so doing, he elevated his writings to the level of human fables (*Lion in the Garden*, 255).

One might summarize Mishima's plight as follows: If one is too keen an observer, too deep a perceiver of the ultimate absurdity of existence, one cannot be absorbed blindly in the immediate problems, pleasures, and routines that fill the consciousness of ordinary people. Without these ordinary modes of response, the nihilist cannot present himself as an integrated being. However, as long as he exists in an assigned space and time, he is under an obligation to strive to become a seemingly integrated whole. As the first person narrator in *Confessions of a Mask* says:

> From the very beginning, life had oppressed me with a heavy sense of duty. Even though I was clearly incapable of performing this duty, life still nagged at me for my dereliction. Thus I longed for the great sense of relief that death would surely bring if only, like a wrestler, I could wrench the heavy weight of life from my shoulders. (*Confessions of a Mask*, 127)

One can be freed from this duty and relax into original non-being only by becoming physically non-existent. Therefore, death is always a sweet temptation for him. Mishima, shortly before his death, wrote:

> If the only natural world for me was one in which death was an everyday, self-evident matter, and if what was natural to me was very easily attainable, not through artificial devices, but by means of perfectly unoriginal concepts of duty, then nothing could be more natural than that I should gradually succumb to temptation and seek to replace imagination by duty. (*Sun and Steel*, 57)

He added: "All we are left with is the freedom to choose which method we will try out when brought face to face with that void in the progressive tense, in the interval while we await the 'absolute'" (*Sun and Steel*, 69).

Recollecting his own adolescence, Mishima has his narrator in *Confessions of a Mask* choose words carefully in forming his mode of response, for he cannot bear anything which is not clearly presented in tangible form. The boy feels, therefore, that he can express himself better in writing than by talking face to face. It is natural for one who lives in words to become a writer, for writing allows one to change the relation between the world and himself and, at the same time, reinforce that relationship. Mishima later confessed, in one of his many essays, that he was envious of people who can enjoy listening to music in a state in which intelligence and the senses are happily fused into one. He himself could hardly bear the uneasiness of succumbing to music because, in music, meaning and content cannot be pinned down. A researcher of himself by means of words, he decided to erect a well-disciplined, logical, but artificial illusion of himself to combat the larger illusion of human existence.

Mishima repeated throughout his literary career that he wanted to make his life into a poem. Here a poem was not a mere figure of speech but indicated an actual artistic form. How could this fluid existence, though, which is always "in the progressive tense," be made into "a poem," an artistic form composed of tangible, static words? The aged writer in *Forbidden Colors* is keenly aware that:

> form is lacking in human experience and in influence on human life. . . . Form was the inborn destiny of art. One had to believe that the human experience within a work and real-life human experience are different in dimension, depending on whether form is present or not. Within real-life human experience, however, there is something that is very close to what is experienced in a work. What is it? It is the impression accorded by death. We cannot experience death, but we sometimes experience the impression of it. . . . In sum, death is the unique form of life. (*Forbidden Colors*, 136)

According to this notion, art can only present itself in stylized forms, forms that mirror the stasis of death. The beauty of art is achieved by straddling reality, forcing it to a halt, and stopping its breath at its root, according to Mishima's own summary.

Mishima's quest for selfhood through the pursuit of a literary career began with *Confessions of a Mask*. The idea of a "mask" confessing suggests that he does not know his true face—even wonders if such a true face does, in fact, exist. It is in this state that he searches for this true face, working through his mask. Here, Mishima's narrator is unable to react spontaneously to the events that happen around him as time passes. However, the boy wishes to react as others do. He says:

> I studied many novels minutely, investigating how boys my age felt about life, how they spoke to themselves. . . . As a result, my only recourse was to infer from theoretical rules what "a boy of my age" would feel when he was all alone. (*Confessions of a Mask*, 108)

He finds, for instance, that it is because of his homosexuality that he lacks any urge toward the opposite sex. Realizing his inability to react spontaneously, he thus attempts to participate in reality by giving names to the responses of others. Once he has done this, he can create a mode of behavior for himself through that name—by causing the concept to appear, by embodying it. When he tries to personify normality, for instance, he says:

> My "act" has ended by becoming an integral part of my nature, . . . It's no longer an act. My knowledge that I am masquerading as a normal person has even corroded whatever of normality I originally possessed, ending by making me tell myself over and over again that it too was nothing but a pretence at normality. (*Confessions of a Mask*, 153)

Unable to trust the will or the response which could define him, he feels he is non-existent, deprived of identity. Though he physically exists: "The pain proclaimed: You're not human. You're a being who is incapable of social intercourse. You're nothing but a creature, non-human and somehow strangely pathetic" (*Confessions of a Mask*, 230).

In this struggle the war comes to his rescue. During the war, death is for all young Japanese an inescapable reality. The possibility that he might achieve a heroic, romantic, young death gives Mishima a reason to sustain his masquerade: "It was a rare time when my personal sense of termination and that of the age and of society at large was one and the same" (*"Watashi no Henreki Jidai,"* 434, trans. mine based on John Nathan's). During the war, the boy—already inherently and incurably afflicted with the "disease" called romanticism—enthusiastically responds to the voice of the Japanese romantic school that teaches the elevation of a dark destiny into a sublime, heroic fatality and preaches the beauty of dying. Most ostensibly, it was Zenmei Hasuda, who shot himself when Japan was defeated, who made an indelible impression on the young Mishima.

When the war ended, then, Mishima felt himself again sentenced to life, to ordinary, mundane living. Deprived of his "destiny" of death, his original existential horror of feeling bereft of identity returned to haunt him. Under pressure to choose some mode of existence, he plunged into desperate self-affirmation by making his "romantic disease" his standard. This commitment to romanticism was Mishima's next attempt to combat his feeling of nothingness. Rejecting the reality of a human experience which lacks form and style, Mishima's romanticism turned its eyes not on the self as it exists in the present, but on the past and the mysterious area beyond. By so doing, and by making beauty an absolute, it escaped from the present, which consists of the mundane business of living.

In ancient times in Japan, the concept of beauty seemed to involve little contradiction between reality and art or between life and beauty. With the Middle Ages, though, beauty for its own sake came to stand above life. Japanese Medieval art tended to exclude the affirmation of life that humanism inspired. Almost all art originating in this period attempted to escape from reality, from the turbulent war-torn society around it. The more barren the outside world became, the more strongly the artists tried to deny reality by withdrawing into an aesthetic order of their own creation.

These artists, who did not have an absolute conception of God and who, therefore, did not need to struggle against it, shut themselves up and sharpened their sensibilities. Instead of joining to form a coordinate axis, each of them became the center of his own axis. They created and crystallized beauty by continuously manipulating the data of their own senses. Their beauty had to be perfect in its every detail; a single dissonance would destroy the harmony of the whole. Thus, a sense of crisis was always prevalent, with a kind of stoicism hovering over every form of art. By splitting physical living from the aesthetic or spiritual life, they forfeited the organizing principle that might have given order to the multitude of details of expression. To cover that basic weakness they tried to shape their creations into well-balanced, static forms sustained only by an intense attention to detail.

With Mishima's own comments as a guide, let us make a brief review of several forms of art originating in the Muromachi Era in order to better understand these principles. Let us begin with Japanese gardens:

> the most direct statement of esthetic Japanese thinking . . . in the extreme artificiality of their skillful copying of nature, they attempted to betray nature. Between nature and the work of art, there is a secret rebellion brewing. . . . These famous old gardens are fastened by the cord of a passion for the invisibly faithless female known as the work of art. (*Forbidden Colors*, 183)

The flower arrangement:

> Nature's plants were brought vividly under the sway of an artificial order and made to conform to an established melody. The flowers and leaves, which had formerly existed *as they were*, had now been transformed into flowers and leaves *as they ought to be*. The cattails and the irises were no longer individual, anonymous plants belonging to their respective species, but had become terse, direct manifestations of what might be called the essence of the irises and the cattails. (*The Temple of the Golden Pavilion*, 145)

The tea ceremony: The mere act of making and drinking tea was made into a ritual based on paying intense attention to every single movement of the body. And in *yokyoku* (the scripts of Noh): "one found an aesthetic resistance by words poignant of decadence. The manipulation of extremely artificial, gorgeous words should be inevitably backed by despair" ("*Watashi no Henreki Jidai*," 430-31, trans. mine). Lastly, the *Shinkokinshu*: The eccentric aesthetics of this anthology of poems compiled by *Teika Fujiwara* had, to Mishima, the quality of artificial pearls. For Teika, the well of creation was the cultivation of an artificial madness based upon clear self-consciousness and cold calculation. This cultivated madness was at one with the aesthetic sense, which sustained his poetry.

This cultivation of madness culminated when Mishima, seven and a half centuries later, terminated his life as he did. Mishima willfully isolated himself from daily life in the Japan of his time; through self-restraint and an indulgence in introvert decadence, he elevated his senses to the realm of art. Mishima, to a more intense degree than others, was aware of the poison within his culture:

> Shunsuké's eastern vision sometimes leaned toward death. In the
> Orient, death is many times more vivid than life. The artistic
> work . . . was a kind of refined death. It had a peculiar power to
> permit life to touch and experience death in advance. (*Forbidden
> Colors*, 136)

Faulkner would have been astounded at this proclamation. In spite of sharing a
nihilistic view of life with Mishima, Faulkner valued the confusion of human life
above all. In Faulkner's view: "The aim of every artist is to arrest motion, which
is life, by artificial means and hold it fixed so that a hundred years later, when a
stranger looks at it, it moves again since it is life" (*Lion in the Garden*, 253).

Mishima knew, though, that it was madness to create artistic works which
were a kind of refined death, and he thus eventually became the most severe critic
of his own earlier aesthetic approach. His recognition of his own half-mad
perversions appears in his intense ridicule of Shunsuké, the writer in *Forbidden
Colors* and at least half a representation of Mishima himself:

> It is a shame, but the *Complete Works of Shunsuké Hinoki*, from
> their first lines, renounced war against reality. As a result his
> works were not real. His passions simply brushed against reality
> and, repelled by its ugliness, shut themselves up in his works. . . .
> His style, peerlessly ornate in its decorativeness, was, after all, no
> more than a design for reality; it was no more than a curious,
> worm-eaten figure of speech in which reality had consumed
> passion. (*Forbidden Colors*, 28)

> Artificial gardens from which every value which did not ridicule
> every practical purpose was strictly excluded . . . He persistently
> debased and laughed at every humanistic value. (*Kinshoku*, 542,
> trans. mine)[1]

> He wished to create art which looked like physical existence, but,
> ironically all his works smell of corpses and their structures give
> the impression of extreme artificiality, like exquisite golden coffins.
> (*Kinshoku*, 545, trans. mine)

As Mishima was aware of, his own works suffer from his chronic obsession with stasis as a means to perfection. His world is always closed and self-contained, with characters that do not grow. He confessed, even boasted, that he did not start writing unless he had the last line firmly set in his mind. His narratives were preoccupied with stylistic unity and, as a consequence, failed to flow. This was also partly due to the nature of his means of expression, the modern Japanese language. Using Japanese, a writer can easily tend to fall into the pitfall of a stylistic stasis since Japanese words tend to have a static quality even when expressing movement. In modern Japanese, beauty is achieved mostly in its pauses; it is not a fit language for depicting the motion of human life. Some writers fight to make their words plastic by first eliminating traditional stylistic beauty from their language, as did Kenzaburo Oe. Mishima, however, never attempted to fight against the Japanese tradition of an ornate style.

After writing innumerable novels, plays, and essays in which every humanistic value was sneered at, Mishima ended his period of romanticism by writing *Kyoko no Ie*.[2] In this novel he divided his inner world into four characters, each of whom tries stoically to exist in his own way in anticipation of the coming destruction of the world. Shunkichi, a boxer, lives exclusively by actions, trying not to think for even a moment. When he is disqualified from boxing, for instance, he joins a group of fanatic nationalists in order to remain in motion. Natsuo, an artist, sees, feels, and paints. Having a belief that an angel guards him, he is not afraid to change the living, moving world into static, pure phenomena consisting only of shape and color. Osamu, an actor, is always tormented by the question of whether he really exists. He begins by sleeping with women in order to verify, if only momentarily, his physical existence. This he finds insufficient, but ultimately he discovers a more substantial and certain verification of existence in physical pain: "The blood flowing from his body was an indication of the peerless accord of the internal and the external" (*Kyoko no Ie*, 351, trans. mine). To live that moment of pain he commits double suicide with an ugly woman. The fourth character, Yuichiro, a businessman, exists by means of his determination to obey that which he despises. If he despises customs, he is loyal to those very customs. If he despises public opinion, he is loyal to that public opinion. He establishes himself by means of this "social adaptability."

Mishima's view of his internal self is thus split into four characters in *Kyoko no Ie*. At that point, though, Mishima became aware that he had to affect the integration of his split self if he was ever to shape his existence more sharply against the background of the void. His commitment to romanticism gradually became too weak to crystallize his being. As a protection against disintegration, he took hold of the ethic of the *samurai*, the warriors of the Edo Era, as being more fit for his purpose. The core of the *samurai* ethic was death, not life. The *samurai* ethic taught the individual how to die, how to make his life a preparation for dying a beautiful death. Mishima once said "ethic and beauty are one and the same" and explained why a man should be "associated with beauty only through a heroic, violent death" (*Sun and Steel*, 54). Moreover, the *samurai* ethic (at least as Mishima interpreted it) required of one a strictly classical physical body as a vehicle for a heroic death. To this end, Mishima trained his muscles to make his body fit for heroism.

To achieve this end, he also felt that he had to die before physical deterioration began. The age limit Mishima set for himself was forty-five. Mishima's next concern was to find an appropriate place of death. He felt that death should really take place on a "battlefield," but on a battlefield of his own creation. When he thought of heroic death in the real world, he rejected the reality of "such things as mud, blood, shit and vermin which enter into the game of making war" (Miller, 45). His search for his own battlefield in the Japan of his time led him to an interest in terrorism. Terrorism became the battlefield for which he had been searching.

Mishima, who knew so well the impossibility of dying for some concept, had made up his mind to die for the traditions of the old beautiful Japan, the core of which was the Emperor, the descendant of the gods. He skipped over the contradiction between the conceptual "Emperor" and the conceptual *samurai* (a *samurai* was to die for his feudal lord not for the Emperor). Indeed, to achieve his purposes, Mishima was never afraid of making contradictory speeches. When he spoke of "dying for the tradition," it was not a figure of speech. He saw his death as the only way to crystallize his existence into beauty, into "a poem." In so doing he felt he was keeping faith with the tradition of Japanese art, a tradition in which beauty of form is achieved by halting change, by dying: "I was beginning to plan a union of art and life, of style and the ethos of action," a union which was to be achieved only at the moment of death (*Sun and Steel*, 47).

He continued by explaining that there were:

two contradictory tendencies within myself. One was the de-

termination to press ahead loyally with the corrosive function of
words, and to make that my life's work. The other was the desire
to en-counter reality in some field where words should play no part
at all. (*Sun and Steel*, 9)

We can surmise from these quotations that Mishima wished to join the sword with
the pen, his life with his art, to be both a *samurai* and a writer. Mishima had never
before dreamed of the possibility of combining words and actions in one person,
of being a man of letters and a warrior, or both a seer and a doer.[3]

In Mishima the horror was that his absorption in physical activities, his
decision to become a fanatic nationalist, and his frantic advocacy of the unity of
art and life, which were for him incompatible except at the moment of death, were
all being watched by his own cold, objective eyes—eyes which were always
aware of the utter uselessness of his frantic attempts. Toward the end of his life,
he publicly proclaimed that human existence should not be "in the progressive
tense" because the process of becoming inherently lacks stylistic perfection.
Proclaiming that only the weak allow them to be time-bound, he wrote:

The fact that life dilutes expression, robs the real preciseness from
expression, everybody is aware of. . . . When living men are driven
to hopelessness in trying to express this, again and again it is
beauty that comes rushing in to save them. It is beauty that teaches
that one must stand one's ground firmly among the impressions of
life. (*Forbidden Colors*, 400)

He condemned the Japan of his day for persisting in "stylistic confusion." For him,
every phenomenon should be precise and perfect in its presentation. He, who had
suffered from the "sickness" of perfection in his theory and in his works, could
not perceive the possibility of opening himself to imperfection by the act of living
and writing in the real world. As a writer, Mishima had never dreamed of the
possibility of catching life in its fluidity as Faulkner attempted to do.

To catch life in the process of becoming, Faulkner consciously avoided
making his writing stylistically perfect. He aimed to open his writings to imperfection, desiring to make his "failure grandiose by attempting the impossible."
In this respect, also, these two writers are at opposite extremes. Mishima's
obsession with perfection had imprisoned him within his own world and led him

to deny every humanistic value except beauty, and even that was seen as stasis. On the other hand, Faulkner's commitment to imperfection left him open to accepting life with all its stylistic confusion and enabled him to create literary works that tried to help man pursue living.

The Sea of Fertility, Mishima's tetralogy, forms his epitaph for himself. In the four novels, an observer, Honda, watches the transmigration of the hero through four characters. The first character personifies romanticism; the second, fanaticism; the third, sensualism, and the fourth, an ever-conscious objectivism. Finally, all are absorbed into nothingness, into the inner "sea of fertility." In *Spring Snow*, the first novel in the series, Mishima crystallizes his romanticism into an extreme stylistic beauty. Kiyoaki, the hero, is determined to live only for his emotions: "The only thing that seemed valid to him was to live for the emotions—gratuitous and unstable, dying only to quicken again, dwindling and flaring without direction or purpose" (*Spring Snow*, 15). Only by attempting the impossible—specifically, by breaking the prohibition against loving Satoko, engaged to a prince of the imperial family—can he give shape to his emotions and elevate them to the level of passion. He becomes a doer for the first time in his life and dies as a beautiful young warrior on the battlefield of love.

In *Runaway Horses*, the second novel in the series, Isao, the incarnation of Kiyoaki, lives only to act out the idea of purity; his world is filled with action. To sustain his purity he feels that he has to die for the Emperor, the moral center of Japan. Failing in this experiment to personify purity, though, he kills himself after assassinating Kurahara, a minor character who is a successful businessman: "Death in success, death in failure—death was the basis of Isao's acts" (*The Temple of Dawn*, 87). The third incarnation in *The Temple of Dawn* is in the form of a Siamese princess, Ying Chan, symbolizing absolute flesh, one who drifts from one sensual experience to another. Each of the three dies at the age of twenty, their young deaths emphasizing their eligibility for reincarnation.

In the fourth book, *The Decay of the Angel*, however, we meet a character not eligible for reincarnation—Toru, the adopted son of Honda. Toru, like Honda, is an observer, but unlike his father he is motivated by contempt. He views himself as aligned with the gods of evil. When, though, it is proven that he is not the chosen of the gods of evil, he tries to commit suicide. However, he survives, deprived of his eyesight, the moral center of his existence. Such a mere observer is not entitled to die young. In this final book of *The Sea of Fertility*, the reader also learns that the whole tetralogy is really the story of Honda, who has always suffered from the "illness" of objectivity and self-awareness. A cursed observer, he has always been excluded from action, always unable to participate in life.

In *The Decay of the Angel*, Mishima reaches the place where he can no longer believe even in his unchangeable point of reference, beauty. In this novel, for instance, a mad girl who is extremely ugly believes that she is beautiful. What, then, is beauty? Mishima concludes that there is no absolute standard by which to judge beauty:

> Toru always enjoyed her absence. When such ugliness became absent, how did it differ from beauty? Since the beauty which had been the premise for the whole conversation was itself absent, Kinué continued to pour forth fragrance after she was gone. (*The Decay of the Angel*, 83)

Mishima abandons his stronghold of "beauty," the only principle by that he has lived and written.

In the final pages of *The Decay of the Angel*, Honda seeks out Satoko, now an aged reverend nun. She denies ever having known Kiyoaki. The whole story of reincarnation and transmigration thus crumbles:

> He spoke loudly, as if to retrieve the self that receded like traces of breathes vanishing from a lacquer tray. 'If there was no Kiyoaki, then there was no Isao. There was no Ying Chan, and who knows, perhaps there has been no I.' (*The Decay of the Angel*, 235)

Is human existence, then, a shadow, a phantom, remembered only in the hearts of those who choose to remember? There is only nothingness in the last scene of the tetralogy. When Mishima says, through Honda, that "Perhaps there has been no I," he includes himself as well as Honda.

Mishima, bereft of any means of coping with the void, determined to act with madness in order to exterminate himself by dying a warrior's death, by dying for the conceptual Emperor. Mishima handed the manuscript of the last volume of the tetralogy to his editor on the day he killed himself: "That is the ultimate vision, the denial at the end of all seeing, the eye's denial of itself" (*The Decay of the Angel*, 146). After his death, his bloody corpse, beheaded according to the *samurai* tradition, hardly looked poetic. No one can tell if Mishima felt finally existed at the moment of death.

Mishima endeavored to grasp his selfhood in isolation and to make himself exist in relief, as it were, against the background of death. He wished to cut himself off from everything that conditioned his existence, an existence that proved to be nothing when consciousness tried to catch it. He refused to admit that human existence is fluid, always incomplete, and that it can be shaped only by growing into the outer world. He rejected the only possible way of verifying existence—through relations with other beings even though any hope of succeeding in relating with others is uncertain. Mishima lived and died true to a tradition devoted to order, obsessed with stylistic perfection, and therefore devoid of any space for hoping and searching. No other writer so personified the difficulty of living as a Japanese person than Mishima. Through his death and dying, he presented himself as a self-sacrificing lamb, a self-immolating martyr to negativity.

3.   Masks and Unmasking in O'Neill
From *The Great God Brown* to *The Iceman Cometh*

> For what, at bottom, is the new psychological insight into
> human cause and effect but a study in masks, an exercise in
> unmasking? . . . One's outer life passes in a solitude haunted
> by the masks of others; one's inner life passes in a solitude
> hounded [sic] by the masks of oneself. "Memoranda on
> Masks," 3.

In *The Great God Brown*, written in 1925, O'Neill uses actual masks. By manipulating those masks, O'Neill studies the nature of human character as it is formed in the dichotomy of one's masked self and one's real self. By moving the mask, he also dramatizes the transference of a part of one's personality to another. The manipulation of masks becomes disorganized, however, and the playwright's idea begins to become a muddle. Fearing that people would not understand his intentions, O'Neill sent a poetic explanation to the press. Below I will touch upon the salient features of this letter.[1]

The play is made deliberately unrealistic not only by the use of masks, but also by having one character frequently address another in the third person, serving to distance the action. This technique is employed to show that a man cannot communicate directly with others since he is alienated from others by the mask he wears. Each locked behind his own mask, humans live in a hostile world. Of the four characters who wear masks, Dion Anthony and William A. Brown are presented as composites of conflicting forces, while Margaret and Cybel are symbols, as will later be explained by O'Neill himself. The use of the device enables O'Neill to show, for instance, the conflict between the opposing forces embodied in a person through the study of the discrepancies between Dion's mask and his real face and dramatizes the transferability of human personality by showing the visual transference of Dion's mask to Brown.

Dion Anthony wears a mask—or, rather, he has two faces, that of Dionysus and that of Saint Anthony. Of Dion, O'Neill says that in him "the creative pagan acceptance of life" is "fighting eternal war with the masochistic, life-denying spirit of Christianity" (Clark, 105). Under the influence of Nietzsche, O'Neill first names these two opposing forces Paganism and Christianity. O'Neill projects himself onto Dion, a young artist in revolt against the defeatism that Catholicism has deeply embedded within him. O'Neill tells us that a man's character is formed in the conflict between these two opposing tendencies within him. If one has to transcend oneself, the split of his or her inner being is inevitable. In a way, a conceptualized being is at war with a real being, an earth-bound creature that has given up all aspiration to live a creative life. When the upward movement of creativity ceases, the resultant reality brings a deathlike sterility. Thus, in this drama, an inner struggle between two masks is the destiny of all creative people, especially of male artists.

Dion was born hypersensitive: "Why was I born without a skin, O God, that I must wear armour in order to touch or to be touched?"[2] In order merely to exist in society, he has to protect himself with a skin, a mask. To give a face to his sensitivity, Dion first wears the mask of Pan. As O'Neill explains: "Dion's mask of Pan which he puts on as a boy is not only a defense against the world for the supersensitive painter-poet underneath it, but also an integral part of his character as the artist" (Clark, 105). Dion tells us, "When Pan was forbidden the light and warmth of the sun he grew sensitive and self-conscious and proud and revenge-ful" (67). Dion as Pan originally aspires to become a painter, one who paints the beauty of nature, but this aspiration is distorted; instead, he becomes an architect who designs commercial buildings, thus becoming a servant of material success. As his mask undergoes a change from Pan into Mephistopheles, Dion's architectural designs become a skillfully concealed blasphemy of every faith.

In the first scene:

> *The mask is a fixed forcing of his own face—dark, spiritual, poetic, passionately supersensitive, helplessly unprotected in its childlike, religious faith in life—into the expression of a mocking, reckless, defiant, gaily scoffing and sensual young Pan.* (11)

The polarity between the two faces grows as the scenes unfold: ascetic and Mephistopheles, saint and Satan. The more the inner face becomes resigned and fixed in its resolute withdrawal from life along the path of Christian retrogression, the more defiant, mocking, and devilish becomes the outside mask needed by Dion to confront the world.

Dion wishes Margaret, his love, to be his skin and his armor because if she was he would be able to throw away his mask of defense. However, Margaret loves Dion's mask of Pan and refuses to recognize the naked sensitivity underneath it. As O'Neill explains:

> Margaret is my image of the modern direct descendant of the Marguerite of Faust—the eternal girl-woman with a virtuous simplicity of instinct, properly oblivious to everything but the means to her end of maintaining the race. (Clark, 104)

Margaret ignores Dion's real suffering face—the one that forces him to wear Pan's mask as a defense, since only the mask, the Pan part of him, represents the pagan, life-giving force that is the means of "maintaining the race." The result is that only through the mask of Pan can Dion communicate with Margaret. She watches Dion's outer Pan mask being slowly transformed into Mephistopheles. She accepts the mask's change with bewilderment, but still with love. (Why Dion as Satan still loved and admired leaves me not quite convinced).

Only in the company of Cybel can Dion expose his inner self:

> Cybel is an incarnation of Cybele, the Earth Mother doomed to segregation as a pariah in a world of unnatural laws, but patronized

by her segregators, who are thus themselves the first victims of their laws. (Clark, 104-05)

An Earth Mother wearing the mask of a prostitute shows nature segregated from society in this unnatural world, as is a prostitute, with whom men try to find life-giving power in temporary sexual ecstasy. In Cybel, to whom he can reveal his real face, Dion finds a sanctuary. However, Cybel comforts Dion by promising that he will find peace in dying, not by endowing him with the energy to navigate the maze of life. Here Cybel seems to personify the comfort of death rather than "the creative pagan acceptance of life." Yet, under the influence of Cybel, Dion's inner face is supposed to reflect a new quality, the ultimate spiritual value of love and peace.

Still, it is only by means of his proud mask that Dion can communicate with others; it is his pride that sustains the mask. He sustains his mask by proud assertion, by making himself into Mephistopheles. The dying Dion tries to laugh proudly since proud laughter is "Man's last gesture"(70). However, he cannot sustain his proud, Mephistophelean self so he finally reveals his Christian martyr's face and asks for forgiveness.

While Dion, with his two faces, lives alienated in an antagonistic bourgeois culture, Brown is:

> the visionless demi-god of our new materialistic myth—a Success—building his life of exterior things, inwardly empty and resourceless, an uncreative creature of superficial preordained social grooves, a by-product forced aside into slack waters by the deep main current of life-desire. (Clark, 105)

The fact that Brown does not wear a mask is natural because he has only one face, that of social conformity. He is always envious of Dion's creative power and his ability to be loved. It is ironic that Brown gives Dion creative power by forcing him to wear the mask of Pan to protect himself from Brown's cruelty. Brown, who has tried at every possible opportunity to steal everything from Dion, inherits Dion's mask.

If one's particular mode of behavior presents itself as that of a particular character or a personality—fluid and in continual transformation—one can present different personalities by borrowing or stealing different modes of interaction. As O'Neill remarks of Brown, "When he steals Dion's mask of Mephistopheles he thinks he is gaining the power to live creatively" (Clark, 105). Yet, to adapt the mask of creativity, he also has to inherit the self-splitting agony of creation. The mask holds a magic power over the wearer; indeed, the mask possesses the owner. Brown now has come to have three faces: Dion's mask, that of a successful businessman, and his real face, *"tortured and distorted by the demon of Dion's mask"* (79). Moreover, Brown does not have a comforter to console him because Cybel presents only her mask of a prostitute to him. Through Margaret, whose love Brown desires, he comes to hate his uncreative, unloved Brown self. The tension of living with three faces results in a laughter, which grows increasingly neurotic. His laughter is a sign of his inner suffering. As he says, "Man is born broken. He lives by mending. The grace of God is glue!" (100-01). Brown, who has lost faith in material success, has no glue with which to mend his broken self.

Brown, in dying, suddenly comes to believe in life, that man must go through pain to find God: "in the end out of this anguish his soul is born, a tortured Christian soul such as the dying Dion's, begging for belief, and at the last finding it on the lips of Cybel" (Clark, 105). O'Neill's bold experiment in using masks to probe the depths of the human soul is drowned in the complexity of mask manipulation. The study of the opposing forces within man half-forgotten, the play ends in an abrupt affirmation of God: "I have found Him! I hear Him speak! 'Blessed are they that weep, for they shall laugh!'" (108). By having both Dion and Brown die as Christian martyrs, however, O'Neill did not mean that "the masochistic, life-denying spirit of Christianity" has won over "the creative pagan acceptance of life." In this way Cybel is intended to personify "certainty in life for its own sake"(Clark, 104). O'Neill seems to have found the "pagan acceptance of life" in Christianity; we are left in mid-air at Brown's abruptly finding the Christian God, hitherto considered to be life-denying and uncreative, and at his "finding it on the lips of Cybel," the pagan Earth Mother (Clark, 105). In *The Great God Brown*, O'Neill certainly made an in-coherent affirmation of God.

When, in 1946, O'Neill comes to produce *The Iceman Cometh*, he abandons the use of actual masks and instead developed a successful exercise in symbolic unmasking. The characters do not have masks but illusions about themselves, "pipe dreams." O'Neill questions what is left when one is deprived of one's illusions. *The Iceman Cometh* is a profound orchestration of unmasking, with its themes and variations beautifully interwoven. In this unmasking exercise, O'Neill confronts the nature of human existence.

Harry Hope's saloon, O'Neill's "lower depths," is a symbolic universe in which people work to exist behind their pipe dreams. Each character lives from day to day, striving to maintain a self-image nourished by his pipe dream. As Larry, a former anarchist, says, "The lie of a pipe dream is what gives life to the whole misbegotten mad lot of us, drunk or sober. . . ."[3] When this illusory self-image is ripped off, what is left? Nothing. Only by acting according to a self-image and by accepting the illusions others have of themselves can we manage—barely—to sustain the appearance of life having purpose.

Harry Hope and the patrons of his saloon provide many examples of the basic theme that is being orchestrated. All of them are human derelicts who retain dreams that keep them going. Each had been apprenticed to an ideal, a cause for which he had worked: politics, the circus, power, law, gambling, reporting, commanding battles, or anarchism. Each having pursued human possibility in his or her own way, and each having lost in his or her endeavors, each has become a failure. They are now sojourners in "the Palace of Pipe Dreams." Each is distinguished from the others only by his particular pipe dream. (No woman is found in this universe except whores, and only Parritt's mother, who vaguely reflects Emma Goldman, is presented as not having been confined to the relationships with men).

The roomers keep up their spirits by identifying themselves with what they are called—the "one time" such-and-such and, therefore, the "future" such-and-such. Rocky and the two prostitutes add a slight variation to this theme. Rocky claims to be a bartender, not a pimp, while the girls say they are not whores, just "tarts." Chuck and Cora also can deny that the one is a pimp and the other a whore by maintaining the illusion of becoming husband and wife some day. By so naming themselves, they can create what they consider a warm relationship. Names have a magic power that takes possession of their owners.

In order to shape the life he conceives of as most desirable, each of them glorifies or distorts the past because each has memories he wants to erase from his consciousness. This memory of the adjusted past enables each to dream about a tomorrow which never comes, a tomorrow in which they will be restored to the past glory as it is given form in the distorted images of their past selves. They see the lie in the dreams of others, while failing to see that in their own. Yet, each has a secret knowledge of what he really is; he knows he is lost and finished. Each lives in the tension between his real self and his wished-for self. Each keeps up appearance by pretending to be something he is not. Joe, a former gambling joint owner, says: "Don't you get it in your heads I's pretendin' to be what I ain't, or dat I ain't proud to be what I is, get me?" (97). Yet, after all, is it not that human existence is given coherence by one's endeavor to become what he is not? Each of their endeavors embodies the paradox that is man.

They avoid solitude, which would force them to face their real selves. Only in the company of those who tolerate their self-images, their wished-for selves, are they able to sustain their illusions. The sustenance of self-image is made possible by mutual understanding and cooperation. Hugo, the one-time editor of anarchist periodicals, for instance, has served ten years in prison. Even if disdain for his beloved proletariat occasionally surfaces, his self-image as a hero who has sacrificed his life for the cause is tolerated by the others. They consider Hugo to have earned his dream. He is, they feel, entitled to dream away his remaining life as a former hero. In this community where each accepts the other's dream in mutual tolerance, there is "the beautiful calm in the atmosphere" (27).

Thus, in the agreement to call each other by the names each wishes to be called, they live in reasonable harmony. This harmony is, however, destroyed when Hickey, a hardware salesman, comes into their world with a challenge that makes them face their grim realities. When Hickey brings them face-to-face with what they really are, their masks fall away. If their memory of the past is proved to be false and unsustainable, they can no longer build a dream of tomorrow. Today, no longer protected by the memory of a glorious past, is therefore cut off as the root of "tomorrow's movement"; their present selves become meaningless.

Only by the act of reaching out to tomorrow, by conceptualizing themselves in terms of the future, can they have the sense of living in the present; only by having "lousy pipe dreams about tomorrow" can people live today. Hickey brings with him an inhuman doctrine, the peace of death; he has denied them the sense of being alive. Joe, the one-time proprietor of a Negro gambling house, voices the feelings of them all: "Scuse me for livin'." The objectivity which Hickey has brought with him proves to be death, a sense of the nothingness of human existence.

Hickey comes to sell the peace he thinks he has found by killing his own pipe dream, which for him was personified by his wife. She never gave up the pipe dream of his being reformed tomorrow, and her eternal forgiveness reduced

Hickey to the state of a dirty sinner unable to find a moment's peace with himself. His wife represented Hickey's conscience. By killing her, by killing her pipe dream, Hickey claims he can be his real self. Hickey believes that he has killed his wife to save her from the pain of loving him. Since his professed motivation is love, his act of murder seems to have been an act of love. The sense of having risked his own life in an act of love, even if it is an act of murder, allows Hickey to elevate himself to the role of a savior.

Yet, instead of finding peace by killing the illusion that haunted him, he has, in fact, acquired the still greater illusion of having sacrificed his life in an act of love. Imposing upon himself the image of a savior whose time is short, Hickey forces the others to face their present situation, promising, "You'll be in a today where there is no yesterday or tomorrow to worry you" (131). The elevated sense of being a savior enables Hickey to live in the present, denouncing his past and thus killing the future. When his unconscious hatred of his wife rises to the surface, Hickey's self-image crumbles. He is an unpardonable murderer. After a momentary recognition of his having lost his pipe dream, he jumps to yet other illusion—that he was mad at the moment of murder. Even on his way to his execution, Hickey cannot accept his being a murderer, a murderer whose motivation was hatred.

Larry, the one-time Syndicalist-Anarchist, warns his fellow roomers against the peace Hickey preaches: "you'd better make sure first it's the real McCoy and not poison" (81). He knows people need illusions about themselves. Larry is one who was "born condemned to be one of those who has to see all sides of a question. When you're damned like that, the questions multiply for you until in the end it's all question and no answer" (32). His ability to see the two faces of everything keeps him standing paralyzed, unable to choose between them. Larry, however, euphemizes this state of paralysis into a position of philosophical detachment.

His self-image is that of a detached philosophical bum: "I took a seat in the grandstand of philosophical detachment to fall asleep observing the cannibals do their death dance" (16). Larry takes himself to be an exception, one who does not need his own version of illusion. However, he has the grandest of all illusions—that he has no illusion. Therefore, he imagines himself free from any participation in the "death dance" of living. In reality, though, by the very fact of his being alive under his chosen mask, he is, as are we all, a participant in the mad dance of death.

In his conscious effort to be a noncommittal observer, Larry constantly fights back impulses to pity others. Jimmy, the one-time Boer War correspondent, says to him, "You pretend a bitter, cynic philosophy, but in your heart you are the kindest man among us" (45). At this point, Parritt enters to force Larry to choose between living and dying. Larry's damnation of Parritt as a Judas to the anarchist movement ends in showing his own enduring belief in anarchism. Furthermore, out of pity, Larry is forced to sentence Parritt to death. In so doing, he interferes with another's life, an act that is the most serious decision one can make. Realizing that his mask of detachment has been ripped off, Larry has no alternative illusion to turn to. He now has no way to create a life-sustaining mask: "Be God, I'm the only real convert to death Hickey made here" (222). He is left unmasked, facing death in life.

O'Neill acknowledges that humans have to fight not for something but against nothing. Self-image and self, as the dream and the dreamer, equal zero; they come to nothing. In this struggle to shape existence in the face of an all-absorbing nothingness, all one can do is to choose the mask which one wishes to wear, the one which nourishes one's own particular illusion. A man is forgiven when he justifies his past and thereby gives the appearance of meaningfulness to his present self. Yet there is a limit to the forgiveness that one can accept. If one's past contains something deadly, such as murder out of hatred, one cannot be pardoned. Parrit, for instance, who has, out of hatred, killed his mother's soul by his treachery, is not allowed to conjure up any face to exist in the present. As long as their dreams are harmless, though, they are left to create their illusory self-images out of anything they can manage. O'Neill has Larry say, "To hell with the truth! As the history of the world proves, the truth has no bearing on anything" (15). At the same time as he denies all ideals as illusions, he admits the necessity of ideals to keep people alive. If an ideal or illusion gives form to human existence, the illusion becomes the man; the quality of illusion becomes the quality of the man.

In this most nihilistic of his plays, O'Neill provides us with a glimpse of human potential by giving Harry the last name of Hope. As O'Neill says, "Goodness surmounts anything." Harry is not a hero, but he is good. He never feels superior to anyone, never refuses a drink to anyone in desperate need. O'Neill, who no longer believes in the moral superiority of any ideal, now puts simple goodness above all other values. In the community Harry presides over, people help others to exist behind the masks that each has acquired in pain. He runs "the Palace of Pipe Dreams," a communal place maintained by the mutual tolerance of role playing, of the mask each person wears. Just as Harry Hope's saloon verges on a utopia for this group of lost souls, hope can be found only in our mutual understanding and compassion.

If masks help each of us to pass through this vale of tears and sustain our today, let us wear them, however illusory they are. Such masks are to be more valued than a truth that kills; human life is to be valued for its own sake, a stand similar to that which O'Neill seemed to take at the end of *The Great God Brown*. If the truth of human reality kills, O'Neill affirms life after a life-long struggle and search for truth. Young Dion's real face, "helplessly unprotected in its child-like, religious faith in life," is glimpsed in the darkest of his plays. O'Neill, who made incoherent affirmations about God in *The Great God Brown*, in *The Iceman Cometh* succeeded in approaching God through negation. As Meister Eckhart said: The affirmations about God are incoherent, but the negations are true. In brief, God is known (that is, best known) by negation, for He is incomprehensible. (Eckhart, 27)

O'Neill must have caught hold of the attention of the young Faulkner, as he wrote an anonymous article, "American Drama: Eugene O'Neill" in *The Mississippian* in 1922, before O'Neill's major plays appeared (*The Mississippian* 5). O'Neill's religious belief in life also caught the attention of the present reader in her teens, in a land where "death is many times more vivid than life" and where writers tend to find more beauty in dying than in living in stylistic confusion (Mishima, *Forbidden Colors*, 136). O'Neill, along with Faulkner, encouraged me to hope in spite of everything, through negation.

4. *Pylon*
Faulkner's Splendid Lumber Room

Of all the neglected non-Yoknapatawpha novels of Faulkner, *Pylon* is usually considered the most unquestionable failure. Faulkner himself did not regard it highly, classifying it as a tour-de-force he wrote as a respite from the rigorous work demanded by the writing of *Absalom, Absalom!*, which he wanted to put aside for a while.[1] We have to admit that *Pylon* resists all analysis based on the presumption of canonical status and literary importance. Yet, when read with professionalism aside, one finds it a treasure house stuffed with Faulknerian elements in a state of near anarchy. Readers are allowed to have a look at his backstage area, out of which he brought forth his many brilliant performances. In this lumber room we recognize several themes not well digested or fully developed but destined to be more fully pursued in *The Wild Palms*, *As I Lay Dying*, *The Sound and the Fury*, *Light in August*, *Absalom, Absalom!*, and *A Fable*.

At the center of *Pylon*, the author places the problem of language as an inevitable condition of humankind, as he does more specifically in *As I Lay Dying* and *Absalom, Absalom!* Here, though, almost as if to embody the unstable, illusory quality of language, the narratives proceed haphazardly, with floods of imagery. It cannot be denied that *Pylon* lacks the craftsmanship of Faulkner's major works. Yet this very lack of focus and polish enables the reader to glimpse the multiple phases of Faulkner, including his moralistic element, which distinctly surfaces in his Nobel Prize acceptance speech. *Pylon* is the work of a genius with all his glittering contradictions laid bare.

A story of barnstormers, seemingly fit material for a film, *Pylon* was indeed made into a film as *Tarnished Angels* in 1938. These barnstormers, "a fantastic and bizarre phenomenon on the face of a contemporary scene, of our culture at a particular time"[2] are, however, allegorical characters. Normally little concerned with the creation of realistic characters, Faulkner tried to write prose poems that resisted visualization. Though financially supported by Hollywood, Faulkner still did not find film making attractive. For one whose literary style equated with the content of what he wrote, he must have known that film was not a fit medium for him. Therefore, in writing this story of commercial air racers, he did not tell his readers their story.

Today's readers, too, may be inclined to take the barnstormers as the central characters since the author's sympathy is more for those who live in action than for those who live in language. Words, part of the inescapable human condition before they became the medium through which works of literature were created, could do harm to humans who exist only physically, who are unable to live in abstraction. The more deeply involved one is in language, the more urgent becomes his need to confirm his physical being.

Pylon was written at the time when Faulkner was enthusiastically flying his own airplane. He did not give up flying even after his youngest brother, Dean, was killed in a crash. Much later, switching back to livestock because airplanes had become too mechanized for his taste, he jumped horses until the year he died at the age of sixty-four. Thus he kept challenging the limits of his physical capacity along with challenging the impossible in the field of literature. Hemingway, who had to shoot himself when he found himself getting immobilized, has paid homage to *Pylon*.[3] The two writers could have shared their understanding of the erosive quality of language in human life, of the difficulty of striking a balance between words and actions. I cannot imagine Faulkner with his dangerous hobbies all forbidden and no concern for such pressing social issues as human rights and nuclear war, limited only to the operation of language.

Faulkner often repeated that he was a farmer who happened also to write. Farmers support human bodies, which occupy particular spaces at particular times, while artists work in the hope of giving nourishment to their souls. "One cannot live by bread alone" paradoxically says that, without food, no soul can survive. To find moral support for his creative activity, which enabled him to pose as a farmer, Faulkner needed to say that he was primarily a farmer. In his obstinate insistence, we can see that he was a writer in peril of losing his physicality—that is, his life. To support himself and his family Faulkner was forced to sell literary works as consumer goods, to take part in what he called "orthodox prostitution."[4]

The question arises here whether literature can be distinguished from other kinds of commercial writing, other sorts of prostitution. In *Pylon* the author masochistically projects himself upon the reporter, who aspires to become a writer. In reporting, manifest in the language of journalism, what happens in human life becomes an account dedicated to create "any reaction excitement or irritation on any human retina."[5] Not only reporting but any professional writing carries a risk: "without knowing it you listen and see in one language and then do what you call writing in another" (43).

In *Absalom* the validity of language as narrative, as a tool for telling stories, is discussed extensively; the question is whether or not overlapping narratives can form a coherent story. The author only said he had a need to get away from *Absalom* by writing another book, but the fact is that *Pylon* shows us how the sharply focused *Absalom* came to be written. The author freely stuffs his multiple themes in *Pylon*, thus deflating himself, as it were, so that in *Absalom* he could concentrate on narrative. The space was also narrowed down to Yokna-patawpha, his own cosmos, which he knew from corner to corner. He was to rewrite almost all of *Dark House*, the predecessor of the present *Absalom, Absalom!*, in which every narrator cries, "I am here!" each in his own style, and in which telling becomes living.[6]

Pylon tells what happened in the five days before Easter. A quasi-omniscient narrator, through the use of rather unstable, wavering points of view, tells the story. Mardi Gras, a festival no longer part of the official Church calendar, is chosen as the background of *Pylon*. By using the Easter calendar as his framework, New Valois (modeled after New Orleans) is metamorphosed from a Southern city into a metropolis of the modern world; a regional tale thus becomes an Apocrypha.

In this apocryphal world, Mardi Gras, its true meaning lost, does not proceed to Easter. Faulkner, concerned with this century's separation of words from deeds, accepts Jesus, the word incarnate, and his Christian legend as "It's just there."[7] He also said: "No one is without Christianity, if we agree on what we mean by the word."[8] In Faulkner, the resurrection of Christ would be equated to the birth of an artist whose tool is language. Yet, whereas Dilsey in *The Sound and the Fury*, one who can exist in deeds with no interposition of empty words, can rejoice in the coming of Easter, here the reporter gets only a glimpse of words that can be resurrected into action, into body.

City people, having lost contact with natural time, which flows according to the rotation of the earth and the moon, act on the basis of the schedules and routines of their occupations; without coffee and the morning paper, for instance, another day cannot begin for reporters. Sundays are times for barnstormers to earn their living by racing. The earth paved, the sea filled with all mounds of refuse from the big city—earth and water have ceased to nourish humans. Only a well-controlled nature survives in the suburbs where the rich live, and in "the country life" depicted on commercial posters, all urging people not to produce but to consume. *Pylon* opens with riding boots displayed in a show window, boots that entice a misplaced natural man, Jiggs, to destroy his partners.

Money having taken the place of God, the chairman of the sewage board presides over the carnival of New Valois. Sightseers, airshow contestants with their mechanics and families, announcers, reporters—they all gather at Feinman Airport, named after its owner, the chairman of the sewage board, to serve the God of the present day. Sightseers pay to enjoy watching other people risking their lives, while racers strive to earn prize money to support themselves and their families. The voice resounding through the loudspeaker, explaining and interpreting the race everyone can see, becomes the modern environment fabricated by journalism and manipulated by corporate money. The news considered fit by the powerful is reported in the way they want it to be reported. News of a death in a racing accident is printed in bold black gothic type in order to make the oncoming races more exciting, more sensational. The reporter, incapable of bringing in the news required, stands or runs in the center of this apocryphal world.

The reporter is not identified by his personal name, but is, rather, called a "scarecrow," "apparition," "skeleton," or "corpse." He moves:

> without contact with earth, like one of those apocryphal nighttime
> batcreatures whose nest or home no man ever saw, which are seen

only in midswoop caught for a second in a lightbeam between nothing and nowhere. (77)

By giving this "batcreature" the name "X," signifying the unknown, the author seems to have equipped him with some unknown, ghost-like capacity of turning into a figure who, like a ghost, goes beyond other humans with their "restrictions of flesh and time" (171). Also, the names of such anti-heroic heroes as Don Quixote and Lazarus—one a moralist in action though weak and foolish, the other risen from the dead—are casually mentioned in connection with the reporter.

Rushing about the city in "a last and cheerful stage of what old people call galloping consumption," the reporter is found wherever most people are (41). Shumann recognizes in him a "patron (even if no guardian) saint of all waifs, all the homeless the desperate and the starved" (183). The reporter tries to help Laverne, a boy, and Shumann, not only because all these non-human-like members fascinate him, but also because he is basically one who cannot say "He aint our brother" even if he wants to (238). Faulkner seems to be telling us that, in this Quixotesque chivalry, the reporter's impulse to do something for those in despair, hides the embryo of his growing into a writer, a writer with a "mindless and unflagging optimism to explain to someone" that he can communicate by means of the inadequate tool of language (262). Hagood, a graduate from an elite university, confines his creative activity to golf courses. This editor, against his own desire, helps the reporter when he is unable to bring in the information needed because he too recognizes some moral force in him which Hagood has somehow lost in the pursuit of his trade.

The reporter has not even a room that can be called his residence, but only a room like a theater morgue, filled with impractical, useless junk. Only after he has met the barnstormers, whose nights' lodgings depend on the prize money they earn that day, does he realize that one needs a place to live, a place to stay, if one is to create something. He learns that a residence is not a place meant for dreaming beyond the horizon, but one in which to endure today and tomorrow. Here, the author, in his poetic language, touches on another big issue of creating and living:

It would be there—the eternal smell of the coffee the sugar the
hemp sweating slow iron plates above the forked deliberate brown

> water and lost lost lost all ultimate blue of latitude and horizon . . .
> the ten thousand inescapable mornings . . . the thin black coffee,
> the myriad fish stewed in a myriad oil—tomorrow and tomorrow
> and tomorrow; not only not to hope, not even to wait: just to
> endure. (284)

Faulkner, "a vagabond by nature," worked and died in the land where he was born. He felt the need to have a permanent residence if his creative activity was to flourish. Not only did he need a residence, but also, I am compelled to believe, that Faulkner used his family for his writing career. Shumann, a barnstormer, damned and with no ties, could be the author himself; Faulkner had his need to create a friendly ghost named X in the vague hope of someday his (the author's) entering into "the range of God."

The reporter and Jiggs, a mechanic, form a Don Quixote-Sancho Panza-like partnership in the "Lovesong of J. A. Prufrock" chapter, one is a knight who hitches his wagon to a star, while the other serves as that knight's hands and feet. If the reporter is words not fully embodied, Jiggs is pure body with little spirituality. This Jiggs also represents one side of the author, for he succumbs to the temptation of liquor when he knows he should not:

> All he heard now was that thunderous silence and solitude in
> which man's spirit crosses the eternal repetitive rubicon of his vice
> in the instant after the terror and before the triumph becomes
> dismay—the moral and spiritual waif shrieking his feeble I-am-I
> into the desert of chance and disaster. He raised the jug . . . (118-
> 19)

Jiggs' treasured riding boots are transformed into a huge box of candies and three magazines: *The Ladies' Home Journal* for the homeless Laverne, *Boy's Life* for an orphan, and a pulp magazine of war stories for a jumper. Jiggs' love and sacrifice take the form of useless, unwelcome gifts, as useless and unwelcome as writers' gifts sometimes are for readers.

The reporter and Shumann form a contrast:

> the one volatile, irrational, with his ghostlike quality of being
> beyond all mere restrictions of flesh and time; the other single-

> purposed, fatally and grimly without any trace of introversion or
> any ability to objectivate or ratiocinate, as though like the engine,
> the machine for which he apparently existed . . . . (171-72)

In short, the reporter embodies words, while Shumann embodies actions. The
reporter externalizes himself in words to excess—impotent, only a shape without
substance, like a balloon blowing in the wind, a scarecrow about to disintegrate. If
he joined force with Shumann, whose very existence is externalized in action, the
two could form a perfect union, a union capable of changing the impossible into
the possible.

However, this union of the reporter, who aches to act, and Shumann in
desperate need of money, brings about disaster. Upon Shumann's death, the
reporter has an irrepressible urge to explain himself. Here, he wishes to have a
language with which to communicate. When he acquires "that mindless and
unflagging optimism" that people will understand if he just explains, the reporter
begins to turn into a writer (262). If this appeal for understanding moves artists to
express themselves, each through his or her chosen method, the creation of art
will be a love song sung in various styles.

In the process, a man of words with little physical substance comes to
know the taste of tears—the water in which inner feelings are externalized
without any recourse to words. The reporter is gaining physicality in the process
of growing into a writer; he begins to live in his body. Moreover, if he is to live
totally in the money-oriented world, he has no way but to make an offering of
himself in the form of dollars.

Paper money, the sacrificial offering of the reporter and of many others, is
burned to ashes by the enraged might-be-grandfather of the boy. With it dis-
appears the reporter's wish to see Laverne and her grown-up son again. With his
sacrifice, the denial of his whole being, all he *did* and *is* comes to nothing. Drunk,
after a whole day's abstinence, the reporter writes two articles on Shumann's
death: one in the flowery language of literature, the other as a modestly accurate
account of the incident. Throwing the literary one in a wastebasket, he leaves the
news account along with a demand for an advance on his salary on the editor's
desk when he leaves for a drinking spree. His determination to endure this day
destroyed, he closes with his own hands the gate to becoming a real writer.

Two decades later we find him in *A Fable* as the runner, again with no
personal name, but again as one who tries to "do something" in the face of the

reality of a world at war. The reporter is a forerunner of the Christ figure who rose on the battlefield of the First World War and the indomitable runner who carries on this Christ's peace movement (Tao, 208-29).

Laverne, the complete woman, neither wife nor mother in any family, attracts every male who comes in contact with her. Faulkner often equates femininity with passiveness, and masculinity with activeness. Typically, only once does Laverne take the initiative, and that time is in lovemaking. Her presence shows that the goddess of fertility—Eros incarnated—can prove her fertility by becoming a mother. To live the contradictory roles of goddess and mother, she has no way but to damn herself as a bad woman and a bad mother; in turn, she spoils every one around her. Her femininity can thrive in her transitory life, moving from race to race, but motherhood requires a place to live. She aspires not to have the airplane that the reporter goes to much trouble to get for them, but rather a place of her own: "And all I want is just a house, a room; a cabin will do, a coalshed where I can know that next Monday and the Monday after that and the Monday after that . . . " (165).

Her child's name, Jack Shumann (combination of the jumper's first name and Shumann's family name), tells us that he does not know who his father is. This child is more or less motherless as well as fatherless. He, a born orphan, has to talk of each of the three adults near him in the third person, not by means of any term of relationship. When Laverne acts out "the bright plain shape of love," she has to desert her son (235). The author casually has this boy meet a fate no less tragic than that of Joe Christmas, who also does not know who he is in *Light in August*. The author's vision seems to become blurred when he is trapped in his male aspiration for the eternal woman.

The reporter also is a born orphan, one who does not know his father and who gives his mother a present for her third or fourth marriage. Fatally attracted to Laverne, he is drawn to this orphan born in a hangar, a child in whom cylinder oil, not human blood, is supposed to flow. The reporter's mother, another earth mother (of "the rich foul unchaste earth"), spends all her locomotive-like energy in repeated marriages (93). As Olga Vickery has pointed out in 1959 before the rise of the feminist movement, Faulkner admired woman as earth goddesses, an admiration that encloses women within their relationships to men (Vickery, 153).

Faulkner has long been obsessed with the basic contradiction of human love. Caddy is Eros incarnated in *The Sound and the Fury*, her presence and absence shaping the lives of her three brothers, but damned after she grows into sexuality. Eula in the trilogy is another goddess of fertility, both beautiful and damned.

In *The Wild Palms*, written right after the completion of *Absalom*, Faulkner treats this contradiction by focusing on two types of love: Eros and ethos. The story of Eros and that of ethos are told in parallel fashion, never intersecting with each other, unlike passages in a fugue. We can see that the author's sympathy is more for those who lose everything in their wish to keep Eros in its pure form. In *The Wild Palms*, Charlotte chooses to abort the fruit of her erotic love in her attempt to keep the spirit of Eros intact. The question posed and left unanswered in *Pylon* is relentlessly and beautifully developed in *The Wild Palms*.

Faulkner describes the time of the barnstormers as:

> That time of those frantic little aeroplanes which dashed around the country and people wanted just enough money to live, to get to the next place to race again. Something frenetic and in a way almost immoral about it. That they were outside the range of God, not only of respectability, of love, but of God too. That they had escaped the compulsion of accepting a past and a future, that they were—they had no past. (Gwynn and Blotner, 36)

In *The Sound and the Fury*, the author presents his metaphysics, his idea that, for humans, living is to fill the present moment with deeds. Here he says one with no past is outside the range of God. Why are those who stake their lives on a few minutes in the air, who live for only the present moment, immoral? The author has the reporter, a batcreature with no nest, explain that barnstormers are almost immoral because they have no place to go back to: "They aint human, you see. No ties; no place where you were born and have to go back to it now and then even if it's just only to hate the damn place good and comfortable for a day or two" (46). Faulkner went through the rigors of living as a heretic in his own homeland, while Henry James, T. S. Eliot, and Graham Greene chose to live their entire adult life as exiles. Even Hemingway and F. Scott Fitzgerald are considered to have been exiles for crucial periods in their adult lives. Faulkner feels entitled to define one with no ties, no responsibility for his people and land, as immoral.

Roger Shumann's father is a country doctor whose calling is to cure other people's bodies and to help new life come into the world with his dependable medical arts. Against his father's wishes, Shumann stakes his life on pursuing speed in a risky vehicle. Speed achieves a beautiful shape of living in an instant, but flying for the sake of speed is self-conclusive, an act which does not reach others except as something to be watched. Those who strive to achieve beauty for beauty's sake, without desiring communication with others, reside not in the domain of God, but in that of the Devil. At the same time, though, the author, considering speed as a human achievement, aspires for this domain where language cannot enter.[9] This ambivalence in his approach makes *Pylon* inaccessible. The author puts himself in a complex position when he stands with his "modest Q.B. wings" innocently pinned on the lapel of his coat.[10]

Shumann's span of time contracts to an instant in the air; he spends all his remaining hours preparing for it. Basically self-conclusive, he does not have and does not need human ties if he, a medical doctor's son, takes good physical care of his partners. As Laverne is just another of his co-workers, one who happens to be a woman, Shumann is little affected by sharing her with Jack, a jumper. If he eventually succumbs to the titles of husband and father, he yet remains a group leader. Human ties and institutional roles often overlap each other. He lives the role of a man, but he refuses to play the roles assigned to him as a member of a family. Thus, he provides two possible fathers to little Jack, a situation more devastating than no father at all, and leaves a possible grandson to his aged father.

Since a tie comes from accepting responsibility for those who come into one's life, he who negates natural ties has no place to occupy. Shumann's decision to fly a defective airship to earn prize money prepares the way for him to turn his place over to Jack, who fathered the child-to-be. Shumann knows that Jack, unable to allow the reporter to come near Laverne, is ready to accept natural ties, to take up the roles of husband and father. When his airplane disintegrates in the air, Shumann uses his last ounce of control to crash into the water instead of shooting down onto the stands packed with people. A barnstormer condemned by the author as outside the range of God finally does offer himself, sacrifice himself for others. His sacrifice prompts many people, at least for a while, to do something for others.

Ord, now a partner in an aircraft corporation, also flies an airplane he has himself assembled, but without risking his life for prize money. He builds a home, a place to confirm family ties, and enjoys keeping records of his flight. He uses language only to support his actions and does what needs to be done with what he has at hand. In him Faulkner might be presenting his own impossible dream of becoming a well-balanced person.

In 1950, a year in which Faulkner was making slow progress with *A Fable* and in which he received the Nobel Prize for Literature, Faulkner made it clear that the reporter in *Pylon* is Everyman:

> He had no name. He was not anonymous: he was every man. I think that every young man, no matter how ugly—dwarf, freak, cripple, halitosis, all—has once in him the capacity for one great love and sacrifice for love, to a loved one, a beloved. . . . That: what he did. Tragic, sad, true; but better than nothing. In fact, the best is not to be loved, but to love . . . . (*Selected Letters*, 301)

In the "Lovesong of J. A. Prufrock" chapter, everyone vaguely anticipates "the midnight bells from town which would signal the beginning of Lent" (247). Those touched by Shumann's sacrifice all sing tenderly to their fellow humans. The photographer and a policeman take gentle care of the reporter, understanding his needs; Ord lets the check signed by Shumann's father's name burn; sightseers in their automobiles turn their head lights to the water where Shumann's airplane fell, the line extending for almost a mile along the shore without break; Jack, expressing thanks for the first time, offers half the money he has earned jumping to be sent to Shumann's father; the proprietor of a restaurant stand won't let Laverne pay and loans a tarpaulin to the reporter for warmth; Hagood offers a large sum of money, with little hope of recovering it; the alcoholic Jiggs turns himself into "a man trying to herd a half dozen blind sheep through a passage a little wider than he could span with his extended arms," becoming a Christ-like figure, and the reporter makes himself into an offering (251).

We pass through this life in an instant and are forgotten. None knows if it is worth the trouble to endure the agony and sweat. As if to answer this, in the final chapter the author has the reporters join in singing a love song in chorus, though not quite in unison: "They were trying to do what they had to do, with what they had to do it with, the same as all of us only maybe a little better than us. At least without squealing and bellyaching" (290). Similarly, Faulkner did what he could with what he had when he wrote *Pylon*. He exposed his heart, so in conflict with itself, to be seen by every stranger. Allowing us to look into his lumber room, this giant Everyman gives his readers another of his gifts, *Pylon*.

5. *The Wild Palms*
Two Types of Love

In *The Wild Palms*, one of Faulkner's non-Yoknapatawpha tales, two stories having no seeming connection with each other are presented in sequence. This has frustrated, even outraged, many readers, as was demonstrated in the reviews that appeared immediately after its publication (Inge, *The Contemporary Reviews*, 186-206). Criticisms finding it to be an integrated story have, however, appeared since the separate publication of the "Old Man" sections by Malcolm Cowley. The criticisms by Joseph J. Moldenhauer[1] Olga W. Vickery (Vickery, 156-66), and Hyatt Waggoner (Waggoner, 121-47) seem to be most distinctly focused. However, Moldenhauer's brilliant analysis, which finds that both stories criticize the Puritan morality of the American South, appears a little hysterical or monomaniacal to this reader, whose society is not only non-puritan but also non-Christian. Similarly, Vickery's approach, with society, individual, and nature as its keys, is quite neat, as is her wont; its very neatness seems to have somewhat distracted her from her usual meritorious reading—close to the text, not using it for critical performance. Waggoner bases his analysis on Faulkner's own concept of the story as illustrating "two types of love."

I presented an earlier paper with "two types of love" as its subtitle;[2] now, two decades later, I am inclined to wonder if the subtitle ought not to be called "two types of love by men." *The Wild Palms* now seems, that is, the story of two types of men and their loves, or rather the dual aspects of male love embodied respectively in the cerebral man and the physical man. The two women, who are only watched, listened to and touched by the men, similarly represent two types of females—the mentally oriented woman and the physically oriented woman— destined to be admired by or to amaze men respectively.

Two men, a medical intern named Harry Wilbourne and a tall convict without name, live not exactly unhappily, but at least safely, in a strictly ordered world. Driven out of their respective havens, one from his hospital and the other from his prison, they are thrown into a storm, metaphysical for one and physical for the other: Wilbourne by being chosen by Charlotte Rittenmeyer as her partner in her enterprise of love, and the tall convict by receiving the order to rescue a woman from the flooding Mississippi River, "Old Man." Each is thus exposed to a world of disorder and unpredictable changes because of a woman; each becomes prey to natural forces, of which a woman constitutes one vital component. Not only Wilbourne and the tall convict but all the men in the novel, from the "provincial" puritan doctor in the opening section through Charlotte's husband Rittenmeyer, to the plump convict in the last section, appear to be "aligned, embattled and doomed and lost, before the entire female principle."[3] Indeed the book ends with the tall convict exclaiming, "Women—!"

The Wild Palms includes both the "Wild Palms" story and the "Old Man" story. Palm trees which bear no fruit, offer no shade, and only make a dry, wild, bitter sound, provide readers with the essential background to the whole novel. About the unnamed tall convict and the woman in the "Old Man" section, Faulkner has said:

> To me the story was simply for background effect and they didn't need names, they just needed to be people in motion doing the exact opposite thing to the tragedy of Harry and Charlotte in the other story. (Gwynn and Blotner, 171)

Wilbourne and the tall convict, both sheltered from "Nature the unmathematical, the overfecund, the prime disorderly and illogical and patternless spendthrift," achieve peace at the price of liberty, honor and pride, all of which make two-legged animals into humans (105). They share the same trust in words, not in their natural senses, as women do. Wilbourne has to convince himself of the idea first; only later can he act according to his ideas conceptualized in words. The tall convict, to the best of his ability, prides himself on doing what is demanded of him through the words of others (105).

Life for Harry Wilbourne, in the strictly controlled world of his hospital, is like lying "passive and almost unsentient in the womb of solitude and peace" (101). It is as if "life were to lie passively on his back as though he floated effortless and without volition upon an unreturning stream" (29). He is active only in so far as he mentally manipulates his thoughts; this poor intern's peace is kept by means of resignation, verbally disguised as free choice: "*I have repudiated money and hence love. Not abjured it, repudiated*" (30). Obsessed with time's flow as is Quentin in *The Sound and the Fury*, Wilbourne is also confounded by its numerical progression. Perhaps he is more afraid that he will fall out of step with his time since, unlike Quentin, Wilbourne has been trained to deal with the physical welfare of humans; therefore, he is unable to seek peace or perfection in death: "*You are born submerged in anonymous lockstep with the teeming anonymous myriads of your time and generation; you get out of step once, falter once, and you are trampled to death . . .*" (48).

This Wilbourne, a novice in the business of love, is chosen by Charlotte as a partner in her enterprise of love: the endeavor to keep Eros alive between man and woman. Charlotte has a spirit more "manly" than a man, encased in an intensely feminine body; she is often described as hard in her honest stare and with her strong touches. Far from being a nymphomaniac, as has been alleged by some critics, she abounds in distinctly altruistic qualities; Faulkner entrusts to Charlotte "the courage and honor and hope and pride and compassion and pity and sacrifice which have been the glory of [man's] past" (Nobel Prize acceptance speech). Instead of defiling love by pursuing the mere fulfillment of carnal desire, she chooses to fly "full-winged from the haven of respectability, into untried and unsupportive space where no shore is visible" (48).

For her, love is something hard and solid, something achieved between man and woman, hoisted into air, so to speak, outside of themselves; to keep it in its purity, they must eliminate even tenderness from their relationship. Love, shared and supported by two worthy fighters, has to be kept fresh until one of them dies. If one of them fails in the match, even for an instant, love goes stale, begins to smell bad. It is not love that dies, though, but something of value within thè man and the woman; when this dies, they no longer deserve the chance to love. As Charlotte, ever a fighter for love, says:

> 'Listen: it's got to be all honeymoon, always. For ever and ever, until one of us dies. It can't be anything else. Either heaven, or hell: no comfortable safe peaceful purgatory between for you and me to wait in until good behavior or forbearance or shame or repentance overtakes us.' (76)

(One wonders if ever there was a woman who has never wished to eliminate everything prosaic or down-to-earth from her love, from her life, if not as definitely as Charlotte.)

Drowned in the "yellow stare" which betrays Charlotte's unbearable honesty and masculine sobriety, Wilbourne leaves the hospital to join her, with another four month of his internship unfinished. If he were more experienced in love, he might not have made such a commitment: "he might have discovered that love no more exists just at one spot and in one moment and in one body out of all the earth and all time and all the teeming breathed . . . " (38).

They are condemned from the beginning because Charlotte's project is made possible only by the money which Wilbourne has found in a dustbin—that is, through making themselves into criminals. She has to go a back alley, a back alley she refused to enter for their first rendezvous. Ever knowing Charlotte to be "a better man" and "a better gentleman" than he, Wilbourne tries to match her, but he finds himself clinging to her rather than holding her in his arms. Trying to abandon himself to her faith in love, he cannot overcome his habitual fear—the fear of being afraid: "he seemed to see their joint life as a fragile globe, a bubble, which she kept balanced and intact above disaster like a trained seal does its ball" (84).

Beginning in Chicago, Charlotte lives their life and "situation as though it were a complete whole without past or future"; she is totally engaged in her present life, body and soul, with no concern for the future and no regret for the past (84). In a studio room built rather to hold love or creation than to hold roomers, she makes figurines for fun, tangible objects one can touch and weigh in one's hands, and which in time find their way into the marketplace. Wilbourne, failing to keep a medically related job, spends his time secretly keeping a record of their dwindling money.

Then, with all their remaining money converted into one hundred dollars'
worth of food, they move to a Wisconsin lake. There, Charlotte spends the
"golden interval between dawn and sunset" swimming, sunbathing in the nude,
and painting, trying to catch the motion and speed of living things. Meanwhile,
Wilbourne, who is color blind, is secretly engaged in drawing up a calendar and
mentally calculating their decreasing supply of food. He feels happy only once—
when he is given a path to take, facing "the path straight and empty and quiet
between the two fifty-dollar rows of cans and sacks" (94). His life becomes
equated with "blotting the cans one by one in steady progression," and when he
eats, all food tastes like the money it represents (105). Wilbourne shares with the
tall convict a distaste for "Nature the unmathematical"; Wilbourne, too, cannot
live without a framework to give direction to his time. Finding himself bored to
extinction, not needed even by Charlotte, he thinks of sending her back to
Chicago and retiring to a solitary penitent's life. Charlotte, of course, rejects this
plan.

Driven out of Wisconsin by the cold, they come back to Chicago and settle
into a life with a middle-class income. Charlotte is paid by a department store for
her window displays, while Wilbourne writes stories about female troubles for
true-confession-type magazines, though at first he pretends this is only his hobby.
The day Charlotte is offered a permanent position, Wilbourne finds himself turned
into a husband, and their life together becomes like that of any long-married
people. Though he concludes that social respectability has destroyed their love
life, the truth is that he cannot be at ease with the physical comfort brought about
by the income that has made them respectable.

When sinning has become routine, he loses the ground on which to build
his daily life in expiation of his sin (116). They have to be damned or punished in
order to find love in its pure form, all cold edges. Exactly like Quentin in *The
Sound and the Fury*, he is drawn to the idea of himself and Charlotte being two
damned souls, doomed, and isolated from the world and from God (75). As for
the act of love, he finds his life lost in time, though not in space, and feels himself
sucked into "the hot fluid blind foundation—grave-womb or womb-grave."

Instead of condemning himself for his own inability to love, Wilbourne
condemns the world for having no place for love (129). To revive their love
through self-punishment, he deliberately chooses the cold and poverty of a
mineshaft in Utah for their home, to which they move in mid-winter. For the first
time in their relationship, Wilbourne takes the initiative.

Charlotte getting pregnant in the cold of this mine, they leave for the South to eliminate the new life in her. The fruit of their erotic love is regarded as an intruder, as an alien that has little to do with love. In order to return to being just the two of them, she demands that the hesitant Harry get rid of the unborn child. First, Wilbourne tries to erase the fact of her pregnancy by means of a medical man's verbal manipulation; then, he seeks pills in a brothel, buys some obscure medicine from a druggist, and finally performs an abortion on her. Trying to rid themselves of the alien in their house of love, he fails and ultimately loses Charlotte herself.

When he tells himself that his hands trembled because he loved her, it is half-true. Basically being a man of words, he is not good at acting through the channel of flesh, through the channel of love. The fact that he, a surgeon, is not good with his hands is exemplified in scenes when he, like the tall convict, rolls a cigarette. Even if he had completed his internship as a doctor instead of leaving the hospital midway through the course, he would inevitably have destroyed his career some day, somewhere, unless he had changed his field to something like mental care, a form of medicine not requiring the use of his hands.

Charlotte, with no split in her time and space, fully united in body and soul, has been ready to suffer for love from the onset, believing: "that love and suffering are the same thing and that the value of love is the sum of what you have to pay for it and any time you get it cheap you have cheated yourself" (43). The operation having failed, and Charlotte, now ready to pay for the price of love with her life, asks Rittenmeyer not to punish Wilbourne after she is dead. It is Wilbourne who reconstructs the scene between Charlotte and her husband in which she pleads for her cause, not for herself:

> '*For the sake of all the men and women who ever lived and blundered but meant the best and all that ever will live and blunder but mean the best . . . if any of us were ever born strong enough and good enough to be worthy to love or suffer either. Maybe what I am trying to say is justice.*' (207)

She also tries to comfort Wilbourne, saying: "Jesus, we had fun, didn't we," and makes him promise to get out, escape, before other people come (264).

Charlotte dies a warrior's death, but bereft of all the burden of desire, pride, courage and independence which has made her, she leaves Wilbourne nothing to hold on to. Wilbourne pleads guilty, leaving it to Rittenmeyer, the paragon of respectability, to make a plea for him, presenting both of them as co-victims of the female principle. A tablet of cyanide offered by Rittenmeyer prompts Wilbourne to choose life instead of death, to keep his flesh alive for the memory of love to be titillated by, thus not allowing the love he shared with Charlotte to be wasted:

> *Because if memory exists outside of the flesh it won't be memory because it won't know what it remembers so when she became not then half of memory became not and if I become not then all of remembering will cease to be.—Yes,* he thought, *between grief and nothing I will take grief.* (300)

Faulkner often repeated this phrase—"between grief and nothing I will take grief"—and he always did so with pride and sympathy. As an admirer of Faulkner, I once followed his lead, but now I wonder if Wilbourne made as worthy a choice as the author seems to have believed. True, Wilbourne is finally at peace with himself, using his body not to act, but to keep the memory of love: to live on, not to live in, love. For the verbal Wilbourne, memory still consists of words not remembered through "the physical striving with which alone the flesh can try to capture what little it is ever to know of love"(205-06). If he uses his flesh as a mere container for the memory of love, though, he will still not be truly to know of love. Indeed, grief is better than nothing, but his love turns inward for him with scant possibility of its extending to others, of its growing into an offering. No wonder the doctor in the opening section sees in Charlotte's eyes "profound and illimitable hatred" aimed "at the race of man, the masculine," those who are not worthy of the gallant challenge of her love (8).

The tall convict, with his absolute respect for power and, therefore, his limited yet firm moral standard, knows how to engage actively in day-to-day life, though he is sometimes irked by the passing of time. He takes pride in doing what is demanded of him to the best of his ability; he takes seriously:

> his good name, his responsibility not only towards those who were responsible towards him, but to himself, his own honour in the doing of what was asked of him, his pride in being able to do it, no

matter what it was. (153)

Determined to do his best in the fluid world of time, under the control of some authority, he is afraid of disorderly nature and of women, the unpredictable embodied, which threatens his neatly regulated world with collapse. He is no longer enraged either at society or at the judge who sent him to prison; now, he is enraged at the writers of the paperback novels he spent two years counter-reading and counter-calculating in order to make a plan for his chosen gambit, the train robbery. In spite of his having followed "the printed authority to the letter" he feels that he was betrayed both by the writers and by the girl who led him into crime.

Sheltered from the disorder and illogic of human affairs, he enjoys the peace and safety of the prison, tightly governed by its rules and orders. Inserted at this point is an episode of a plump convict who accepted the sentence for man-slaughter even though he committed a lesser crime; he did not want to face the rage of his woman accomplice. Life in prison bestows on the tall convict a greater possibility than living free outside, for there he would have to cope with the arbitrariness of human affairs all by himself.

While doing forced labor on the penitentiary farm, he has been hearing the Mississippi River, "a sound so much beyond all his experience and his powers of assimilation," a sound within range of which he runs his plough through soil hitherto tamely trod by generations of men (65). Ordered to rescue a man and a woman, and so driven out of his haven into the flooded river, he is more amazed and exasperated by the raging water, which follows no rules and has no method in its movements, than he is afraid of it.

Rescuing the pregnant woman by pulling her into his boat, the first thing he tries, exactly like Wilbourne, is to erase the fact of her pregnancy by not seeing it, by wrenching his gaze from her "monstrous sentient womb." After resigning himself to her presence in the same boat as he, he is determined to get rid of her "in the right way," and so he refuses the offer of the men to help him escape on the condition that he burn up his prison uniform; he cannot do that because it is government property. He runs away from the lawmen shooting at him, wanting only to surrender her, together with the government-owned boat. In the water, he feels doomed by life's "folly and suffering, its infinite capacity for folly and pains which seems to be its only immortality" (160).

All the tall convict wants to do is to hand the woman over to the authorities and then return to the safety of prison life: "turn his back on her for ever, on all pregnant and female life for ever and return to that monastic existence of shot-guns and shackles where he would be secure from it" (141-42). Fighting with the water, he takes excellent care of the woman, all the while determined never to be-come emotionally involved, ever ready to flee from the person for whom he does "*what he has to do, with what he has to do it with, with what he has learned, to the best of his judgement*"—that is, to be exact, the act of loving (237). After helping deliver her child, he looks down on the new life he has helped bring into the world and realizes that it is life that he has been afraid of and trying to flee from—life with its lack of definite shape and its unpredictable changes, with all its unreason and loss:

> *And this is all. This is what severed me violently from all I ever knew and did not wish to leave and cast me upon a medium I was born to fear, to fetch up at last in a place I never saw before and where I do not even know where I am.* (212)

The tall convict is carried on by the stream, with the woman and now her baby. For a while they stay with a Cajun Indian, where the tall convict is reminded of the joy of pitting his will and strength against a task (here, hunting alligators for their hides), having for seventeen years on the penitentiary farm been permitted only to toil but not truly to work. Temporarily he is so lost in peace and hope that he forgets his duty to go back to the prison; it takes the power of the state government, dynamiting the region, to drive him and the woman out of the swamp.

After having been brought together by the flood, and thus suffering together for nearly two months, a bond has naturally developed between them: "they had jointly suffered all the crises emotional social economic and even moral which do not always occur even in the ordinary fifty married years" (233). Still determined not to get involved with the female race, he goes back to prison as ordered, clad "in a faded but recently washed and quite clean suit of penitentiary clothing" (255). He reports to the officer: "'Yonder's your boat, and here's the woman. But I never did find that bastard on the cottonhouse'" (256).

In spite of his fulfilling the order exactly as given, and even accomplishing more than had been ordered, he is sentenced to ten additional years' imprisonment for supposedly attempting to escape. Unmoved, he quietly accepts the verdict, saying, "If that's the rule" (307). He is still more at ease being given orders and following rules than being left to act on his own; he is back to enjoy the safety and peace of the prison. The tall convict, who has succeeded in escaping from love, and Harry Wilbourne, who has chosen to live a memory of love in seclusion, end equally protected from life—the unmathematical, the unreasonable.

No one in this novel can be said to love if the word "love" is taken as signifying commitment, words incorporated in deeds, in giving. This is a theme which Faulkner, in his Nobel Prize acceptance speech, expounded upon as every writer's duty and privilege to explore. Wilbourne ends by killing Charlotte and the new life in her, while the tall convict, acting solely through duty, saves a woman and helps a child to be born. Some critics find in the convict a noble savage or a Saint Joseph. Yet, did Faulkner really approve of love practiced as a duty?

In this story, starting with the might-have-been doctor Wilbourne, several doctors appear, doctors whose duty it is to save human lives. That, without question, should be love. A doctor and his wife in the opening section, however, perform their act of love purely out of Christian duty, with no heart-felt sincerity or pity. Faulkner almost curses them as lifeless, exposing his nearly allergic reaction to the act of love performed as an obligation. The doctor is, he says:

> the puritan who some would have said was about to do what he had to do because he was a puritan, who perhaps believed himself he was about to do it to protect the ethics and sanctity of his chosen profession . . . (257)

Similarly, his gray-colored, gorgon-like wife is described as having: "that grim Samaritan husbandry of good women, as if she took a grim and vindictive and masochistic pleasure in the fact that the Samaritan deed would be performed" (7). Two other doctors later in the novel, each capable in their profession and occupationally kind, are concerned only with the patient's disease, and not with the total person.

Evidently Faulkner's sympathy is more for the couple who attempted the impossible in love and failed. Here, though, the reader should not be led to take the author as being against Puritanism or Christianity as is often alleged. He criticizes those who use religion to crucify each other in *Light in August*, and in

The Wild Palms he condemns the Puritan morality, which does not love but instead performs acts of love with a "masochistic pleasure" out of some self-imposed sense of duty. What he most severely criticizes, though, is the absence of love in the specific conditions of the American South he knows so well. Though this Japanese reader can sympathize with Faulkner's frustrated fury at his own culture, his condemnation of Puritan morality sounds excessive, for most Japanese people almost do not value any form of morality. If asked to choose between cold, Puritanical morality and no morality at all, this reader would take morality, even if heartless.

Faulkner tells us that *The Wild Palms* is basically the story of Charlotte Rittenmeyer and Harry Wilbourne:

> That was one story—the story of Charlotte Rittenmeyer and Harry Wilbourne, who sacrificed everything for love, and then lost that. I did not know it would be two separate stories until after I had started the book. When I reached the end of what is now the first section of *The Wild Palms*, I realized suddenly that something was missing, it needed emphasis, something to lift it like counterpoint in music. So I wrote on the "Old Man" story until the "Wild Palms" story rose back to pitch. Then I stopped the "Old Man" story at what is now its first section, and took up the "Wild Palms" story until it began to sag. Then I raised it to pitch again with another section of its antithesis, which is the story of a man who got his love and spent the rest of the book fleeing from it, even to the extent of voluntarily going back to jail where he would be safe. They are only two stories by chance, perhaps necessity. The story is that of Charlotte and Wilbourne. (Meriwether and Millgate, 247-48)

This statement provides a key to pinpoint the fault of this novel, which, even if it is not Faulkner's masterpiece, is yet one of my favorites. *The Wild Palms* admittedly has a certain laxness in the link between its theme and its method. The Puritan couple introduced in the opening section is created to contrast with Charlotte and Wilbourne, and the section provides a physical or metaphysical locale for the novel. Upon finishing the first section, Faulkner must have found that, even though the section might help readers have sympathy for

Charlotte and Wilbourne, this puritan couple did not quite function well enough; their presentation seems too negative. When the author started to write "Old Man" in counter-point to the "Wild Palms," he should have re-written the opening and second-to-last sections, in both of which this couple appear.

Also, in the "Wild Palms" Faulkner is too involved with the lovers to have sufficient aesthetic distance, especially from Wilbourne as is exemplified by his long speech before departing for Utah. On the other hand, in "Old Man" the author seems to enjoy his writing, relaxed and his sense of humor being evident. Certainly "Old Man" can be read as an independent story with its comical rendering of the tall convict's struggle against the powerful forces of nature. Still, when read with the binding theme of "two types of love" in mind, the very craftsmanship exhibited in the "Old Man" story seems to hinder the reader from grasping the theme of the work as a whole. "Old Man" is too well written to strike a balance with "Wild Palms." These two stories, running parallel and in counter-point to each other, do not quite harmonize as does a Bach fugue, for example.

Nevertheless, *The Wild Palms* is one of Faulkner's most gallant attempts to treat the gigantic theme of love, pursued boldly with a contrapuntal technique. In spite of—nay, because of—having this fault, we can hear Faulkner breathing as a fellow human creature.

6. Reading *As I Lay Dying* as a Fable
Words and Deeds

> The aim of every artist is to arrest motion, which is life, by
> artificial means and hold it fixed so that a hundred years later,
> when a stranger looks at it, it moves again since it is life.[1]

Indeed, half a century later when a stranger from Japan looks at the printed words on the pages of *As I Lay Dying*, "it moves again since it is life." In human life, while physical motion has forms which can be easily recognized, metaphysical motion takes on no definite shape until it is fixed by language. Given direction and some consistency in movement, the immeasurable motion of the inner life forms a recognizable person. Without purpose and system in its movement, "the clotting which is you had dissolved into the myriad original motion."[2] Thus, every inner self carries within it the ever-present possibility of crisis, of dissolving into its original motion. Faulkner equates this precariousness of human existence, all of which may be an illusion, with a cluster of buzzards circling in the air: "High against it they hang in narrowing circles, like the smoke, with an outward semblance of form and purpose, but with no inference of motion, progress or retrograde" (156).

Furnished with individual form and purpose, the assemblage of life's immeasurable motion is given its identity and individuality as an integrated whole. The crisis of suffering the bereavement of self, the loss of identity, is more imminent than the inevitable coming of death, the loss of one's physical body:

> I can remember how when I was young I believed death to be a phenomenon of the body; now I know it to be merely a function of the mind—and that of the minds of the ones who suffer the bereavement. (27)

In *As I Lay Dying* the flow of the consciousness in fifteen characters, arrested by language, is told in fifty-nine monologues. Each monologue reveals the inner motion of the narrator, together with the apparent motions of others as the narrator perceives them. All of their lives' motion revolves around a death, a corpse in the process of decaying. Death works as a catalyst to make each life take its shape against the passage of time, constantly enticing all that exist into non-being.

Yet, every human creature is obligated to create some illusion of self in the face of this all-absorbing void. As Yukio Mishima pointed out, only the tension confronted in the crisis of self-disintegration creates what is entitled to be called one's personality.[3] Against this basic void of human existence, each of us struggles to draw a picture of the self by means of words and actions, the components of his or her life. In *As I Lay Dying* the fragmented motions caught in each monologue are finally assembled to form the total picture of a particular person. By the end, fifty-nine monologues have been laid out before us; we can now collect the individual pieces, or tiles, with which we are to build the total mosaic.

Every human creature lives more or less in the toil and agony of his or her assigned time and space. In Addie's father's words, "the reason for living is getting ready to stay dead" (118). Addie has found her reason for living in the duty to be alive, to be blood and flesh. If one's being is formed only in relation to the outer world, she is to make her blood and that of others flow as one stream, thus violating the aloneness of each being as it lays dying, imprisoned in its isolated body. Words, like other means of communication reaching out from isolated selves, pass without ever really touching actual life:

> I would think how words go straight up in a thin line, quick and harmless, and how terribly doing goes along the earth, clinging to it, so that after a while the two lines are too far apart for the same person to straddle from one to the other . . . . (117)

In this fable of words and actions, each character endeavors to straddle the distance from his and her words to actions, thus—hopefully—forming an integrated identity.

Addie listens to "the dark voicelessness in which the words are the deeds, and the other words that are not deeds . . . fumbling at the deeds . . ."(117). Deeds in this passage are words incarnate, the basic concept of Christianity. The Gospel according to John opens with, "In the beginning was the Word, and the Word was with God, and the Word was God."

For Addie, Anse dies in her mind as the echo of his words. Whitfield, her one-time lover, is also a man of words: "to whom sin is just a matter of words, to them salvation is just words too"(119). He believes his sin is forgiven because he, a professional man of God, is eloquent in wording prayers asking for His forgiveness. Yet committing adultery with this minister of God gives Addie the feeling of life being lived in its fullness because she is doubly damned—in her sin and in her violation. After the affair has ended, the child born in sin saves her by helping her to re-construct daily life in "an acknowledgement and expiation of [her] sin"(112). Thus Jewel, the living emblem of her sin, becomes her cross and, by being her cross, her salvation.

Addie has given birth to five children, and Cash was still in her womb when she "learned that words are no good; that words dont ever fit even what they are trying to say at"(115). At Cash's birth, Addie's "aloneness had been violated and then made whole again by the violation . . ."(116). Addie and Cash could thus communicate without words. When she had Darl by Anse, she realized that she had been tricked by empty words older than Anse. Darl was her unloved, unwanted child, for whose birth his mother had to take revenge. While she refused Anse, she got Jewel, her treasure, from her godly lover, and no words were needed between mother and son. To expiate her sin, she gave Anse a daughter, Dewey Dell, to make up for the "Jewel," and Vardaman to replace the Jewel she had robbed Anse of.

To take revenge upon Anse or words for the birth of Darl, Addie made Anse promise to bury her in Jefferson when she died. A "promise" may be mere words, but to keep it Anse has to leave Frenchman's Bend and go to a far-away town, despite his usual reluctance to move. Thus, the dead Addie forces the living members of the Bundren family to go through flood and fire to bury her corpse in Jefferson. During this funeral journey, an Exodus flight to the Promised Land of Canaan, the flows of various lives—Anse's, Cash's, Darl's, Jewel's, Vardaman's and those of neighboring farmers—become evident in both words and actions:

> I would think about his [Anse's] name until after a while I could see the word as a shape, a vessel, and I would watch him liquefy and flow into it like cold molasses flowing out of the darkness into the vessel, until the jar stood full and motionless: . . . I would be I; I would let him be the shape and echo of his word. (116, 117)

Anse's words do not touch or change reality; they only embellish and support his own sense of being. For example, when he keeps repeating, "If the bridge was just up, we could drive across it," he is re-confirming to himself that he has no intention of crossing the river; his words hold no promise of movement toward action, such as repairing the bridge or swimming across the river. His way of life dictates that he avoids any physical movement because movement would result in sweating, and he never sweats.

Instead, Anse's being consists entirely of threadbare Christian cliches, often misused, and a plausible self-pity able to satisfy his egoism and make him appear pious. He himself confesses that he cannot put any heart into his words. His face, deprived of words, is seen by Darl thus: "carved by a savage caricaturist a monstrous burlesque of all bereavement flowed" (50). On the other hand, Anse plays the role of the chief mourner with dignity. He fits in well with the funeral; actual death is stylized into a ceremony that involves more shape than content.

He is good, too, at manipulating others through overtly expressed self-pity and self-restraint. Others are conjured by his words into helping him—made to feel guilty if they don't. As Tull says, "Like most folks around here, I done holp him so much already I cant quit now"(20). Anse accomplishes the funeral journey by exposing others, not himself, to disaster. After burying Addie's odorous body, and after purchasing a set of false teeth with money robbed from his children, he picks up a new wife. Thus, having fulfilled his promise to Addie, he transforms her revenge into something for his own benefit. Throughout the journey from Frenchman's Bend to Jefferson, he has never changed, remaining merely the shape and echo of his words.

In contrast to his father, Cash speaks little and, as a good carpenter, uses his own hands to build tangible objects. He does not mind having his clothing stained with sweat. His name, 'Cash' (money), suggests action in the form of convertibility. Also he is a good carpenter, one who builds things after careful measurements, keeping a balance in any circumstances he is placed. Every time he verbalizes something, he expresses his concern for measurement and a good balance. For example, in his opening monologue, he recounts how to build a coffin by listing a series of steps. This list signifies the way in which his consciousness is occupied with a builder's vocabulary. He embodies his mother's recognition that words are no good, meaningless. His hands, impervious to outer conditions such as the weather, never stop functioning. Darl sees that Cash's rain-drenched "arm functioned in a tranquil conviction that rain was an illusion of the mind" (49). This person has no fear of self-disintegration as long as he has tangible materials to handle.

Cash expresses his love for his dying mother by building her a good, comfortable coffin before her eyes. She accepts it with mute satisfaction; they can communicate without words. Only after he is disabled and cannot use his hands does he begin to fumble for words. When he begins to handle words as tools to reach others, his first utterance is to express his sympathy for and understanding of the suffering Darl. He understands why Darl has to set fire to other people's barns, since he himself agrees that it is against God's will to carry a decomposing corpse to the far-away town of Jefferson:

> how it would be God's blessing if He did take her outen our hands and get shut of her in some clean way, and it seemed to me that when Jewel worked so to get her outen the river, he was going against God in a way . . . . (160-61)

However, Cash, the carpenter, has to solve all problems with only careful measurements and good tools, by means of a sound method. The means are the ends in him; a good cause does not justify a bad method:

> and then when Darl seen that it looked like one of us would have to
> do something, I can almost believe he done right in a way. But I
> dont reckon nothing excuses setting fire to a man's barn and
> endangering his stock and destroying his property. (161)

He reasons that Darl has to be punished because he has lost balance in doing right.
Where no one is absolutely right or absolutely wrong, it is the balance of things
that matters. Cash's last monologue speaks of Darl with sympathy and understanding: "But it is better so for him. This world is not his world; this life his life"
(182).

Dr. Peabody's diagnosis, bringing together the balance and the imbalance
that is to be Cash's life and predicting his life symbolically, says he will "have to
limp around on one short leg for the balance of [his] life" (165). Deprived of his
functioning hands, Cash is obliged to seek out another means of communication
—words. His opening monologue is built around the vocabulary of building a
coffin, while in his last monologue he deals with the metaphysics of distinguish-
ing insanity from sanity:

> Sometimes I aint so sho who's got ere a right to say when a man is
> crazy and when he aint. Sometimes I think it aint none of us pure
> crazy and aint none of us pure sane until the balance of us talks
> him that-a-way. It's like it aint so much what a fellow does, but it's
> the way the majority of folks is looking at him when he does it.
> (160)

Some critics consider Cash to be as affirmative as Dilsey in *The Sound
and the Fury*. Still, Cash has his own limitations just because he is a man of
balance. Never seeing beyond the object before him, he is incapable of doubting
the material that he has carefully measured and that is lying before him. On some
occasions, he measures far more precisely than needed; at other times, his habitual
careful measurements fail to work out well. He passively weighs matters within a
given framework. He will, for example, be an obedient, accommodating son to his
new mother, who is "a kind of duck-shaped woman all dressed up, with them kind
of hard-looking pop eyes like she was daring ere a man to say nothing"(181). A
good worker at the hard task of living, he is not one to take the risk of doing

something that might better the condition of his fellow man. If given a little pleasure after his day's hard work, he endures with no ambition of prevailing.

Cash is a man of his hands, Darl a man of his eyes. Keen perceptions caught in language, his monologues occupy about one-third of the entire book. He provides the greatest amount of information both about himself and about others. Too much of a seer, he describes in his often poetic language even scenes from which he is absent. His eyes reflect life's myriad original motions as they really are, before being given a unified sense of direction. By transcending all modes of response, he stands paralyzed, with his eyes wide open.

Looking beyond what he actually sees, Darl's very perceptibility disables him from having contact with time's flow. Having no center of self to act upon, he cannot fill his consciousness with the immediate events thrust upon him by time. He is ever conscious of his extreme opposite, Jewel, who looking right in front of him and always reacting with violence, somehow leads a seemingly clear-cut existence.

Darl himself knows that the self is expressed only by reacting to the outer world, to others: "It takes two people to make you, and one people to die" (25). This man has never known the love of a mother, the original, basic other. He calls his mother "Addie" and speaks of her in the third person, not by any term of relation. Here, the relationship between mother and son lacks the force to enable him to define himself as his mother's son. He does refer to Anse as "Pa," but because Anse is a man of words and not action, Anse cannot provide Darl with a human other to love, and so Darl has no basis for defining himself as his father's son. A constant observer of events outside of the circle, this essential orphan can never be a participant, one who loves or hates, one who commits himself. Unable to gather his dispersed being either to love or hate, his feelings amount to no more than a vague sympathy or antipathy.

Unable to be actualized into a particular person with a particular mode of response, he always wonders if he really exists: "I dont know what I am. I dont know if I am or not" (51). In his anxiety, he establishes his being in the negative; if he *will not be*, that means he now *is*. Unable to embody himself centrifugally around some core, by seeing all simultaneously, his existence is endlessly dispersed in fragments: "That's why I am not *is*. *Are* is too many for one woman to foal" (65). Between his existing body and the non-beingness in his conscious-ness, he aspires to be dispersed into time, a multi-fractured, scattering motion, unburdened of any of life's obligations:

> How do our lives ravel out into the no-wind, no-sound, the weary
> gestures wearily recapitulant: echoes of old compulsions with no-
> hand on no-strings: in sunset we fall into furious attitudes, dead
> gestures of dolls. (141)

Darl goes insane when he begins to exist entirely, perfectly, outside him-self, referring to himself in the third person and thus completely objectifying himself. When he makes himself into a perfect other, he is liberated from his obligation to integrate his dispersing selves into one person. Darl, who has been utterly incapable of judging between affirmation and negation, finally repeats "yes," but only after he becomes a total other to himself.

Darl strongly reminds me once again of Yukio Mishima, who, just before he killed himself, wrote of "the denial at the end of all seeing, the eye's denial of itself" (*The Decay of the Angel*, 146). If there can be one with the unrealized possibility of doing something not done before, to change the world and make it a little better, that person is Darl, and this possibility propels Darl's insanity. Realizing the futility of carrying Addie's decomposing corpse, Darl, for the first time, takes a decisive move to right the wrong—only to destroy himself.

Contrary to the ever-seeing Darl, Jewel, with "that unmistakable air of definite and imminent departure that trains have," is always doing something (176). He is all Addie's—one for whom words are no good. Both Jewel's legal father and his natural father are men of empty words, incapable of fathering a man of action. Darl says of Jewel, who harbors no anxiety about dissolving into non-being: "Jewel knows he is, because he does not know that he does not know whether he is or not" (51).

Jewel rarely opens his mouth to relate with others, but when he does, he offers mostly curses, using a mobile language akin to action. His violent language, when used in cursing his beloved horse, is transformed into obscene caresses. His horse, constantly inviting him to physical motion, thus helps him carve out a seemingly solid existence. Vardaman is right when he comments that "Jewel's mother is a horse." Horses and all horse-like things, in so far as they invite him to physical movement, nurture Jewel's being. Named Jewel, his mother's treasure, he loves only his mother and his horse—so much so that he hates all those who go near either of them. Hate gives shape to his aggressive nature.

Unlike Cash and his carefully weighed, measured actions, Jewel jumps into violent motion whenever an occasion arises. He is fundamentally passive because his motion is often purely reactive. If he does not repeat "Something is going to happen to me," his actions are yet as passive as those of Joe Christmas, who does not know who he is. Jewel's heroic acts seem only to shape his heroic being; they do not function to better his life or that of others. Instead, he guards his beloved mother's putrid body through flood and fire with a meaninglessness that goes against the will of God. Ultimately confined in his *being*, his actions never grow into the sort of action that God meant for human creatures to do. He hates Darl's eyes, for they probe the basis of his own being by seeing through the meaninglessness of his acts and his existence, given shape only by a series of meaningless actions.

Dewey Dell, her name signifies the misty valley of the female body, also hates Darl's eyes. They hasten the dissolution of her inner world, "a little tub of guts" with no "room in it for anything else very important" (37). Her "smouldering" world of senses will crumble if she allows the invasion of a consciousness pinned down by language: "I feel my body, my bones and flesh beginning to part and open upon the alone, and the process of coming unalone is terrible" (39). She is constantly running from self-recognition by means of language.

She does not admit her pregnancy, for example, because by verbalizing it even to herself it would be solidified into incontrovertible fact. She is afraid of Darl's knowing eyes, since a known fact is verbalized into evermore concrete knowledge. Wishing that the fact of pregnancy would disappear along with Darl's knowing of it, she wants to kill Darl. More aggressive than Jewel, she tries to catch Darl and send him to the lunatic asylum. She cannot consult Dr. Peabody about an abortion because if she does, the fact of her pregnancy will take solid shape by his knowledge of it. Rather she goes to a pharmacist in the big city who does not know her because if only a stranger knows of it, it can be ignored as long as she herself tries not to remember.

Running from the invasion of language into her wordless world, she cannot help but feel a black nothingness blowing over her: "*it was wind blowing over me it was like the wind came and blew me back from where it was I was not . . .*" (79). Still, with the author's usual male approach to female flesh, he has Darl define Dewey Dell as possessing "those mammalian ludicrosities which are the horizons and the valleys of the earth" (110). In other words, she is the earth mother. The author's romantic tendency to see women as aspects of Mother Nature becomes even more easily visible in *Light in August, The Sound and the Fury*, and The Trilogy: *The Hamlet, The Town*, and *The Mansion*.

Vardaman, the youngest, can acknowledge his experience and his own being only in relation to others. The dead fish laying in the dust and Vardaman's perception of himself as a seer still require the verification of others who have also witnessed the same fish. The actuality of a horse seen alone in the darkness threatens to scatter into its components, along with the reality of the seer himself, as Vardaman loses the integrity of his being:

> It is as though the dark were resolving him out of his integrity, into an unrelated scattering of components . . . an illusion of a coordinated whole of splotched hide and strong bones within which, detached and secret and familiar, an *is* different from my *is*. I see him dissolve . . . and float upon the dark in fading solution; all one yet neither; all either yet none. (36)

Vardaman realizes that Cash has broken his leg, while the others have kept their two legs intact. Unable to accept and digest the fact of his mother's death, he tries to alter it to the more acceptable death of a fish and urges Tull, with whom he saw the dead fish, to agree to his confused conclusion that his mother is a fish. Whenever things threaten to make him feel non-existent ("I am not anything"), he buttresses his being by ascertaining his relation to others; by repeating "Cash is my brother" and "Jewel is my brother, too," he can identify himself as Cash's brother and Jewel's brother. In this respect, Vardaman is unlike Darl, who cannot define himself as his mother's son. Even after Darl has gone completely insane, Vardaman does not reject his relationship with this brother, accepting the fact he has a brother who has gone mad. Crossing the flooded river and holding Tull's hand with all his might, Vardaman makes Tull feel that he can, by staying with the child, accomplish the impossible.

Still, because Vardaman always identifies himself in relation to others, his existence is not built upon moral judgement soundly chosen. Vardaman's cause involves risk since only circumstances determine whether it will work in a lifegiving or a life-denying direction. As with all children, Vardaman holds not only great potentiality, but also the danger of conforming to the wrong framework. He needs to develop his own way of judging between affirmation and negation; he must establish a method of his own, one which can bear comparison with Cash's carpenter's tools and, by extension, the carpenter tools of the young Jesus.

There remain Tull, Armstid, and Samson, who, like Cash, strike a balance between words and actions. The difference is that the carpenter Cash's materials are inanimate, while these men are all farmers who deal with living things. Their habit of caring for crops and cattle naturally extends to their neighbors, so long as doing so does not cause irreparable damage to themselves. With little personal concern for justice, they do everything habitually. Customs are formed by habit, and dwellings are lived in by habit; the farmers take no risks that require them to do things not done before. As with the weather, they accept whatever God sends in their direction with the indispensable optimism of men who nurture living things.

Doing hard work everyday is the most important thing for them, and they speak only when there is a need to do so; thinking is done only when necessary. Helping others when requested, the farmers are wise enough to approve of Tull's wife Cora, who elbows heavenward with absolute self-righteousness and imposes her help on others. Tull silently argues that he and the farmers can at least pretend to have respect for such self-righteous people as Cora since they are often useful in an emergency.

In *As I Lay Dying*, Faulkner succeeds in carving many different types in relief, often through caricaturization. The people in this fable appear rather comical and a little sad, as all human creatures do. Our own lives would never fit into any one type; we take turns being Anse, Cash, Darl, Jewel, Dewey Dell, Vardaman Bundren, and Vernon Tull. The author lets each give shape to his or her life in his or her own distorted way, yet all fall within the God's range of love.

Faulkner played out a fable of words and actions, about the human aspiration for words incarnated into deeds, into *Agape*, into the love of God. Thus, the author has transformed a story of poor whites in the American South into a universal human fable. This genius of literature, our fellow creature, gazes with sympathy and with pity upon human beings as they carry a deep abyss within them and yet have courage enough to commit themselves to the absurdity of existence.

7. *The Sound and the Fury*

> To-morrow, and to-morrow, and to-morrow,
> Creeps in this petty pace from day to day,
> To the last syllable of recorded time;
> And all our yesterdays have lighted fools
> The way to dusty death. Out, out, brief candle!
> Life's but a walking shadow, a poor player
> That struts and frets his hour upon the stage
> And then is heard no more: it is a tale
> Told by an idiot, full of sound and fury,
> Signifying nothing. (*Macbeth*, V. v. 19-28)[1]

Part 1: Prelude

Faulkner took the title of *The Sound and the Fury* from the famous soliloquy in *Macbeth*; he also made substantial use of other materials from the play and even its spirit, in this novel and other works. Later, in a question-and-answer session, Faulkner said that the writer is completely amoral in taking whatever he needs from the best of his predecessors. With the exception of the Bible, which Faulkner said was "just there"[2] in the culture, he must have taken most from Shakespeare. We can also see traces of Shakespeare in, for example, *As I Lay Dying* and *Absalom, Absalom!*. Faulkner might not, though, have always been conscious of his borrowings from Shakespeare, with whom he not only shared the same language, but also the culture with Christianity as its core.

In one of the colloquies at the Nagano Seminar of 1955, Faulkner said he had a complete Shakespeare in one volume that he carried with him and might read at almost any time. We can safely assume that he read more Shakespeare than he watched on the stage. Reading is the royal road to Shakespeare since, unlike modern plays, the action is not only acted out but also verbalized in Elizabethan drama; for example, Macduff's son cries out, "He has kill'd me, mother" (IV. II. 86). Reading Shakespeare must have greatly helped the young Faulkner grow into a writer. Faulkner adopted not only Shakespeare's language, but also his method; Faulkner relied more on having characters talk in each own style than on describing them from the point of view of an omniscient narrator.

Faulkner often relied on monologues, as in *As I Lay Dying*, where fifteen narrators present fifty-nine monologues. In *The Sound and the Fury*, three dissimilar monologues relate the failure of three different characters as they try to cope with time; the last chapter, in contrast to the previous three chapters, is written more nearly in the 'omniscient' style. However, the narrative in the fourth section, presented from a vaguely authorial point of view, sounds more like the author's own monologue rather than a description.

Macbeth ends with a proclamation of victory by Prince Malcolm, the rightful heir to the Scottish crown. His recovery of the throne signals the re-establishment in the land of a universal moral code; through the victory of the rightful heir, the time—that is, the whole world—is to be liberated. In this tightly structured framework, Shakespeare's language often is more sharply focused than Faulkner's utterances. *Macbeth* is like a flower garden blooming with words in action, each uttered with its own finality, with none of the impatient searching for words we tend to find in Faulkner.

For Shakespeare, the opening of the Gospel according to John is taken to be a fact, not the ideal state of language as it is for Faulkner. In *Macbeth*, God defines every phenomenon and names it as He did light, heaven, earth, seas, and so on in Genesis; in other words, God gives everything existence by naming it.

Witches, outside of the divine order, are therefore undefined by God; they function only in the service of destruction and denial. They are apparitions without substance, without sex, unable to occupy time and space physically. Not defined by God in terms of who they are, all they can do is "deeds without names": "you should be women, / And yet your beards forbid me to interpret / That you are so" (I. III. 45-47).

As apparitions incapable of telling right from wrong, beauty from ugliness, their language lacks moral judgement, as is aptly put by the witches themselves in a chorus in the first scene: "Fair is foul, and foul is fair"—words that Macbeth himself will echo in the third scene as he comes upon the witches: "So foul and fair a day I have not seen" (I. III. 38). By being given names and thereby defined, humans come to "be" and can begin their life's actions, actions based on the ability to judge between affirmation and negation, between fair and foul: "Let your 'Yes' mean 'Yes,' and your 'No' mean 'No.' Anything more is from the evil one." Understanding without judgement, however deep it may seem, leads only to a denial of life.

Banquo also is moved by the witch's words, but he is able to check himself by his self-admonition: "But, hush, no more." Thereby he can will his return to God's system: "Merciful powers, / Restrain in me the cursed thoughts that nature / Gives way to in repose!" (II. I. 7-9). He contrasts well with Macbeth, who after the murder of Duncan, cannot pray when he wants to: "But wherefore could not I pronounce 'Amen'? / I had most need of blessing, and 'Amen' / Stuck in my throat" (II. II. 31-33). What separates Macbeth from Banquo is Banquo's will power, the power of judging affirmation and negation rightly. It is only natural, then, that Macbeth, who can only recognize right from wrong, is afraid of Banquo: "He hath a wisdom that doth guide his valour / To act in safety. There is none but he / Whose being I do fear: and under him / My Genius is rebuked, as it is said Mark Antony's was by Caesar" (III. I. 52-56).

Without having a foundation on which to build his being, Macbeth acts according to the aesthetics of his mascurilinity, a manliness enacted in its most easily recognizable form of violence. Introduced as "valor's minion," but taunted by Lady Macbeth as "quite unmann'd," he, who boasts that he dares "do all that may become a man; / Who dares do more is none," feels that he has to prove his masculinity by assassinating King Duncan (I. VII. 46-47). His determination to fight to the very end is supported also by his warrior's aesthetic, which binds the parts of his divided-self through action. He takes himself to be approved or cursed on the basis of violence; in other words, this concept of masculinity decides his destiny. (Only once in *Macbeth* is the term "man" used referring to humankind, and this is by Macduff after he hears that his wife and son have been slaughtered by Macbeth.)

In Shakespeare's Christendom, kings are endowed with the power not only to govern, but also to love like God. Resistance to a king's authority is taken to be a sin against God, while personal virtue is approved only insofar as it does not contradict the sovereignty of the royal institution. When Banquo says that "In the great hand of God I stand," he recognizes God's divine order and the natural law that is upheld by the king (II. III. 129). For an Elizabethan, there seems to have been no division between religion and the royal sovereignty. Thus a good king, standing at the center of his community, is seen as a loving father to his subjects. As embodied by Duncan, the sovereign king is equated with the natural force that gives life to every living thing under heaven; he is presented to us as one more dedicated to cultivating and giving than to dominating: "I have begun to plant thee, and will labour / To make thee full of growing" (I. IV. 28-29).

Macbeth, "valor's minion," unlike Banquo, allows the language of the witches to invade his consciousness; by so doing, he slips out of life's order, out of the natural moment of the eternal present. By assassinating King Duncan then, he destroys nature's harmony; he murders its blessings, the pleasure of wholesome sleep and eating: "Methought I heard a voice cry 'Sleep no more!; / Macbeth does murder sleep'—the innocent sleep" (II. II. 34-36). By murdering sleep, Macbeth ruins his own daily existence, since every creature, even a king, must have his daily sleep, "Chief nourisher in life's feast," just as he must have nourishment and protection from the elements. Thus, Macbeth destroys his present time in order to establish his future dynasty, not realizing that tomorrow's dynasty cannot be founded on the ruins of today. (Faulkner transplanted this issue of founding tomorrow's dynasty on the destruction of today to the American South in *Absalom, Absalom!*.) Macbeth's world is disjointed at the moment he allows the witches' language to invade his consciousness.

Faulkner divides the disjointed world of Macbeth into three parts: the distorted time of Quentin, "a walking shadow" who is obsessed with time's flow and who finds his peace only in dying; that of Jason, another failure at coping with time and "a poor player, / That struts and frets his hour upon the stage / And then is heard no more"; and of Benjy, who, confined in his frozen time, tells "a tale told by an idiot."

Faulkner, called "Count no 'count" by his neighbors after the First World War, with uncompleted university education, is freer from the conventions of novel writing than many other writers. Yet, he still has to suffer the restrictions imposed by the "fragile thread" of language. Language, when used as a tool for writing, devoid of the physicality of sound—of the voice, tends to transform every phenomenon into abstraction. To counteract the corrosive function of printed words, Faulkner opens *The Sound and the Fury* with the monologue of one "incapable of relevance." Incapable of abstraction, and therefore free from prejudice, Benjy, whose absolute objectivity reflects all phenomena as they really are, proves to be a more reliable narrator than the others, whose prejudices produce distortions. Through Benjy's consciousness, Faulkner begins to tell his "tale told by an idiot, full of sound and fury," trying to make it signify *something*, rather than nothing.

Faulkner is skeptical of every institutional authority and convention. In his search for his own style, he seeks to establish his own moral standard, one that has direction but no termination. His writing begins and ends in a search, a search open to imperfection because it is an eternal process, eternally unfolding and eternally becoming. In spite of the Appendix he later attached to the book in order to make it complete and final, *The Sound and the Fury* if judged by the standard of perfection remains his "most splendid failure."

Macbeth is a character made fully rounded not only through action and dialogue, but also through the exposure of his inner self by the words of his soliloquies. In *The Sound and the Fury*, though, with its three monologues and one descriptive section, the author is more in pursuit of the metaphysic of time than of the creation of characters, so we find no one as fully characterized as Macbeth. Instead, three concepts of time are presented in the monologues of Benjy, Quentin, and Jason, each of whom reveals his consciousness in his own vocabulary. In the last section, featuring Dilsey, the appearances and patterns of behavior are for the first time observed from the outside and told in a vaguely authorial voice. Thereby, it is in Dilsey that everything is externalized through action, and she is most clearly placed in time.

Faulkner puts no trust in institutional order, not even the smallest, most integrated unit—the family. Instead, he entrusts all his hope to the ever-elusive eternal women, creatures who are all embracing as they give, who exist only in men's dreams. Faulkner, in creating Dilsey and Caddy—both embodiments of love, his Martha and Mary—seems to be the last of the romantic feminists. Caddy, Eros incarnate, is full of the promise of life, brave enough to face the truth, and capable both of loving without the expectation of any return, and of falling into degradation. Her presence and absence dictate the motion of times for Benjy, Quentin, and Jason. After writing of the absence of life's promise, Faulkner willfully adds the last section to commend to us love that is enacted in our daily lives. Dilsey acts, thus answering the daily needs of her white family who suffer from the absence of love. The author swings between Caddy and Dilsey, Eros and ethos, cannot but turn his eyes to *Agape*, love in a state of perfection.[3]

When life-giving force is materialized in a little girl who smells like trees and a black nurse of the family, the concept of masculinity also suffers deconstruction and transformation. Quentin, quite masculine in his urge to conceptualize everything into abstraction, cannot engage in natural time through action. Unable to act violently as an aggressive male, he tries to play the romantic role of the knight or the gentleman. Unconsciously assigning himself the role of one who gives up his life for the honor of a lady, Quentin is much concerned with courtesy and proper grooming.

For Jason, masculinity consists of power in the capitalistic world; he is more attached to the power symbolized by money than to the money itself. Therefore all phenomena, from the sun to time, become his enemies, waiting to make of him a loser. He divides people into those he feels able to control and those he cannot control, his enemies. In order to secure his power, he attacks everyone he thinks weaker than himself.

In the last section and for the first time in this novel, Dilsey, a character whose hours are filled with action, is observed by a narrator who hints at being authorial. Dilsey is adorned with such words as "regal," "moribund," "courage," "fortitude," "indomitable," "somnolent," and "impervious." Living through action, she is perfectly externalized as she is presented to us by a traditional third-person voice. The author tells us, indirectly, why only Dilsey can cope with her time and live in the present moment. Rather than reporting what she thinks or feels, he has us watch what she "does." She is not the sum total of her consciousness, but the sum total of her action, answering the daily needs of those around her. Accepting time as it flows through her, she lives in the present moment as it intersects with eternity.

To believe in God is to accept time in a perspective that goes beyond the restrictions of human recognition; it is to commit one's being to the present time.

Faulkner, in one of his later interviews, talks of God in terms of the eternal present:

> I'm not talking about a personified or a mechanical God, but a God who is the most complete expression of mankind, a God who rests both in eternity and in the now. . . . There is only the present moment, in which I include both the past and the future, and that is eternity. In my opinion time can be shaped quite a bit by the artist; after all, man is never time's slave. (Meriwether and Millgate, 70)

Not sharing with Shakespeare an absolute trust in words, and therefore unable to take it as fact that the Word is God, Faulkner believes that poets—writers—should return their crafted words to God.

Part 2: Time in *The Sound and the Fury*

Time is fleeting. The Present now is fluid, and only when it becomes the past does it have shape enough to be told. "[T]here is nothing else in the world its not despair until time its not even time until it was."[4] Man, whose misfortune is his being time-bound, has to live amid this ever evasive "now." Is he destined to be the sum of his misfortunes, "his climactic experiences" or what have you, or must he remain a cynical bystander who "stay[s] awake and see[s] evil done for a little while" (219)? Sartre, in his criticism of *The Sound and the Fury* presents "a metaphysic of time" that he believes to be Faulkner's and concludes by saying, "I like his art, but I don't believe in his metaphysic."[5] In its turn, this paper will try to present Faulkner's fable of time and explore whether or not Faulkner is guilty of believing in a defeatist's metaphysic, as Sartre accuses him of doing.

In *The Sound and the Fury*, Faulkner plunges us right into Benjy's monologue with no explanation: "Through the fence, between the curling flower spaces, I could see them hitting"(1). If Benjy can thus recognize the inter-relationship of objects, spaces, and actions to name them, he cannot be an idiot. The very inability to recognize them would constitute idiocy, as Kenzaburo Ohashi points out (Ohashi vol.1, 191-272). Faulkner himself was concerned "as to whether [Benjy] is believable as I created him." Indeed, he is more believable as "a prologue, like the grave-digger in the Elizabethan dramas,"[6] than as a character. By giving a speechless idiot a voice, Faulkner begins his tale. Benjy is "trying to say" in his section, just as in the story as a whole Faulkner is trying to tell, to make his "tale told by an idiot, full of sound and fury" signify *something*.

Because Benjy is unable to differentiate between the past and the present, his time is a constant present with scenes recalled in exact life size. Because he has no power to conceptualize the events and so distort them in some way, he serves as the most reliable deliverer of information in the novel. After Benjy's monologue, which serves as the prologue of the tale, Quentin offers his monologue, and Jason his, but neither of the other brothers is as trustworthy. Faulkner says of Benjy that he feels "grief and pity for all mankind" and Quentin and Jason, brothers in mankind, are also to be pitied and grieved over. Benjy— confined in frozen time, Quentin—trying to stop time, and Jason—fighting with it—with none of them is time lived to the fullest.

For each, time wheels around the same axis, the memory of the loss of Caddy. Caddy, whom Faulkner calls "my heart's darling," is called "ever-elusive Eurydice" by André Bleikasten. She is something beautiful which is capable of giving love and tenderness and, at the same time, causing dishonor and shame, something like the promise of life. The memory of the loss of Caddy and the subsequent absence of any promise of life makes Benjy moan literally, while it also makes Quentin and Jason each moan in his own way. Indeed, *The Sound and the Fury* is full of moaning. It is Benjy who moans, cries, howls, and bellows to typify the blind "self-centeredness of innocence" (Jelliffe, 103), but Quentin and Jason, too, are innocent. In Faulkner, the word "innocence" connotes something negative and complex. They all are innocently self-centered and blindly narcissistic. In their blindness, the present is filled with helpless moaning in Benjy, Quentin has an absent feeling, and every action is meaningless to Jason. In their crippled time, the sun shines on none of them.

A reader can only struggle to see how time and the idiot created as a vehicle for it are related to one another. For all his thirty-three calendar years, Benjy has never grown beyond a mental age of three. Although his brain is capable of registering events, these events evidence no flow from yesterday or into tomorrow, since his sense of time is frozen. Various catalysts in the present induce him to recall fragments of memories in vivid detail but without forming any history. Incapable of conceptualizing his memories, he loses nothing but remembers only its loss and moans.

For instance, "Caddy smelled like trees and like when she says we were asleep" (5), the ending of a happy recollection, is followed by *"What are you moaning about, Luster said."* The moan is triggered by the memory of Caddy, which triggers the eruption of the memory. All happy memories, remembered only in their loss, illustrate his growing alienation from Caddy. Moreover, all events are encased in death scenes: Damuddy's, Roskus', Quentin's, and Mr. Compson's. In these scenes he howls at every smell of death and at every sign of alienation from the love and tenderness of Caddy. It can indeed be said that Benjy remembers only death and loss. His present-self moans at the loss, and his re-called-self howls or bellows at every smell of death. Evidently, except for his occasional "hushing" at some substitutes of life-giving symbols, he moans throughout his entire life after he loses Caddy. It is as if life were filmed in the negative—consisting only of loss and death. It is symbolic that Benjy's only excursion beyond the fence is to the cemetery and that his playground is a "graveyard."

When seen from outside, Benjy is: "a big man who appeared to have been shaped of some substance whose particles would not or did not cohere to one another or to the frame which supported it" (342). Similarly, internally, his scattered fragments of sense cannot be integrated into a unity. Even his own hunger is not known to him. It is merely that his mouth does the act of eating, while his eyes watch the food in his bowl diminishing. Pain also consists of scattered experiences of his throat, hand and mouth (72). This absence of a central "I" reminds us of Quentin who, in his imagination, watches his own eyes floating up. His disintegration, though, comes about in a direction opposite to Benjy's; Benjy is unable to recognize cause and effect, while Quentin is alienated from reality by over-intellectualization. Benjy has no ability to abstract, so "even eagerness [is] muscle-bound," while Quentin tries to disregard his body, trying to achieve the abstract self.

Nevertheless, in many aspects Benjy's perception shows a striking resemblance to Quentin's. The sun never shines on either of them, but only "slants." In Benjy's fragmented time, the sunlight is sliced into slanting sectors, while for Quentin the sun is merely one of his several chronometers telling the time. Birds also "slant" or poise, but never fly for them. Both brothers are keenly aware of shadows; Benjy, though, simply notices his own shadows without understanding the connection between his body and its shadow, while Quentin is obsessed by all shadows. This shows the similarities and differences between one for whom time has stopped and one who tries to stop time.

The choice of dates also seems to have special importance; Benjy tells his monologue on his birthday, and Quentin, on the day of his own death. The author's sympathy seems to be more for Benjy, who was stricken mindless at birth with no choice, than for Quentin, who lives in a deliberate perversion of self. Benjy's birthday is also the day of the Passion: Benjy's bellowing may thus signify the darkness of the world before the redeemer is resurrected. The author describes Benjy's bellowing: "Just sound. It might have been all time and injustice and sorrow become vocal for an instant by a conjunction of planets" (359).

Quentin embarks on his monologue by explaining, "When the shadow of the sash appeared on the curtains it was between seven and eight oclock and then

I was in time again, hearing the watch" (93). Quentin, like Benjy, catches life as on a negative film; he perceives the life-giving sun in its negative form of shadows which tell him of the passing of time. His world is undermined by the sound of time rushing beneath him. Time carries everything away before it can take definite shape: "a love or a sorrow is a bond purchased without design and which matures willynilly and is recalled without warning to be replaced by whatever issue the gods happen to be floating at the time" (221). A man is defined by the pattern of his reactions to or against the stimulants around him, which are called love, sorrow, joy or despair. In Quentin, "the long diminishing parade of time" does not offer him time enough to react, form his consciousness, and carve the outline of a stable "I." Consequently, Quentin suffers non-beingness in his fleeting time.

As the heir to Mr. Compson's fine collection of words, Quentin surpasses everyone else in the abundance of his vocabulary. He is himself dazzled by the glibness of his own words and cannot check himself. He cannot, for example, help using such language as "the caverns and the grottoes" in place of plain caves. While he is busily pinning down everything into "fine dead sounds," though, the present moment does not wait for him. Quentin always looks back at his static words while time carries him along. Thus: "the present makes its way in the shadows, like an underground river, to reappear only when it has become past" (Sartre, 228). Trying to mold his being upon the concept, he is always behind time, too late to carve an "I" caught in time. He always is in short of time. Unable to "come out even" with time, Quentin finds that for him, time never comes to life.

The loud sound of passing time transforms the whole world into "a gigantic chronometer" (*The Most Splendid Failure*, 124). The child Quentin misses his lesson because he is absorbed in counting time on his fingers. Every shadow turning into a sundial, he can almost tell by it the exact time. His body, too, turns into a clock by means of its slanting shadows in the morning and afternoon sun. In this world of slanting, any phenomena which poises itself in time and space in a secure identity soothe Quentin's racked nerves: "a gull motionless in midair," a trout hanging "delicate and motionless among the wavering shadows," the beauty of his friend's body in motion, which mounts into "a drowsing infinity," the twilight, "that quality of light as if time really had stopped for a while," and so on (110, 145, 209-10). They all give him the illusion of time having stopped.

He wants to negate the fact that his body occupies a particular space in a particular time. His own body is for Quentin a hateful thing which tricks him into doing something that his mind does not want. For instance, he feels bitter about "the business of eating" on the day of his suicide. The problem of space and time in the business of eating confuses him: "Stomach saying noon brain saying eat oclock" (129). He wants to exist only in mind, only in time stopped, but his shadow accompanies him wherever he goes, telling him he exists not only in the mind but also in the flesh.

To solve the confusion of time and space, he tries to make his shadow invisible at every possible moment. He chooses to eliminate it by walking on the shady side of a street and imagines blotting it "into the water, holding it until it was drowned." He treads upon it and tramples it into the concrete. Not only shadows, though, but also bells, chimes, and the persistent clicking of his watch pursue him. He wonders whether he can escape from time "in the bowels of the earth" where no shadows and no watches are to be found. To stop time's flow, to trap time, he turns his watch face down and finally breaks it. A fragment of the glass hurts his finger, but still its minute finger refuses to stop. When he takes the watch to a clock repair shop, he sees that every clock shows a different time. This enables him to convince himself that there is no such thing as "the right time."

As the heir to a family who kept "the principle that honor must be defended," Quentin forms his mode of behavior upon a concept of honor which is high above time. Acting upon the concept though, he becomes, in the eyes of his friends, a "half-baked Galahad" who only serves to get "licked" like a gentleman. For example, the child Quentin fights with his schoolmate when his friend boasts of planning a dirty trick on a female teacher, without giving thought to the possibility of his actually doing the trick, which requires a frog in November. The important thing for Quentin is that he fights and fights nobly for the honor of the female teacher against an opponent who is as big as he. Also, his preoccupation with the orderliness and cleanliness of his clothes on his last day reveals his faithfulness to his concept of gentlemanliness. Similarly, Herbert, the husband-to-be of Caddy, is to Quentin a most despicable person who thinks cheating is not illegal and therefore permissible. For Quentin, cheating is worse than a crime because it negates the concept of honor.

Quentin must value above all Caddy's virginity:

> Who loved not his sister's body but some concept of Compson
> honor precariously and (he knew well) only temporarily supported

by the minute fragile membrane of her maidenhead as a miniature replica of all the vast globy earth may be poised on the nose of a trained seal." (411)

A concept supported by her physical being would prove a concept caught in time, not behind it. When Caddy throws away her virginity, on which she herself places no value, Quentin's being threatens to fall to pieces. To keep the concept alive in some form, in any form possible, he has to say that they have committed incest. As Mr. Compson says, Quentin tries to sublimate "a piece of natural human folly into a horror." To keep Caddy "intact amid the eternal fires" above time, above "the sequence of natural events and their causes," her folly must be made into something clean and hard as "some Presbyterian concept of its eternal punishment" (411): "If we could just have done something so dreadful that they would have fled hell except us. *I have committed incest I said Father it was I it was not Dalton Ames . . .*" (97-98). Yet nothing, no concept, is dreadful enough to stop time.

Quentin is then afraid that Caddy, out of her love for her brother, may actually assent to the act of incest; all Quentin wants is to tell his father they did it, not to do it actually. Actual incest would plunge him right into the loud world of the flesh he wants to escape. When Quentin resoundingly warns Caddy's lover, Dalton Ames, "Ill give you until sundown to leave town," Dalton shows more concern for Caddy than for his own safety and offers Quentin a pistol (198). Furthermore, to help Quentin, whose only concern is to act upon a dead concept, Dalton lies for Caddy's sake, thus showing he is capable of sacrificing the show of masculinity in defense of Caddy. Quentin is doubly defeated by his own incapacity to love and his incapacity to act—that is, to live.

Living in words and capable only of self-love, Quentin is "long divorced from reality." He hopes that thinking is "making of unreality a possibility, then a probability, then an incontrovertible fact" (145). Thus, to change reality by means of mental operation, he wants to live in abstractions. His mind lives in a stopped time—that is, in the constant past: "I was. I am not" (216). While his body fights with Bland in the present, for instance, his mind lives over a scene with Dalton Ames in the past. What his body does is what his mind does not. What he is in his flesh is what he is not in his mind. Thus:

the whole thing came to symbolise night and unrest I seemed to be lying neither asleep nor awake looking down a long corridor of grey [sic] halflight where all stable things had become shadowy paradoxical all I had done shadows all I had felt suffered taking visible form . . . thinking I was I was not who was not was not who. (211)

To heal this unhinged state into that of an integrated person, he has to achieve "an apotheosis in which a temporary state of mind will become symmetrical above the flesh" (220). Nothing but the moment of death can encompass this apotheosis.[7] As death is his predetermined goal, Quentin's life is lived in "a deliberate and almost perverted anticipation of death" (411). Only in death can he find unity and peace, freed from the loud clicking of time: "And then I'll not be. The peacefullest words" (216). He drowns himself in the river, which fuses everything and flows away to the ocean. He feels that only by ceasing to exist, can he escape from time, and yet Quentin is actually drowned in time.

Jason and Quentin are two wheels moving in parallel orbits around the axle of time. If Quentin's fight with time is passive, Jason's is active and aggressive, and they are similar in busying themselves with constant self-justification. The parallelism becomes even clearer when the Appendix is treated as an integral part of the whole novel.

"Once a bitch always a bitch, what I say," Jason's monologue opens with this threadbare cliché, followed by much crude self-assertion" (223). This opening sentence sharply catches the outline of Jason, who tries to coerce his being in "the violent cumulation of his self-justification."(378). Having no time to do anything but borrow ready-made dictums, he is quick to pick up prejudices against women, Jews, foreigners—indeed any other people—and to buttresses his opinions with self-assertion.

His monologue, basically told in the past tense, is spotted with present tense of assertions such as "what I say," "like I say," or "I says." While Quentin's monologue is told in the past tense throughout, Jason is determined to keep fighting with the past tense. Jason, too, uses words to define himself; he is always in haste, always trying to catch up with time. Words constantly pull him to the past, but Jason fights back by violent self-assertion in the present tense. The author has Jason bubble in a self-righteous tone in his section, but his inner disintegration is remembered by the omniscient narrator of the fourth section. If

Jason were to tell how his invisible life fell apart in the past tense, he would become someone else. He has to forge himself in the split of the two tenses, working by means of crude and hasty self-assertion. Thus, his being is founded on words in spite of the frenzy of his actions.

Compulsions of hate and haste make up Jason. Swallows and pigeons are only nuisances, briars prick him, and the sun hurts his eyes. Even "the fact that the day was clearing" is "another cunning stroke on the part of the foe" (382). Hating almost everything and everybody, he is yet keenly conscious that time is slipping away from him. Always obsessed with what time it is, exactly like Quentin, he automatically looks at his watch whenever anything happens. He is constantly afraid of being late and asserts that he never has time, even to be the reproaches to the family which Caddy and his brothers were. His habit of grabbing money and food at every possible chance also reveals his compulsion to try to take a firm hold of everything in time in order not to be too late. He is made dizzy by the flurry of his own hate and haste: "But who can remember anything in all this hurrah" (268). Even he himself cannot help dropping an occasional remark such as "Sometimes I think what's the use of anything" (293). In fact, he achieves very little except making noises.

He conceives of honor in terms of opposition, that is, in terms of its violent negation. He prides himself on negating any traditional moral value which the long line of the Compson family has upheld. Contrary to Quentin, who makes such a fuss over the honor of his sister, Jason chooses to bed "a good honest whore." Any show of pride and decency pricks him into a violent hatred of what he thinks of as hypocrisy. He gloats, for example, over his having tricked Caddy out of her money by the literal execution of his promise to let her see the baby Quentin "a minute"; he literally did as he promised, and so he did not exactly lie. He is satisfied with his not having "the sort of conscience [he has] got to nurse like a sick puppy all the time" (284). Anyone who does not act out of a sense of profit is, in his eyes, "bound to be a crook," a hypocrite. Only Dilsey, the Negro servant whom he cannot force to leave even after he has stopped paying her weekly wages, defies his categorization.

Jason, a peculiar moralist, holds to his choice of what he considers to be honor. He is concerned with the good name of his mother, who asserts she is not a Compson but a Bascomb, and he keeps Benjy for her sake. Also, he frets over clothing dignified enough for himself as a man of position; he professes horror at the thought of himself "without any hat." In a way, in fact, he is far more sensitive to what people think of him and the family than Quentin. Only as far as his sense of honor demands, though, does he act inconsistently with his philosophy.

Denying having any moral code, unlike Quentin, Jason considers the police to be the proper judges of human conduct. He is determined to act mean simply for meanness' sake if it does not constitute a crime. He is engaged in the cotton market, a most un-Compson-like occupation, buying and selling the crop that farmers raise with the sweat of their brows, but without even touching the actual cotton himself. Jason's decision is to end: "that long line of men who had had something in them of decency and pride even after they had begun to fail at the integrity and the pride had become mostly vanity and selfpity" (415).

He is most comfortable in relations built upon business terms. Since he is being paid to work for Earl, any protection or consideration on Earl's part is insulting to him. A woman is an object which needs his managing under the un-written contract of her not imposing her existence when he is not in her company. When Luster cannot buy a circus ticket from him, Jason burns two tickets rather than giving one to him because giving away is against his idea of how a good businessman should act. His mode of behavior, coinciding with the work ethic of the day, does indeed give him the appearance of being rational and practical. His mother, for instance, believes he is the only one of her children with any practical business sense.

For a businessman, though, what Jason does is often irrational. With the one thousand dollars which was to give him a partnership in the shop, he buys a car, which then causes him terrible headaches because of the smell of gasoline. His motive in owning the car is not convenience, but revenge on the memory of Caddy, who deprived him of a position in a bank, a good business opportunity, and who had once owned the first automobile in town. Therefore, his car becomes merely a symbol of his revenge on the past. He hides his money in his room and makes a special trip back from work only to count it. No bank is good enough for his money because "all the rest of the town and the world and the human race too except himself were Compsons" (421). Of all his actions motivated by his hatred of the past, some do happen to coincide with rational businesslike acts. On the whole, though, he is "a philosopher in the old stoic tradition" rather than a businessman.

Boasting of his own cleverness, Jason is mocked for his own triumphing by the old man Job, who says, "You fools a man whut so smart he cant even keep up wid hisself" (311-12). Holding his money in his pocket all the time, and so unable to get his hand out in time to catch himself, the child Jason often stumbles. The adult Jason is robbed by his niece Quentin, his intended victim, not only of the proceeds of his thieving, but also of his own savings. Yet he can neither tell the police nor catch her since then the act of his cunning thieving would come out. All he can do is to grit his teeth, lost in a vain dream.

For him, as in Quentin, a human being exists as an abstraction. His niece Quentin merely symbolizes the past on which he has to take revenge. She and the money, together, have compensated him for the lost opportunities in life. Victimized by his victim, by the very symbol of the past, Jason, a supposedly shrewd business-man, is outwitted by "a bitch of a girl," "his invisible life ravelled out about him like a wornout sock" (391). In his defeat, imagining himself pleading with Lorraine, Jason's self-image completely crumbles. In fact, "Jason" does not exist any more. He has to find another symbol somewhere in order to resume his life. Jason gives the appearance of being down-to-earth, being "here" in the present, but in reality his present is perverted and distorted by the past; his frenzy leads him nowhere. In competition with time, with the memory of the loss of life's promise, he voyages furiously for nothing. He loses his fight with time.

"The day dawned bleak and chill" is not the opening of a monologue by Dilsey to correspond to the earlier monologues of Benjy, Quentin and Jason (300). The author himself makes his first entrance here and presents Dilsey:

> She had been a big woman once but now her skeleton rose . . . as though muscle and tissue had been courage or fortitude which the days or the years had consumed until only the indomitable skeleton was left rising . . . and above that collapsed face that gave the impression of the bones themselves being outside the flesh, lifted into the driving day." (331)

In this fourth section, Faulkner uses a traditional third person narrative, writing only of Dilsey's outer actions and never entering into her consciousness. The character Dilsey thus exists without any self-justification. As she lives her time in answer only to the needs of the time, living only in action, all an omniscient narrator has to do is to write of what she does. In short, what makes Dilsey Dilsey is not her consciousness but her action. Her life is not the sum of the moments of her consciousness, but the sum-total of what she has done.

While the Compson brothers fail to cope with life, Dilsey lives it to the fullest. Her time is lived in constant involvement in answer to the needs of her white family. She does the best she can by doing one thing at a time with all her being. Jason wonders at the way she prepares his supper as if "there wasn't but one supper in the world, and that was the one she had to keep back a few minutes on [his] account" (315). She identifies herself with what time demands. She has no time to waste on self-justification, as her participation is constantly needed.

She and Mrs. Compson make a good contrast. While Dilsey's life consists of "doing," all Mrs. Compson—the mother of the family—does is to verbalize complaints, self-pity, and feelings of rejection. She tries to negate the fact that Benjy is her own child by changing his name. When Caddy is abandoned by her husband, Mrs. Compson harps on her sanctimonious Christian duty not to accept her sinful daughter in order not to corrupt the morality of the family. Everything she does is accompanied with a performance of self-righteousness; she concerns herself only with a performance of morality, not with her own sin of not loving. Quentin feels she is a lightless dungeon, a mother who is incapable of giving love to her children. Therefore, in spite of her pious Bible reading and constant harping on self-sacrifice, she is in truth "a cold and querulous" person.

Dilsey has no time to read the Bible, but she believes in her heart in the affirmation of the life-giving force beyond the need for words. In contrast to the Compsons, she is willing to postpone the assurance of knowledge; she will know "in the Lawd's own time." Busying herself in working for others, she is free of superstition and obsession. She knows that changing a name brings no luck, and Jason cannot scare her out of helping Caddy by mentioning leprosy. Death also cannot frighten her because she knows everyone has to die someday. The clock in the kitchen is three hours slow, but she does not care. She does not need a calendar to change her clothes, as she removes layer by layer as spring progresses. Her Christ not "worn away by a minute clicking of little wheels," she is not obsessed with the passage of time (94).

Accepting time with whatever it brings and directly involving herself in it, she lives in the present. She patiently preoccupies herself with the present, enduring it by being involved in it, "which is the only possible way of living with time" (Vickery, 48). Whatever happens, she will do the best she can, so "Whut kin happen" to her? She knows "whatever happens must be met with courage and dignity in which there is no room for passivity or pessimism" (Vickery, 48). For her, time is eternal and blessed with its possibilities in "de power en de glory." Her timeless patience and unshakable serenity, which Quentin so envies, stem from her conviction that God knows everything and that all she has to say is that "Ise here." She lives fully in time—that is, in daily life.

When one asks if she can save mankind, the answer, however, is in the negative. As Jason says, she cannot even save any of the Compsons. In a world where life is lived "with all its incomprehensible passion and turmoil and grief and fury and despair," one cannot save another unless human nature undergoes a complete change (419). All she can do is to do "something" to make the world a little better than when she finds it, without asking for any reward. She neither escapes from time nor fights with it, but accepts it, with willed actions.

Surely, *The Sound and the Fury* is Faulkner's metaphysic of time, one which is finally affirmative. In order to take an affirmative stand, he must first probe thoroughly in the "turmoil and grief and fury and despair" of man. Indeed, more than the five-sixths of the novel is devoted to presenting time as "the mausoleum of all hope and desire" (93). Still, Faulkner's overall thrust—his final message—is affirmative. Sartre, for all the sensitivity with which he commends Faulkner's skill in arresting motion, complains in his conclusion that Faulkner tries to escape from this world by means of "mythical ecstasies." Really, however, far from wanting to forget time in mythical ecstasies, Faulkner wants human being to do something about his or her condition instead of theorizing about evil. He hopes that man is capable of believing, without proof, reproof, or support, "that man's condition can be bettered" (*Faulkner at Nagano*, 158). I have to say of Faulkner, "I like his art, and I believe in his metaphysic."

8. *Light in August*
Christmas, Our Fellow Country Man

> Thou still unravish'd bride of quietness,
>   Thou foster-child of silence and slow time,
> Sylvan historian, who canst thus express
>   A flowery tale more sweetly than our rhyme:
> What leaf-fring'd legend haunts about thy shape
>   Of deities or mortals, or of both,
>   In Tempe or the dales of Arcady?
> What men or gods are these? What maidens loth?
> What mad pursuit? What struggle to escape?
>   What pipes and timbrels? What wild ecstasy?
>
>   Keats, ode on a Grecian Urn

Faulkner, who called himself a failed poet,[1] is known to have loved John Keats. As he said in an anonymous article called "Verse old and nascent: a pilgrimage" published in *The Double Dealer* for April, 1925:

From this point the road is obvious, Shakespeare I read, and
Spencer [sic], and the Elizabethans, and Shelley and Keats. I read
"Thou still unravished bride of quietness" and found a still water
withal strong and potent, quiet with its own strength, and satisfying
as bread. That beautiful awareness, so sure of its own power that it
is not necessary to create the illusion of force by frenzy and motion.
Take the odes to a Nightingale, to a Grecian urn, "Music to hear,"
etc.; here is the spiritual beauty which the moderns strive vainly for
with trickery, and yet beneath it one knows are entrails;
masculinity.[2]

Indeed, Faulkner, with his impressions stored in his lumber room,
crystallized them into *Light in August* published in 1932. Keats' Grecian urn, that
"still unravish'd bride of quietness," "foster-child of silence and slow time," was
embodied by Lena Grove, on whose quiet surface are drawn the "mad pursuit"
and the "struggle to escape" of those who need "to create the illusion of force by
frenzy and motion." Structurally, Lena round, in an advanced stage of pregnancy,
is being watched in the opening scene, and the story closes with her holding a
baby in her arms and attended by Byron (vaguely a Saint Joseph and the mediator
of the two stories), thus suggesting the roundness of an urn.

It little matters that Faulkner sometimes said *Light in August* was Lena
Grove's story and at other times said that it was the tragedy of Joe Christmas,
since Lena provided the ground on which to chisel the tragedy of Christmas in
sharp lines. If one must choose between these two possibilities, one can say that
Faulkner entrusted all his dream to his heroine, Lena (Helena) Grove, while he
made his hero, Joe Christmas, the bearer of universal human destiny. Lena is
everything celestial that the author aspired to, when not numbered as an earthy
member of the human race.

After he settled on the title *Light in August*, Faulkner came to refer to Lena
as more an embodiment of light than as a Grecian urn. That is, she had been
conceived as a Grecian urn, but she was materialized in the world of literature as
an embodiment of light. Both, however, represent the same life force, "a luminosity older than Christian civilization," one not inhibited by any abstract concept,
of which Christianity can be one. When asked about the meaning of the title *Light
in August*, Faulkner answered:

in August in Mississippi there's a few days somewhere about the middle of the month when suddenly there's a foretaste of fall, it's cool, there's a lambence, a luminous quality to the light, as though it came not from just today but from back in the old classic times. It might have fauns and satyrs and the gods and—from Greece, from Olympus in it somewhere. It lasts just for a day or two, then it's gone . . . and that's all that title meant, it was just to me a pleasant evocative title because it reminded me of that time, of a luminosity older than our Christian civilization. Maybe the connection was with Lena Grove, who had something of that pagan quality of being able to assume everything . . . . (Gwynn and Blotner, 199)

The paths of Lena and Christmas never cross each other. It is Byron Bunch and the farmers and townspeople who provide the common ground, who link Lena's and Christmas' stories, working as mediators between the characters. For example, Byron Bunch introduces Lena and Doc Hines (Christmas' mad grandfather) to Hightower (a defrocked minister). Also, Byron sometimes embodies the authorial point of view; Byron almost introduces Christmas in Chapter 2 by describing how the vagabond impressed Byron when Christmas made his first appearance at the planing mill where Byron works.

Barefoot Lena, with her round belly, placidly walks onto the scene with her shoes in her hand. Faulkner identifies this country girl, who travels looking for the father of her child, with the "still water withal strong and potent, quiet with its own strength," which he found in Keats' ode. Lena, more an image than a character, is an embodiment of the natural stream of life, one for whom time flows toward eternity. She is as quiet and as potent as nature itself, with no anxiety of being, needing no struggle to prove herself.

Lena is another product of Faulkner's male aspiration for the eternal woman, the dream woman who can never exist. Therefore, for a reader with no particular inclination to romanticize women, she is less a woman than an allegorical figure made into a character. That she is allegorical and not intended to be real is made known in the opening section: "Behind her the four weeks, the evocation of *far*, is a peaceful corridor paved with unflagging and tranquil faith and peopled with kind and nameless faces and voices."[3] On the other hand, for Christmas, an embodied human tragedy, the same road runs on barren, always empty.

Lena, considered as a heroine to match the doomed hero Christmas, is far from a Forsterian rounded character. Some critics call her the "vegetable Lena" or, like Hyatt Waggoner, wonder if Faulkner was saying that only fools can prevail after the death of all human intellectuality (Waggoner, 119). Lena, who slowly enters the stage in radiance, sets the tone or provides the ground of the story, but when she reenters toward the end, she justifies the question posed by Waggoner. It must have been difficult even for the author in his prime to form such a "still unravish'd bride of quietness," such a "foster-child of silence and slow time," into a character. Here is another example of Faulkner's attempt to achieve the impossible in literature.

Yet, even considering all this, *Light in August* is entitled to be called Lena's story since Faulkner tried to write (more accurately, he wanted to write) of life in its origin, of light in its origin. To do this effectively, he had no alternative but to create Christmas, the embodiment of darkness, a darkness that can be seen only through light, with Lena shedding enough light to throw Christmas' agony into sharp relief.

When human creatures live close to the earth, their living is shaped by the alteration of night and day and by the change in the seasons in their due course. When cities came to be formed, people, cut from the earth and living in contact only with their fellow humans, felt a need to insist on their individuality, on particularity. Thus, humans came to be doomed "to create the illusion of force by frenzy and motion." Roses smell roses even when called by another name, and cats do not lose their catness by being raised among humans. The basis of human-beingness is, though, far more fragile than those of roses or cats, since humans cannot exist as a collective noun. If raised among wolves, a human wolf is called a wolf boy and can have no human language and no human mode of behavior. This higher animal, standing on its two hind-legs, has both glory and misery.

The human animal exists in its individuality, a fluid individuality that appears only through its contact with the world of others. Faulkner has Byron say to himself, "*you are just the one that calls yourself Byron Bunch today, now, this minute . . .* " (316). If a person cannot give coherence to his image, which appears but for an instant, his individuality is dispersed into the air, plunged into "the deep abyss," "the bottom of hell." With the disappearance of God, people have come to rely upon abstractions: money, organized religion, past glory, almost anything which can bind their scattering selves to their illusory individuality. If people's chosen identities are threatened, they do not hesitate to victimize each other. Simply in being human, they alternate between being victims and those who victimize.

Joe Christmas is a constant victim, because he does not know who he is: "the people that destroyed him made rationalizations about what he was." In Faulkner's own words:

> that was his tragedy—he didn't know what he was, and so he was nothing. He deliberately evicted himself from the human race because he didn't know which he was. That was his tragedy, that to me was the tragic, central idea of the story—that he didn't know what he was, and there was no way possible in life for him to find out. Which to me is the most tragic condition a man could find himself in—not to know what he is and to know that he will never know.(Gwynn and Blotner, 72)

Light in August tells, therefore, the story of a man who has nothing to define himself except his name, Christmas. As Alfred Kazin aptly put it:

> "Joe Christmas" is worse than any real name could be, for it indicates not only that he has no background, no roots, no name of his own, but that he is regarded as a *tabula rasa*, a white sheet of paper on which anyone can write out an identity for him and make him believe it. . . . Joe Christmas is nothing but the man things are done to, the man who has no free will of his own, who is constantly seeking a moment of rest . . . and who looks for an identity by deliberately provoking responses that will let him be *someone* . . . . (Hoffman and Vickery, 248, 252-53)

Faulkner puts this man deep in the American South in the early twentieth century. Any society, a composite body of individuals, comes to have a collective face and assume a collective character. In the world where Christmas' tragedy takes place, if someone calls another "Nigger!" it would make that person much more furious than if he were called "Killer!" One is always made conscious of his racial identity. Another important, specifically local condition was its Puritanical religiosity, which, as the author understands, dwells more on God's wrath than on His love. People have to be black or white in every sense of the word—in the color of their skin, in their judgement, in their behavior. That is to say, nothing is to be done in moderation; there is no neutral gray zone in which to reside:

> Pleasure, ecstasy, they cannot seem to bear: their escape from it is in violence, in drinking and fighting and praying; catastrophe too, the violence identical and apparently inescapable *And so why should not their religion drive them to crucifixion of themselves and one another*? (273)

In this Southern culture, religious faith urges people more to deny life than to affirm it, since they use religion not to love each other, but to persecute each other, dividing themselves into the chosen and the damned. For people to feel secure in their chosen state, they need a constant supply of those not chosen to damn.

Doc Hines, Christmas' grandfather (though this fact is unknown to Christmas) —poor, uneducated, ugly; in other words, having nothing to be proud of but his white skin—chooses to act upon the concept of white supremacy. He has no particular occupation except being a fanatic, a self-appointed preacher who identifies the damned by the color of their skin. He kills the Mexican who is Christmas's natural father, allows his daughter Milly to die in childbirth, and abandons the nameless baby on an orphanage's doorstep. Living in the orphanage as a janitor to fulfill his self-appointed role as the judge of the chosen and the damned, Doc Hines succeeds in making this child with parchment-colored skin wonder if he has black blood in him. By creating such a fanatic to determine Christmas' destiny, the author perhaps over-stretches himself, but the lingering (at least for this reader) episode of the kidnapping of the child might serve to provide a feel for the locality that has produced Hines.

The baby abandoned on the doorstep of an orphanage on Christmas Eve is, as a joke, named Joseph Christmas. He has to carry this unusual name, a sign which causes people to wonder what he will do with his life; a life lived in peace cannot be expected of a man with this name:

> And that was the first time Byron remembered that he had ever thought how a man's name, which is supposed to be just the sound

for who he is, can be somehow an augur of what he will do, if other men can only read the meaning in time. (23-24)

In the orphanage, Christmas, a shadowy child, feels he is somehow different from the other children. His world there operates according to the rule that punishment follows every pleasure. The five-year-old Christmas catches a young female dietician in bed with an intern doctor; she tries to bribe the child, himself waiting to be punished, with a gold coin. The order of his world thus collapsing, Christmas comes to feel a vague fear of women, who seem to act not on principle but on emotion. He also comes to feel a dislike for his own need for food since for the child the dietician is always connected with food. This incident, foreshadowing his abiding distrust of female race and food, fundamentals for any living person, imbued Christmas at a tender age with life-denying inclinations.

Because of this dietician's intrigue, Christmas comes to be adopted by McEachern as a white boy. Mr. McEachern, a strict Calvinist, raises Christmas "to fear God and abhor idleness and vanity." Christmas gradually comes to form himself through resistance to his foster father. McEachern is reliable in that he acts and reacts methodically, on principle, so the boy can form himself into a man by simply contradicting his foster-father; he can, that is, grow in the negative mode, in a relativity which at least provides shape though no substance.

Mrs. McEachern, with all her kindness and care, always acting on emotion, uses Christmas as a means to resist her husband; she tries to bribe Christmas to her side, to turn him into a crying weakling. Knowing this, he resists his foster mother also; for instance, he throws away the dishes which Mrs. McEachern has secretly prepared for him and instead devours scattered food on all fours, like a dog. Similarly, he steals money that would have been given him if he had asked. Food and money—everything—has meaning for him only if they give him a sense of masculinity by the way he gets them.

Even while constantly resisting his father and negating his religion, the boy comes to adopt McEachern's uncompromising approach toward everything. Rejecting Calvinistic religiosity, Christmas makes the Calvinistic thought pattern his own. Thus, under McEachern, he forms himself into a man constantly driven by negation and rejection.

In an encounter with Bobbie, a prostitute waitress, though, the boy can act as a normal adolescent who wants female company without acting out his mechanism of negation and rejection; he can talk quietly while touching female flesh as if no one has ever done such a thing before. He thus comes to know a peace and quiet such as he will never know again. This brief period of suspension ends when Christmas tells her he might have black blood in him; Bobbie shrieks and calls him "Nigger," and the men present beat him up. The youth, with an outlaw's mannerisms and does not know whether he is black or white, finds himself on the streets.

He is doomed by motion because, the moment he gives up his frenzied motion, his being threatens to dissolve. He creates an image of his self by a series of violent, if meaningless, motions, such as fighting with a black man who calls him white or making a white man call him black. Blacks, women, every person he meets who does not prompt him into a fight all form a bottomless abyss that threatens to absorb him into non-existence. When he is quiet, not moving, his stillness is seen by others as that of a non-being: "In the wide, empty, shadow-brooded street he looked like a phantom, a spirit, strayed out of its own world, and lost" (84). He thus has no choice but to keep moving in order to make his external self appear distinct. However, because his every move is made in reaction, in the end he is basically passive. Cut off from any social group or institution, and having no identity other than that of man, he has to rely on masculinity in its most easily recognizable form, violence.

The twenty-odd years Christmas spends on the road are condensed into a few sentences:

> He thought that it was loneliness which he was trying to escape and not himself. But the street ran on: catlike, one place was the same as another to him. But in none of them could he be quiet. But the street ran on in its moods and phases, always empty: he might have seen himself as in numberless avatars, in silence, doomed with motion, driven by the courage of flagged and spurred despair; by the despair of courage whose opportunities had to be flagged and spurred. He was thirtythree years old. (167)

This vagabond, involuntarily returning to the place where he was born, is watched by Byron:

> there was something definitely rootless about him, as though no town nor city was his, no street, no walls, no square of earth his

home. And that he carried his knowledge with him always as though it were a banner, with a quality ruthless, lonely and almost proud. (22)

In contrast with Christmas, who does not know who he is, Joanna Burden is "burdened" by her heritage. Her father, an ardent New England Puritan, taught her how to cope with blacks:

'You must struggle, rise. But in order to rise, you must raise the shadow with you. But you can never lift it to your level. . . . But escape it you cannot. The curse of the black race is God's curse. But the curse of the white race is the black man who will be forever God's chosen own because He once cursed Him.' (188)

These words dig out the channel of her life's stream, and she devotes her life to living out the metaphor.

Christmas can come into contact with her because their encounter involves violence right from the beginning. Joanna has "the mantrained muscles and the mantrained habit of thinking born of heritage and environment with which he had to fight up to the final instant" (174). To seek such a relation as marriage with her would be for Christmas nothing but self-denial: "'No. If I give in now, I will deny all the thirty years that I have lived to make me what I chose to be'" (197). Christmas, who rapes and finally kills Joanna, is no more than a murderer, yet, paradoxically, he is absolutely passive in that he sees himself as reacting in his self-defense because Joanna deprived him of his individuality by treating him as an abstract collective noun, a member of the black race.

In their sexual relations, her pent-up desire cannot find its proper channel without interference by the concept of damnation. In order to be excited, she has to feel that she will burn in hell fire, be damned, let herself be taken by one of the cursed black man. When with the coming of menopause she comes not to need him sexually, she again demands that he play a black man, this time as a shadow she has to raise up, a cross she has to carry. She plans to educate him to make a black lawyer of him, and finally she demands that he kneel and pray to save her from the hell into which she has fallen; she demands of him that he play a black man and accept the religion in whose shadow he had formed himself by hatred and negation. What she demands of Christmas is total self-denial, the absolute erasure of his being.

It is evident that they cannot co-exist. Before he kills her, Christmas murmurs, in total passivity, "Something is going to happen to me." There is no choice for him but, in his turn, to seek to eradicate her:

> he believed with calm paradox that he was the volitionless servant
> of the fatality in which he believed that he did not believe. He was
> saying to himself *I had to do it* already in the past tense; *I had to
> do it. She said so herself.* (207)

He kills Joanna, who is armed with her ancestor's ancient pistol, by cutting her neck with his razor. After killing her, he storms into a black church and curses God from the pulpit. These are both gestures of rejecting the role of a black man that Joanna has forced him to play and of rejecting the God she has forced him to pray to. In killing Joanna in self-defense, though, Christmas only ends by destroying himself.

Even when Hightower sees universal human destiny in Christmas, he, a former minister, fails to come to his rescue. In contrast to Christmas, who is doomed to motion, Hightower, as his name signifies, has escaped into dreaming, into non-action. His father, an austere Puritan who offered himself to the cause of putting an end to slavery, acted as an oppressor of his son. Hoping that nobility will skip a generation, Hightower dreams of the gallant figure of his grandfather, a legendary hero of the Civil War. This grandfather becomes Hightower's pride, that for which he lives—a life made possible only because Hightower never knew his grandfather in the flesh.

Hightower has chosen the church as a career not in order to love people, but in order to be sheltered from "the harsh gale of living" and dying:

> He believed with a calm joy that if ever there was shelter, it would
> be the Church; that if ever truth could walk naked and without
> shame or fear, it would be in the seminary. When he believed that
> he had heard the call it seemed to him that he could see his future,
> his life, intact and on all sides complete and inviolable, like a
> classic and serene vase, where the spirit could be born anew
> sheltered from the harsh gale of living and die so . . . . (356)

As this allusion to a classic Grecian urn suggests, he fulfills a cyclical pattern by marrying the daughter of a powerful figure in the seminary and being dispatched to the very parish where his grandfather died in the battle. He does this in the belief that his salvation lies in returning "to the place to die where [his] life had already ceased before it began" (355). His wife, despairing of the unnatural relation she has with her husband, kills herself in disgrace; expelled from the church, Hightower yet refuses to leave, living on in Jefferson as a self-styled martyr and victim. Thus he succeeds in acquiring a sanctuary where he can dream his life away without having actual contact with flesh and blood people.

This ex-minister of God refuses to get involved with the destiny of Christmas, saying, "I have bought immunity, I have paid." Yet, as a minister of God, still attached to the habit of helping others, he delivers Lena's child; thereby he attains the strength to see himself as he really is. Yet, still unable to take action and rescue Christmas from Percy Grimm, a self-appointed representative of the persecutors, Hightower watches over Christmas' horrible dying to the very end.

Percy Grimm, who lynches and then mutilates Christmas, is not a born cold-blooded killer. Still, as one who can realize himself only in violent self-justification and vehement self-assertion, he cannot be part of the natural stream of life, just as Christmas cannot. The concept of white supremacy and patriotism, made legal by the new civilian-military act, saves him: "He could now see his life opening before him, uncomplex and inescapable as a barren corridor, completely freed now of ever again having to think or decide . . ." (336). The nagging question of how to deal with his life is suddenly answered. His choice is not to endanger the sobriety of the world he lives in, so the society welcomes him. Grimm and Christmas are like twin brothers; both are captives of their situations, too purist to walk the moderate middle road and both find themselves truly distinct only in violent actions. This fraternal wheel revolves until it grinds Christmas to death.

The irony is that the moment Christmas, refusing to play the black man, kills Joanna, those who were hesitant before can now put a label on him; he is now a black who has raped and murdered a white woman. Even Gavin Stevens, the elite intellectual of the town, talks of Christmas' killing as caused by the conflict between the black blood and the white blood in him. All the whites of the town boil up, wanting to damn a black man in order to keep themselves, the white race, as the chosen people. To doubt or pity him might lead them to doubt themselves—or even to find themselves pitied. To validate their chosenness, they need to victimize Christmas as one of the cursed.

Hunted like a wild animal in the fields, Christmas comes for the first time to see the flow of natural time and the pulsating, living things around him. When he thus comes to have direct contact with the earth, Christmas, hitherto doomed by motion, can stop acting in a fury. Abandoning himself to the nature that surrounds him for the first time in his life, he knows the fulfillment of being human without any need to pursue self madly. His thirty-year series of barren motions, like a chained pearl necklace, comes to an end:

> It is just dawn, daylight: that gray and lonely suspension filled with the peaceful and tentative waking of birds. The air, inbreathed, is like spring water. He breathes deep and slow, feeling with each breath himself diffuse in the neutral grayness, becoming one with loneliness and quiet that has never known fury or despair. 'That was all I wanted,' he thinks, in a quiet and slow amazement. 'That was all, for thirty years. That didn't seem to be a whole lot to ask in thirty years.' (246)

A peace he has never known also comes, as he comes to think, from the fact that he does not need to eat. The act of eating equates with the will to continue one's life; as long as he eats, he has to keep up his struggle to give shape to his life: *"Yes I would say Here I am I am tired I am tired of running of having to carry my life like it was a basket of eggs   they all run away"* (250). He finally finds peace with himself when he gives up the struggle to carry his fragile individuality like a basket of eggs, a struggle that for him has been life.

It is not because he acknowledges his blackness that Christmas now sees a black man as his brother. He is in the process of becoming a person, one who can no longer be categorized merely in terms of race. When he is captured in the town in which he was born, Christmas makes the townspeople all the more furious by behaving as neither black nor white, since for them he has to be a Negro who murdered a white woman. When he surrenders his struggle in search of his true identity, the identity given to him is that of a victim, a sacrifice:

> For a long moment he looked up at them with peaceful and
> unfathomable and unbearable eyes . . . the man seemed to rise
> soaring into their memories forever and ever . . . . It will be there,
> musing, quiet, steadfast, not fading and not particularly threatful,
> but of itself alone serene, of itself alone triumphant. (346)

The sacrificial lamb—also "with peaceful and unfathomable and unbearable eyes"—is the symbol of Christ's being. Much criticism has been written
in an attempt to establish similarities between Jesus Christ and Christmas, but
symbol hunting does not seem very productive. Christmas approaches Christ, the
prototype of humankind, mainly in the pain of his life, a life lived in agony and
ending as a sacrificial offering. If Faulkner criticizes Calvinistic religiosity as
practicing a life-denying severity, this does not mean that he denies Christianity.
Those who are most severely criticized here are those who have turned their backs
on Christ, the essence of love and pity, and who use religion to judge and crucify
each other.

Most people identify themselves in terms of where they belong and feel a
sense of belonging through rejecting not-belonging. They are afraid of those who
do not seek their identity in belonging because these outsiders force others to
doubt their own thoughtlessly chosen identities. The seeker for perfection, the one
who does not make easy compromises in his or her search for identity and who is
therefore hard to categorize or label—this is the person who is most hated. When
most people find such a human being, they do not hesitate to assign him or her an
identity they themselves have chosen, to grind him or her into the ground of their
own struggle to escape from doubt. This happens all over the world, differing
only in detail. Christmas, a vagabond in the American South, represents all of us
who might be like him in different times and different places.

9. *Absalom, Absalom!*
A Symphony of Echoing Voices

Absalom, Absalom! has inspired a vast variety of criticisms regarding the central issue: what the author was trying to say. This diversity of opinion on the part of world's readers was, to a degree, encouraged by the author himself when he talked to the students during the now famous question-and-answer session at the University of Virginia:

> I think that no one individual can look at truth. It blinds you. You look at it and you see one phase of it. Someone else looks at it and sees a slightly awry phase of it. But taken all together, the truth is in what they saw though nobody saw the truth intact. . . . It was, as you say, thirteen ways of looking at a blackbird. But the truth, I would like to think, comes out, that when the reader has read all these thirteen different ways of looking at the blackbird, the reader has his own fourteenth image of that blackbird which I would like to think is the truth. (Gwynn and Blotner, 273-74)

More than two decades ago, the present writer wrote a paper on *Absalom* acting upon this advice.[1] I have stuck to my chosen image of a blackbird, disregarding the hunch I had on my first reading—that it might deal with the story of an absence—or with the absence of a story. Now I would like to read *Absalom* not so much as a story as the absence of one, asking if it is a story at all.

I found that of all the criticisms I referred to in my earlier paper Peter Brooks' is the most penetrating (Brooks, 286-312). Brooks discusses Faulkner's narrative along with others by Stendhal, Freud, Dickens, Flaubert, Conrad, and Beckett. Brooks, with this wide range of reading, wrote the most provocative essay on the narrative of *Absalom*; Faulkner cannot be treated with too much specialization.

This time, instead of focusing upon the characters or upon what happens in the story, I want to discuss narratives per se—and also what is not narrated. I will question if a plot in fact exists in this novel; if not, I will try to prove its absence by going through the text chapter by chapter. I find *Absalom* more of an orchestration of narratives than a story told chronologically.

Absalom opens with a narration from the point of view of Quentin. The story of Sutpen, in its most compact form, the skeleton of it, is given by the eternally outraged Rosa Coldfield:

> *It seems that this demon—his name was Sutpen—(Colonel Sutpen)—Colonel Sutpen. Who came out of nowhere and without warning upon the land with a band of strange niggers and built a plantation—(Tore violently a plantation, Miss Rosa Coldfield says)—tore violently. And married her sister Ellen and begot a son and a daughter which—(Without gentleness begot, Miss Rosa Coldfield says)—without gentleness. Which should have been the jewels of his pride and the shield and comfort of his old age, only—(Only they destroyed him or something or he destroyed them or something. And died)—and died.[2]*

The variations of this legend are repeated by several narrators in various tones and colorings, like waves rolling to the shore and then retreating. Estella Schoenberg calls this *Absalom*'s "ripples" quality, taking her cue from Faulkner's own text:

> *Maybe nothing ever happens once and is finished. Maybe happen*

> *is never once but like ripples maybe on water after the pebble sinks, the ripples moving on, spreading, the pool attached by a narrow umbilical water-cord to the next pool which the first pool feeds, has fed, did feed, let this second pool contain a different temperature of water, a different molecularity of having seen, felt, remembered, reflect in a different tone the infinite unchanging sky, it doesn't matter . . .* (261)

Rosa as the narrator is, then, projected in greater relief than the story she tells:

> talking in that grim haggard amazed voice until at last listening would renege and hearing-sense self-confound and the long-dead object of her impotent yet indomitable frustration would appear, as though by outraged recapitulation evoked, quiet inattentive and harmless, out of the binding and dreamy and victorious dust. (7-8)

The first chapter opens with Rosa talking and Quentin listening; then Quentin begins to speak through his imagining, supposing, and compiling what Rosa has said. Yet, his questioning and answering is conducted within himself; his speech forms itself into a monologue. The monologue sections often begin "Quentin seemed to watch" or "it seems," as if he has no confidence in his own imagining, supposing, and compiling. Rosa has chosen the best hearer, one who listens but who never initiates a dialogue because what she needs is not a partner in conversation but a recipient of her monologue. The two monologues—Rosa's and then Quentin's interpretation of what Rosa tells—proceed side by side; the two speakers have no dialogue in this chapter.

Rosa's monologue, contrary to Quentin's, consists of assertions given by an eyewitness. After repeating "I saw" with such decisiveness throughout, though, Chapter 1 ends in a surprise for the readers: "'But I was not there. I was not there to see the two Sutpen faces this time—once on Judith and once on the negro girl beside her—looking down through the square entrance to the loft'" (30). What she has said so far could all be dismissed at this point. The reason she so insists on talking in spite of having no intention of reporting what she saw and so knows to be true is provided by Quentin: "*It's because she wants it told*" (10). The author suggests in this opening chapter that it is the narrative impulse that has prompted her to talk, to tell tales.

Chapter 2 deals with Sutpen's appearance in the town of Jefferson from out of nowhere and his marrying into respectability by choosing Ellen Coldfield as his wife. The townspeople's talk of the legend about them, which has come down through witnesses and is told by Mr. Compson to Quentin. The shift of the narrative voice is signaled only by how they refer to Quentin's grandfather— whether as "General Compson" or "your grandfather." Often, particularly in the former half of this chapter, dotted as it is with words unlikely to be those of either General Compson or townspeople, the narrators are not clearly discernible. What is most likely, though, is that Mr. Compson lets General Compson and the townspeople use his (Mr. Compson's) language; as such, Mr. Compson talks through everybody else's mouth. Only after his speech is placed in quotation marks do his own views, his own prejudices, come more directly into his speech.

Sutpen, the man of action, is cynically analyzed by an avowed by-stander, one who always stands back from the action. Quentin is obliged to listen to his father's opinions on the subject of women and marriage. At the same time, a dilettante over-burdened with knowledge, Mr. Compson depicts Sutpen as a damned hero in a Greek tragedy—good at shooting, subjugating slaves, and marrying not by church ceremony but by walking through torch lights lifted high by slaves standing in rows.

Chapter 3 offers us Rosa's upbringing and the story of the Sutpens at the time of her coming into contact with them. Mr. Compson's introductory remark, "your grandfather told me," appears far less frequently than in Chapter 2. Only a very few characters are known to him; most are created at Mr. Compson's own discretion, with an occasional "probably" or "perhaps." For example, by present-ing Mr. Coldfield, the father of Ellen and Rosa, as a narrow-minded fanatic, he reveals his hatred of puritans. In dealing with Ellen and her daughter Judith, he is inclined to treat those of the female gender as species other than human, creatures who are not men. Helen, the wife of a wealthy plantation owner, is presented thus: "she moved, lived, from attitude to attitude against her background of chatelaine to the largest, wife to the wealthiest, mother of the most fortunate" (69). Similarly, Judith is rather perfunctorily described in terms of a middle-aged dilettante's concept of young virgins:

> where they exist (this the hoyden who could—and did—outrun and
> outclimb, and ride and fight both with and beside her brother) in a
> pearly lambence without shadows and themselves partaking of it;
> in nebulous suspension held, strange and unpredictable, even their
> very shapes fluid and delicate and without substance . . . (67)

Upon Sutpen Mr. Compson imposes his own fatalistic view of life. Wishing to equate Sutpen with a doomed hero in Greek tragedy, he goes so far as to change a name: he insists that Sutpen, out of ignorance, has made the mistake of naming his daughter, begot from a slave woman, Clytie (Clytemnestra) instead of Cassandra because Clytie is to play the role of a dark prophetess like Cassandra. He speaks of Miss Rosa's projecting all the frustrated dreams of her young days on Judith. Yet, Mr. Compson, more faithful to his thinking than to the facts, projects himself on every character who enters into his narration.

Especially in Chapter 4, Mr. Compson characterizes Bon, Sutpen's unacknowledged son, as a fatalist patterned after himself. His tone of cynicism in the previous chapter becomes one of approval, almost praise:

> a certain reserved and inflexible pessimism stripped long generations ago of all the rubbish and claptrap of people (yes, Sutpen and Henry and the Coldfields too) who have not quite yet emerged from barbarism . . . . (94)

Here Mr. Compson indicates that all people except Mr. Compson are uncivilized barbarians.

Bon and Henry are treated as materials from which Mr. Compson can make a comparative study of the refined Latin culture and the barbaric Puritanism of the American South. Dialogues between Bon and Henry, sometimes internal and sometimes voiced, are freely invented. The relationship between Henry and Judith is explained as out-and-out incest since the hearer at this point is Caddy, the object of Quentin's incestuous love in *The Sound and the Fury*. Henry has to match Judith with his half-brother, Bon, for Henry to metamorphose "into the body which was to become his sister's lover" (105).

Not knowing Bon, Sutpen's natural son, Mr. Compson does not understand why Bon wants to marry his half-sister Judith, or why Henry had no choice but to kill Bon: "It's just incredible. It just does not explain. Or perhaps that's it: they dont explain and we are not supposed to know" (100). Here, Mr. Compson has prevented himself from succumbing to modestly admitting the impossibility of knowing the truth. It is more important for him to make a survey of an issue than to know the truth of it; therefore, he quickly abandons every issue from which he cannot make a beautiful vision of his own. The only tangible object, that which can be seen and touched in this chapter, is Bon's letter to Judith, handed by Judith to Mr. Compson's mother.

Mr. Compson, the eternal by-stander, lives for voicing what he thinks he has observed and thought. His whole existence is staked on talking; he has to make a speech about every issue, posing as a detached observer, always sitting one step back from the action. It is only natural that the content of what he says matters far less than the act of talking itself.

Like Mr. Compson, Rosa must also tell tales. In Chapter 5, she tells of Henry's killing of Bon, of Sutpen's marriage proposal to her, and of her acceptance and subsequent refusal. Why she refused, though, the voluble Rosa deliberately refrains from telling. This Rosa, who has spent her earlier life listening to voices behind closed doors, now lives in words. She could love Bon without reserve since for her he existed only in the words of others. She has become an expert on love—"*all polymath love's androgynous advocate—*" without making any actual contact with a partner (146). Even if she buries Bon with her own hands, inside the casket is "*a shape, a shadow: not of a man, a being*" (149). However, as a narrator, she amazes us by declaring that she cannot contradict someone who says that nothing has happened; she knows that her own memory is not to be counted upon: "*there is no such thing as memory: the brain recalls just what the muscles grope for: no more, no less: and its resultant sum is usually incorrect and false and worthy only of the name of dream*" (143). The question of why Rosa tells old tales to Quentin is answered by herself—that she can bear life only by telling tales:

> *like quiet in the raging and incredulous recounting (which enables man to bear with living) of that feather's balance between victory and disaster which makes that defeat unbearable which, turning against him, yet declined to slay him who, still alive, yet cannot bear to live with it.* (161)

Never having lived her own life in action, words are all she lives for, and she knows it. Even though she is a maniac who never stops condemning Sutpen as the devil, though, she may yet be a more reliable narrator than Mr. Compson, who never takes time to observe himself.

Shreve, Quentin's friend at Harvard, is from Canada, a new country with no old ghosts to haunt him. He makes his first entrance in Chapter 6, which opens with Mr. Compson's letter telling of Rosa's death. Then Shreve offers his guess as to why Rosa has refused Sutpen's proposal. This chapter, sprinkled with the deliberately open vocabulary of youth, recounts Sutpen's struggle to found a Southern dynasty of his own, his losing everything, and his seducing Milly, grand-daughter of Wash Jones, a poor white man. Then Quentin's inner voice, prodded by Shreve's crude language, continues to talk about the nature of the relationship between Sutpen and Jones, about Rosa's running away from Sutpen, and about Sutpen's making Milly pregnant and then deserting her because she has not given him a male heir.

Here Quentin introduces the topic of the five tombs that he saw and Mr. Compson's talk of how and by whom each was erected. Mr. Compson cannot help but be tempted into depicting Bon's concubine, a mulatto woman, in a Wildean cemetery scene. At this point, Charles Etienne Bon, Bon's previously unknown son, comes in on his way to Gethsemane, trying to get the answer to his question, '*What are you? Who and where did you come from?*' (203). Chapter 6 ends with the appearance of Jim Bond, the idiot son of Etienne and a black woman.

The basic narrative voice in this chapter is that of Mr. Compson telling of what he has heard from his father, General Compson. Inserted here and there, though, are Quentin's remarks as he responds by means of an intense monologue. As for Quentin, the author makes it clear that Quentin is not an eyewitness of those scenes by adding such remarks as "It seemed to Quentin," "He could actually see them," or "He could see it." Yet Quentin concludes by telling us that he can see better just because he was not there; he can freely re-create past events without seeing or he can re-create them better by not seeing them.

That Sutpen, Henry, Bon, and Etienne have actually lived is proved only by their tombstones, which serve as documentation. What has happened in human life is either absorbed into oblivion or is incorrectly remembered by those who choose to remember. Mr. Compson has the dead Sutpen ask: *" 'What was it, Wash? Something happened. What was it?' and Jones looking at the demon, groping too, sober too, saying, 'I dont know, Kernel. Whut?' each watching the other" '* (186).

Chapter 7, Supten's story told chronologically through Quentin's first person-narration, presents the least difficulty to the reader. For about three pages, though, Shreve intrudes with, "Let me play a while now"; the spirit of play motivates him to participate in the creation of the story (280). Shreve talks with unsentimental sentimentality of his own youth—ashamed of being moved in spite of himself. Sutpen, while of a tender age, encountered a shocking incident which made him determined to have others recognize him as a member of the human race in the South:

> 'You see, I had a design in my mind. Whether it was a good or a bad design is beside the point; the question is, Where did I make the mistake in it, what did I do or misdo in it, whom or what injure by it to the extent which this would indicate. I had a design. To accomplish it I should require money, a house, a plantation, slaves, a family—incidentally of course, a wife.' (263)

Sutpen wonders if he has made "a minor tactical mistake" when Bon, the son of his first marriage, appears as a friend of his legitimate son, Henry. Sutpen comes home after losing everything in the Civil War and is killed by Wash with a scythe he had loaned to Wash, a scythe the goddess of destiny carries; he thus meets a destiny of his own creation.

The tale is told by Quentin's grandfather, General Compson, to Mr. Compson, and by Mr. Compson to his son, Quentin. At each recounting, the tale is deformed or at times totally misunderstood, so in the end little of the original is preserved intact. Also, no one can be sure if Sutpen's first-person narration was really expressed in that form. The only tangible fact is that even Sutpen, the man talked about, begins to talk.

Quentin, willingly or unwillingly, is often put in the position of a listener. He sighs:

> *Am I going to have to have to hear it all again* he thought *I am*

> *going to have to hear it all over again I am already hearing it all*
> *over again I am listening to it all over again I shall have to never*
> *listen to anything else but this again forever so apparently not only*
> *a man never outlives his father but not even his friends and*
> *acquaintances do . . . . (277)*

Recalled to the past by the old tales, Quentin is unable to outgrow his father, to escape from the past. As long as he remains an eternal recipient of other people's talk, he cannot live the present moment, which is life itself.

In Chapter 8, Quentin glimpses the possibility of his escaping from the role of a mere listener. Henry and Bon, youths together fifty years ago, are freely and without reserve invented between Quentin and Shreve. A brief letter Bon once wrote to Judith and Bon's tomb are enough materials from which to create those who might never have existed. The speaker and the hearer becoming one in this chapter; Quentin and Shreve accomplish "some happy marriage of speaking and hearing" (316).

> both thinking as one, the voice which happened to be speaking the
> thought only the thinking become audible, vocal; the two of them
> creating between them, out of the rag-tag and bob-ends of old tales
> and talking, people who perhaps had never existed at all anywhere,
> who, shadows, were shadows not of flesh and blood which had
> lived and died but shadows in turn of what were (to one of them at
> least, to Shreve) shades too, quiet as the visible murmur of their
> vaporizing breath. (303)

Bon, a tool for his mother to take revenge on Sutpen, is sent to the University of Mississippi by a guardian, a crafty lawyer. Bon, who patiently waits for Sutpen's recognition, if only by a sign or a glance, looks totally different from the elegant fatalist created by Mr. Compson. Henry, meanwhile, agonizes over the difficulty of convincing himself of the marriage between his half-brother Bon and his sister Judith. Shreve mentions that Bon loved Judith simply because to do so was incest. Here, though, Quentin cannot join with Shreve in their exchange because Shreve makes so light of using the term "incest," the word that has so much of importance for Quentin.[3]

Sutpen tells Henry that Bon has black blood in him. Bon thus can do nothing but say he will marry Judith in order to get recognition of being Sutpen's son. Henry may be able to justify incest, but he cannot justify mixed marriage. As Henry and Bon go off on horseback side by side, bound for home, Henry shoots and kills Bon at the gate of the plantation. The photograph of Bon's woman and her son is left as Bon's will, his tender message to Judith: "'*I was no good; do not grieve for me*'" (359). Chapter 8, created with "the heart and blood of youth" and with little concern for facts, is so poignantly narrated that it becomes almost irrelevant to ask whether or not it is based on facts: " there are some things that just have to be whether they are or not, have to be a damn sight more than some other things that maybe are and it dont matter a damn whether they are or not?" (322). This is Rosa's "*there is a might-have-been which is more true than truth*" deliberately rephrased in the crude language of Shreve (143). Rosa and Shreve think alike in spite of the distance between them in time, space, and gender.

The last chapter seems to contain the key to the plot: Quentin's confrontation with Henry in Sutpen's dilapidated mansion, a confrontation which binds every fragment together to form the plot of Sutpen's story, which thus fully surfaces for the first time:

> *And you are* —?
> *Henry Sutpen.*
> *And you have been here* —?
> *Four years.*
> *And you came home* —?
> *To die. Yes.*
> *To die ?*
> *Yes. To die.*
> *And you have been here* —?
> *Four years.*
> *And you are* —?
> *Henry Sutpen.* (373)

What is happening here? Is this imagined by Quentin, or was it an actual conversation? Since Quentin is not likely to demand of an emaciated old man if he is Henry Sutpen or not, even if he did see the old man, the assumption is that these words were spoken in the mind of Quentin. It is a kind of palindrome, a dialogue which makes no progress, with no beginning and ending. We are left wondering if anything really happened. If this confrontation forms the pivot around which the whole narratives turn, then the plot has a hole at its very center:

> 'Your old man,' Shreve said. 'When your grandfather was telling this to him, he didn't know any more what your grandfather was talking about than your grandfather knew what the demon was talking about when the demon told it to him, did he? And when your old man told it to you, you wouldn't have known what anybody was talking about if you hadn't been out there and seen Clytie. . . .' (274)

The author here deliberately writes "Clytie" rather than Henry, perhaps to withhold the mystery.

Like a folding fan without a pivot-pin, the overlapping narratives are not bound into a traditional plot. However, there is no question that *something* has happened to drive Quentin to despair beyond all hope of recovery; the dead past has somehow forced its way into the present and made him an eternal captive. At the same time, the collaboration between Quentin and Shreve to create a story comes to an end with Shreve, back to being a youth from Canada, asking Quentin, "Why do you hate the South?" (378). Their happy union of speaking and hearing broken, Quentin is forced back to the position of a listener. The flames of the Sutpen mansion engulf Henry and Clytie, trapped within, as Jim Bond, the idiot scion of Sutpen, is heard howling in the ruins.

Figures reflected in a distorted mirror with their narratives loosely bound, is *Absalom* entitled to be called a novel, or even a story? Schoenberg says the Sutpen story is so full of holes that it is impossible to mend them. Admittedly it is full of holes, but this reader wonders if this novel is really Quentin's story, as Schoenberg contends. Rather, no hero is to be found in *Absalom*, only the resonance of its narrative voices. The power of the narration itself, even in the absence of a sustaining plot, grips the readers' attention from beginning to end. The key to *Absalom* lies more in Judith's words than in the dialogue between Henry and Quentin:

'Because you make so little impression, you see. You get born and
you try this and you dont know why only you keep on trying it . . .
or having to keep on trying and then all of a sudden it's all
over . . . . And so maybe if you could go to someone, the stranger
the better, and give them something—a scrap of paper—something,
anything . . . at least it would be something just because it would
have happened, be remembered even if only from passing from
one hand to another, one mind to another, and it would be at least a
scratch, something, something that might make a mark on something that *was* once for the reason that it can die someday . . . (127)

Judith does not make an issue of the letter's factual content. Here, it is more
important to leave "a scratch" for her existence and her suffering to be remembered.

    Everybody talks in order to be remembered, and yet they do not believe in
the potency of language. Except for the "innocent" Sutpen, who went to the West
Indies, taking written words at their face value, no one believes that language
functions as it should. The author has General Compson, the man seemingly
equipped with more discretion than the other narrators, think of:

the language (that meager and fragile thread, Grandfather said, by
which the little surface corners and edges of men's secret and
solitary lives may be joined for an instant now and then before
sinking back into the darkness where the spirit cried for the first
time and was not heard and will cry for the last time and will not
be heard then either) . . . (251)

If Mr. Compson is obliged to tell what General Compson said to him, he, the man
of words, seems not to have any objection to his father's statement.
    Rosa, who has lived only in words, does not believe that language
communicates. She speaks, for instance, of:

the very simple words with which we were forced to adjust our
days to one another being even less inferential of thought or
intention than the sounds which a beast and a bird might make to

each other. (153-54)

People choose to speak, even knowing that human language functions less well than the sounds made by a beast and a bird. Even Sutpen, a man of action not of words, the subject of much talk, suddenly breaks his silence:

> trying hard to explain now because now he was old and knew it, knew it was being old that he had to talk against: time shortening ahead of him that could and would do things to his chances and possibilities even if he had no more doubt of his bones and flesh than he did of his will and courage, telling Grandfather . . . (261)

Every one is spurred to talk by the signs of "time shortening," striving to be remembered after he or she is gone, striving to leave footprints, to talk against the all-absorbing oblivion.

Faulkner says of what makes the writer write:

> I don't think that he bothers until he gets old like this and has a right to spend a lot of time talking about it to put that into actual words. But probably that's what he wants, that really the writer doesn't want success, that he knows he has a short span of life, that the day will come when he must pass through the wall of oblivion, and he wants to leave a scratch on that wall—Kilroy was here— that somebody a hundred, a thousand years later will see. (Gwynn and Blotner, 61)

Whatever form artists choose by which to express themselves, each creator ultimately cries, "I am here! Remember me!" To talk, to express oneself in the meager and fragile thread of language, is to live. In this, *Absalom* is more like music than literature. It is a grand symphony of narratives, with the Sutpen motif often recurring. Amid the reverberation of many voices, this reader also joins in to talk what she has seen of, her own image of the blackbird.

10. A Huge Parable on Peace
Faulkner's War and Peace

'It will be a War and Peace close enough to home, our times,
language.'   To his editor, Robert Haas, referring to *A Fable*.

A Fable is still the most unpopular of all Faulkner's works. The author himself was, to a degree, prepared for its poor reception. "It is a fable, an indictment of war perhaps, and for that reason may not be acceptable now"[1] and twenty century has continued to be one of wars. In 1955, the year following the book's publication, the author as a cultural ambassador sent by the State Department told Japanese scholars of American literature at the final session of the Nagano Seminar that "one state, one precinct has no business compelling another state or precinct to correct its ills; that never works, but the precinct, the state itself must correct those ills." This reader of *A Fable* wonders if the Korean War, the Vietnam War, and the Gulf War "worked." So is it not unlikely that some force has been working to confine Faulkner in a totally apolitical, aesthetic domain and to disregard him as a writer who has argued against the old problem of war and humankind? It was not a sudden shift for him to write about war, that "fatal vice which man has invented."[2] The radical individuality shown in his earlier works found a natural course of development in *A Fable*. Only a very personal writer can be truly political without being merely ideological. In Faulkner, to be personal is to be political.

Right after its publication in 1954, favorable reviews appeared by Heinrich Straumann[3] and Delmore Schwartz[4]: the one a defeated German and the other a son of Jewish immigrants escaped from Rumania. Before Abner Keen Butterworth wrote his Ph.D. thesis, *A Critical and Textual Study of William Faulkner's* "A Fable"[5] in 1970 and even after, however, it still tended to be neglected or ignored by critics and readers alike. At the 1985 International Faulkner Symposium *Faulkner after the Nobel Prize*, held in Izu, Japan, Noel Polk read his paper titled "Enduring *A Fable* and Prevailing."[6] André Bleikasten complained that Faulkner, a private man, played an expected public role after winning the Nobel Prize.[7] Kenzaburo Ohashi, who reads *A Fable* as a continuity and accomplishment of his earlier works, belonged to a small minority.[8] Joseph Blotner who has devoted decades to his biography of Faulkner lamented the time and energy Faulkner spent on the book.[9] In 1989, though, Joseph Urgo valued it as the greatest of the author's achievements.[10]

Faulkner received the Nobel Prize in 1949, when the Cold War was already in full swing. His acceptance speech assumes a backdrop of a destroyed globe after a nuclear war in which no country wins. That voice echoes in *A Fable*. During his three-week sojourn in Japan, whose people had suffered nuclear bombings, "His every utterance was charged with utmost seriousness and simplicity" avoiding "the least trace of flippancy or superficiality" (Preface to *Faulkner at Nagano* v). He appeared on the Japanese horizon more as a writer whose "duty" and "privilege" was "to help man endure by lifting his heart" than as a modernist or a chronicler of the American South.

Faulkner, though he talked as a son of those defeated in the Civil War, could not react quite positively when Tomoji Abe, a noted writer, wanting to introduce *A Fable* to the recently defeated Japanese people, asked for permission to translate it. Abe wrote that Faulkner's answer was something like, "translate or not translate, either is all right . . ." Abe's translation, with a commentary by Kenzaburo Ohashi and a promotional band around the cover with the catch phrase "Anti-war Literature," appeared in 1960. Unfortunately, though, that was the year of the Mutual Security Pact signing and the suppression of the concurrent wide-spread protest movement. The US, immediately after the war, had brought us a

Constitution that makes a pledge of everlasting peace, the dream of humankind, but soon changed its policy in the context of the Cold War. To my knowledge, in the '50s, only Abe, Ohashi, and Takako Yamaguchi were capable of reading this hard-to-read book since the scholars who participated in the Nagano Seminar chose *Sanctuary* as Faulkner's best. My contemporaries and scholars of the younger generation, with few exceptions, have taken an aesthetic approach under the sweeping influence of New Criticism and so have paid little attention to *A Fable*.

Faulkner had, in his "little postage stamp of native soil," material that he could not exhaust in his lifetime. He watched people who live and die in the Deep South, his Yoknapatawpha, with understanding and compassion. All of his works are sustained by his chosen desire to attach the utmost importance to the life and breadth of humankind, a species of animals which moves on its hind legs. Yet in the so called Yoknapatawpha saga, the Civil War is not exactly presented as killing each other. He volunteered for the British Air Force in Canada in the First World War, with his proper share of youthful heroism. At the opening of the Second World War, he, a writer of over 40, seeking his livelihood outside of Hollywood, tried to be accepted by the US Air Force.[11]

Yet, nevertheless, he was also the writer who started his career with *Soldiers' Pay*. After the young people around and close to him had gone to war and the young faces of war casualties began to appear in Lafayette County papers, Faulkner gradually became immersed in the argument over war and humankind. As the ideology of the '30s apparently passed by without touching him, he was moved only by and through his personal experiences. Personally involved in World War II, Faulkner's eyes naturally moved beyond Yoknapatawpha to the world at large. After all, he had pursued throughout his career as a writer the universal in the individual and the individual in the universal.

A Fable is the story of humankind as it moves on its two hind legs. Faulkner continued to develop an argument for a decade, which ground down not only the author but his readers as well. Right after setting to work, he wrote to Robert Haas of Random House, whose airman son had been lost in action off Casablanca:

> The argument is (in the fable) in the middle of that war, Christ

(some movement in mankind which wished to stop war forever) reappeared and was crucified again. We are repeating, we are in the midst of war again. Suppose Christ gives us one more chance, will we crucify him again, perhaps for the last time. . . . I am not trying to preach at all. But that is the argument: We did this in 1918; in 1944 it not only MUST NOT happen again, it SHALL NOT HAPPEN again. i.e. ARE WE GOING TO LET IT HAPPEN AGAIN? now that we are in another war, where the third and final chance might be offered us to save him. (*A Biography*, 1154)

In the Yoknapatawpha saga, the institutionalized religion of the area is severely criticized. When the author published this heavy book with crosses on its cover, many were puzzled or embarrassed. In *A Fable* Faulkner for the first time summarized his own understanding of Christianity. His approach seems to be close to that of the Catholic Church after the Second Vatican Council. Faulkner, alone in the south of the Bible belt, argued over the dynamics of Christ and His church as an institution. "God is"[12] voiced in all his works, in his own way; only in *A Fable*, which has Christ rise a second time on the battlefront of the First World War, however, was he able to express God's being.

Jesus, the Dreamer, chose to entrust His church to Peter—Peter, who followed Jesus from the first encounter but in the end denied him three times, a very weak man but one with passion and possibility. Jesus said to Peter, "*On this rock I found My church*" (364). The rock here was an unstable, inconstant human heart and the church, the nebulous, airy faith of man. It was not Peter but Paul, a Roman, only one-third dreamer, who realized His dream, who established the visible church that was not "*snared* in that frail web of hopes and fears and aspirations" of man (364). Paul gave man "a morality of behavior inside which man could exercise his right and duty for free will and decision" (364). As Olga Vickery rightly points out, it cannot be denied that individual faith is in need of systematization and dogmatization in order to be evangelized (Vickery, 209-27).

Yet, once an institution is founded on absolute goodwill and necessity, it inevitably begins to exert its force to absorb or disregard individual differences. Yet, "the salvation of man is in his individuality" not in his membership in a group.[13] The Church as an institution should, 'as a traveler on this earth,' be a fluid unit, "some movement," composed of individuals who pursue the unattainable dream of loving each other. Moreover, the first commandment of love is to recognize and understand the variety and differences among humankind. In the horse theft episode of *A Fable*, a dreamt-of-church and its community, which accepts individuals as they are, is presented with one stroke of the brush, as a part of the legend.

Joseph Urgo sees Christ as a rebel against every human institution. Yet, since rebellion is, in a way, a reactive move, passive almost, not based on free choice and decision, it operates only momentarily. If Christ had acted in the relativistic domain of rebellion, Christianity would not have endured. Camus, after his "I rebel—therefore we exist," adds, "if only for a moment."[14] Individuality can obtain its place not in rebellion but in the dynamics of individuals and the institution to which each belongs. When this dichotomy is lost, every institution, including the family, the smallest unit, immediately becomes regimented.

Faulkner develops his argument on the basis of reality, the ever-durable power structure, and of dream, the union of free individuals. Dreams are born of mundane, grim reality. Reality without dreams can exist; without reality, though, there can be no dreams—and only dreams born of reality can change the world. History is created and colored by those who dare to go beyond reality. Therefore, in *A Fable,* the Corporal, who staked his life on bringing peace to the battleground of Europe, confronts his father, the General. "Corpus" in the Christian context is the "body of Christ," so the Corporal can mean one who embodies Christ. The confrontation is related by the General:

> we are two articulations . . . which . . . must contend and—one of them—perish: I champion of this mundane earth . . . you champion of an esoteric realm of man's baseless hopes and his infinite capacity—no: passion—for unfact. (347-48)

The way in which the General is interpreted determines one's understanding of the entire work. Butterworth misses the point by interpreting him as the embodiment of civilization. Joseph Urgo, by taking him as the embodiment of institution, is inclined to underestimate the author's Yoknapatawpha pieces. If the reader takes the General as the champion of the earth, as related by the author, there still remains a problem. The author had no recourse but to make the Marshal, the champion of the earth, playing the role of God the Father who sacrifices his only begotten Son to realize his Son's and his dream, and also the role of the father-reality who gives birth to the son-dream. The author, conceiving the General as "an implement"[15] to frame the structure of the fable, has ended in burdening him with incompatible multiple roles, leaving many readers con-fused—and many critics enraged.

The general has no name; a name would signify individuality. His earlier life was spent in escaping from the doom of the chosen. He exiled himself to a post in "the black hole" of the earth, where he succeeded in avoiding warfare, but only through tricking another into dying for the nation. Now, he is the old general at the top of the army hierarchy, one who, like a priest, calls everyone "my child," knowing all and believing in nothing. When he is alone, he looks like a toy, a child immobilized under the glitter of stars and braid.

The Corporal is a shadowy character who speaks little and whose life, in fragmented Biblical analogies, is loosely told by others. The Corporal's sister Marthe, as Holy Mother, continuously makes speeches. Those who bear a Biblical analogy unquestionably fail to emerge as characters. The runner, for example, who carries on the movement started by the Corporal, an imitator of Christ, can-not be rated an aesthetic success as a central character who might be expected to carry this huge parable through.

On the other hand, sharply chiseled out with a master's skill are those not loaded with allegorical meaning. They justify what the author told Harold Ober, his literary agent of long standing, four or five years after he began the work: "It was a tragedy of ideas, morals, before; now its getting to be a tragedy of people."[16]

The army, the arena in which *A Fable* is played out, is a miniaturization of the state, where hierarchy is functionally systematized. War is embedded in the mechanism of the nation, the last resort to save it from bankruptcy. War as a complex chronicle is reduced to "a simple regimental attack against a simple elevation of earth" where people engage in killing each other. To justify killing on an individual basis, to make a vice into a virtue, abstract concepts like the glory of the Fatherland have to be trumpeted. Killing becomes for the individual "A vice so long ingrained in man as to have become an honorable tenet of his behavior" (344). Men die en masse and are enshrined as unknown soldiers. Enshrined in the tomb are not people whose nameless bones are buried but the nation:

> a plan, a design vast in scope, exalted in conception, in implication

> (and hope) terrifying . . . the vast solvent organizations and
> fraternities and movements which control by coercion or cajolery
> man's morals and actions and all his mass-value for affirmation or
> negation . . . finding its true apotheosis then, in iron conclave now
> decreeing for half the earth a design vast in its intention to
> demolish a frontier, and vaster still in its furious intent to obliterate
> a people . . . . (232)

The characters in *A Fable* are divided into two broad types: those who
have sold their birthright in humanity to be promoted and those who remain
human within the system. Army professionals are identified only by their ranks,
with the General at the pinnacle of the hierarchy. The Group commander, who is
called only by his nicknames, Mama Bidet or General Cabinet, treats human
beings as functioning machines. He is an excellent supervisor, quite good at
making an army function well because he understands that the essence of control
lies in not letting the controlled know their hidden capacities. The army is a
miniature of a modern nation in that those who are promoted are men like him,
not brave soldiers like Gragnon. The corps commander, Lallemont, a cool
professional, uses the army to climb the institutional ladder. The German general
is concerned more with how to be a good soldier than with how to win the war.

This group is joined by a comfortably regimented army priest who has
turned his back on Christ, whose dream is to bring peace on earth. This military
priest is a living contradiction since a soldier deals with death, and a priest, with
life. The Corporal calls him Sergeant, not Father.

The division commander of the mutinied regiment is given a full name,
Charles Gragnon, emphasizing his individuality. Completely institutionalized in
the army, where no privacy is provided, he, a born orphan, has abandoned every
natural desire that is born of privacy. He even thinks officers have to be hated by
their troops. Not knowing that modern war doesn't require brave soldiers, he
pursues his individual moral code of honor and pride in the army structure. His
promotion is stopped simply because he is a perfect soldier, not a cold-blooded
supervisor; he is not a good commander.

Gragnon, knowing only how to obey and give orders, does not know how
to fill the empty hours before he is summoned to the headquarters. Presented with
silence and privacy for the first time, he recognizes himself as a natural man and

listens to nature alive around him. The unfortunate commander, walking into a grassy field full of cordite to find a cicada, is watched closely with sympathy and pity.

The second type of those who remain human is subdivided into three species. Later, the author names them "the trinity of consciousness":

> The same trinity [Faulkner compared his own trinity to that of the three mates of *Moby Dick*] is represented in *A Fable* by the young Jewish pilot officer who said, 'This is terrible. I refuse to accept it, even if I must refuse life to do so,' the old French Quartermaster General who said, 'This is terrible, but we can weep and bear it,' and the English battalion runner who said, This is terrible, I'm going to do something about it. (Meriwether and Millgate, 247)

Levin, the first of the trinity, is an English pilot officer still in his teens. His Jewishness makes his Jewish mother both protest her son's going to war and at the same time urges him to go. He is put in the same situation as young Japanese-Americans who were released from concentration camps to fight for their adopted country, America. In Levin's chapter, his native country, England, is a motherland, not a fatherland. A boy wishing to be recognized as a son of England, never having endured the silence of thinking alone, is easily moved by the slogan, the glory of the nation, especially when added to this is a natural urge to show his masculinity.

When a cease-fire strangely comes to the war before he is able to experience actual combat, Levin, like Gragnon, never having endured the peace of daily life and not knowing what to do, is made to face the mechanism of war and the true nature of nations. After burning his Sidcott, his aspired-for flying uniform, in the latrine—the place where no one can act heroically—he thumbs off the safety of his pistol. Refusing to accept the reality, including his own, he has no alternative but to terminate his life.

In contrast to Levin, who is chiseled out with loving care, the Quarter-master General comes on stage as "a gigantic peasant" with "a sick face" and "hungry eyes." He expects the General to reappear "in the shape of man's living hope" since the General, as one born into wealth and fame, is free from rapacity.

Yet, the author lets the General say that it is rapacity that makes man immortal. With respect to his inner motivations and depiction, the Quartermaster General is rather perfunctorily created. His role is to represent those who observe but do not act, the majority in almost any society. His resignation, like the Corporal dying to bring peace to the battle ground and the General sacrificing his only son to endure and realize his dream, is only "a gesture" to show his ability to recognize evil.

The dustjacket blurb written by the author and turned down by Random House, begins with "This is not a pacifist book":

> On the contrary, this writer holds almost as short a brief for pacifism as for war itself, for the reason that pacifism does not work, cannot cope with the forces which produce wars. In fact if this book had any aim or moral . . . it was to show by poetic analogy, allegory, that pacifism does not work; that to put an end to war, man must either find or invent something more powerful than war and man's aptitude for belligerence and his thirst for power at any cost, or use the fire itself to fight and destroy the fire with; that man may finally have to mobilize himself and arm himself with the implements of war to put an end to war . . . . (*A Biography*, 1494)

Private soldiers "do something" to stop the war when they do not leave the trenches at the order to attack. If, when taken from peaceful lives to become killing machines, they act out of a natural desire called self-preservation, a hatred of killing, or just the wish to go home, it is mutiny. It is the soldiers at the front, who act on the natural instincts of man without any specified ideology or slogans, who cause the runner to recover his hope and his belief in man.

Not only the soldiers but also those who work with their hands and have their own Yeses and Noes are entrusted with hope. These "people" (the author's favorite word) vividly populate the stage more than those who play allegorical roles. Crossing the stage are preachers who do not belong to religious institutions; a farmer who feels despair for the devastated earth; a dressmaker who aspires to be a writer and who dies to save strangers; a young farmer who says "No!" to an order to assassinate; a lock-picker who takes a risk for the sake of a dead soldier's mother; a man who, having lost his son, becomes a father to all soldiers; mothers who never stop lamenting, and good thieves who are shot on either side of the Corporal—an idiot who never gives up his dream of going to Paris and a pickpocket who dies for his friend. With the exception of Judas, a city intellectual, all these twelve disciples are mountain men, farmers and fishermen. This reader senses the author's message to be that only those who make use of their own bodies and skills can act independently and therefore carry forward the possibility of humankind.

The runner, who continues the Corporal's movement by taking the absolute risk of believing in man's capacity and hope, is an architect in peacetime, signifying his belief in human creativity. He changes himself through his own search for the rediscovery of the lost hope in humankind. In contrast to Cash in *As I Lay Dying*, whose change is shown in his monologues and closely watched from outside, the runner's conversion is explained only by his inner voice while the surface shows him forcing his decision on others—acts, which can justly be categorized as cruel and egoistic.[17]

Butterworth, condemning the runner as didactic and cruel, tries to prove his point by frequently using the word "unpitying" with regard to him. However the same word "unpitying" is also often attached to the life-giving, witless sister of the Corporal, Marya, signifying that the word "unpitying" is given a positive connotation in *A Fable*. The author is the one who urges man to "use the fire itself to fight and destroy the fire with"; the man of pity, Christ himself, "has come to the world to throw his sword in." To love, to give life to oneself and others, one sometimes has to act on the basis of will and not on the basis of the emotion of pity.

Surely the runner is not provided with a charm capable of carrying this huge book. However "an imitator of Christ" lives in a different domain from that of charm; charm is a power outside of the Divine system, belonging to the Devil. Thomas a Kempis' *The Imitation of Christ* comes across to this reader as totally devoid of poetry and depresses her in spite of its aim to encourage readers. In *Quo Vadis* by Sienkiewicz, the Epicurean Petronius is far more convincingly presented than Peter, the leader of the twelve disciples. The personification of an 'attractive' imitator of Christ in literature is close to impossible. In the English sentry, the author has narrowly escaped by defining him as a dirty, morose, foul-mouthed character. Faulkner, characteristically, has attempted the impossible in the creation of the runner. Indeed, *A Fable* also might well, as a whole, be ranked as a magnificent failure, magnificently attempted.

The architect, unable to cope with the absurdity of having absolute control over the life and death of soldiers just because he is an officer, has succeeded in demoting himself to a private soldier, a runner. This is not because he loves men but because through living in the midst of soldiers he wants to inspire despair without reservation and to deprive himself of the foolish habit of having hope for humankind, "of having to perform forever at inescapable intervals that sort of masturbation about the human race people call hoping" (62).

By watching the process that leads to the mutiny and its aftermath, the runner realizes that one can act only through believing in human capacity without proof or support; he could have recovered his lost hope by just believing. Like Paul, who had never met Jesus, the architect chooses to carry on the movement started by the Corporal; again like Paul, he tries to give men "a morality of behavior inside which man could exercise his right and duty for free decision." The runner, "one furious saffron scar," disturbs the General's national funeral and dies in the arms of the ex-Quartermaster General, the pacifist and the eternal by-stander.

One third of the way through *A Fable,* which begins with billowing mob scenes and ends in "tears," Faulkner inserts the horse theft episode, an episode told in an entirely different tone. The stage is suddenly shifted from the European battleground to the American Deep South hinterland, and the narrative is present-ed in 'tall-tale' fashion. Lifted for a while by this tender legend encased in a gray fable, the reader can follow its grinding argument. The author describes this episode as "one single adjectival clause describing a man."[18] In fact, it has more weight than an "adjectival clause" when seen as counterpointing the dream, the American dream, against the reality of a world at war.

A man, an English sentry and a money lender, acts out the pageant in and out of Mississippi as Harry, a groom. Sutterfield, the black groom who has shared the dream with Harry, tells the runner that Harry has a mystery in him, or rather is Mystery itself. Sutterfield is a fantasized embodiment of the author's dislike for institutionalized religion. The author has this man, an unauthorized minister of God, say that he believes in man rather than in God. This does not mean to deny God, but to believe in God, to hope and to preach; all stem from the same root, a belief in man. The old soldier who informs the runner of the second coming of Christ also acts as a lay preacher, a night watchman, a nurse and now a prophet.

In contrast to these private, unauthorized preachers, the author has the regimental preacher, a military priest, kill himself. Faulkner himself is a lone preacher who finds it necessary to argue with himself. This quality in him made him, a very private man, declare in public that a writer's duty and privilege is to help man not only to endure but to prevail.

Harry, the English sentry, links Mississippi with the European battlefield. Every payday, privates make long lines to borrow money, at an outrageous rate of interest from a "stupid, surly, dirty, unsocial, really unpleasant man" (59). Not only that, they make him the beneficiary of their soldiers' life insurance. The deal gives soldiers the hope of coming back alive because the lender's and borrowers' death rate are exactly the same. The sentry acts on "ethics" and the only word that can explain their relation is "love" (147, 59). Hope and belief in man: love is hidden in this dirty man. When they are barraged from both sides in no man's land, for the first time in his life the sentry refers to himself as "we," not "I." The groom, who lived a love story with the horse in Mississippi, can now join the human race:

> the immortal pageant-piece of the tender legend which was the crowning glory of man's own legend beginning when his first pair-ed children lost well the world and from which paired prototypes they still challenged paradise, still paired and still immortal against the chronicle's grimed and bloodstained pages . . . . (153)

This "immortal pageant-piece" has to be played out in America, where not only Harry but the American people are the heroes. Descendants of those pioneers who crossed the ocean for freedom, they are capable of challenging reality and uniting themselves by free choice. In the country they founded, a human worth is to be judged by how well one copes with one's dreams, how one goes a little beyond human reality. The horse and the men are pursued by the railroad company, the insurance company, the horse's owner, the Federal police, and finally by the prize of the "sheer repetition of zero" for the crime of horse theft. The theft, committed to keep the horse—the symbol of possibility—from becoming mere breeding stock, becomes "a passion, an immolation, an apotheosis" (153). The law, buttressed by money, pursues the passion for infinite possibility.

In the country developed not with kings and lords but with the law as its core, the courthouse rises in the center of every county seat. With the law of the people, by the people, for the people becoming God, the country brings forth great many outlaws just because it is so law-conscious, so law-abiding. Noel Polk is convincing when he says, "we thus assert our freedom by choosing to obey."[19] Yet, in this legend, deputies, sheriffs, lawyers and, most of all, farmers, choose the dream of pursuing infinite possibility and so protect criminals by law.

In the legend, the author has created a hand-made Utopia cut out with the sharp edge of his pen. The people in his Utopia, in their Civil War, don't belong to either side or rather they have changed partners for their own cause of equality between the races. The community forms no hierarchy but accepts a stranger, a foreigner, as he is. The minister accepts one who needs to share his prayers but who is not accustomed to join groups into his church, and he is not afraid of defining war as "murder and sudden death." The community center serves also as a gambling joint where a "jug full of white mountain whisky" is on a shelf. Gambling and drinking are not worth condemning, compared with committing the unpardonable sin of abandoning one's dreams. To act on possibility, one is in need of a gambler's moral fibre. In this pageant centering around horse racing, only those who join in the gambling carry the hope of humankind.

This tender legend parallels the author's resounding essay, "On Privacy. The American Dream: What Happened to It." Before publication, one chapter was read by Faulkner near the close of the Nagano Seminar and impressed participants as being an "affirmation of the American spirit."[20] When read with *A Fable*, this essay can be seen not merely as a condemnation of the invasion of privacy by journalism, but as a protest against a society that has lost the founding dream of America. Faulkner, the mythmaker of the American South, was also a son of those settlers who left their old countries in search of freedom.

Privacy for him means basic human right: to be born, to think, and to die alone. Only in the privacy of time and space can one muster one's energy before one acts and creates. Without privacy, one cannot arrive at one's own judgement, that core of individuality which makes true communication possible. He condemns war not only because it kills people, mostly the young, but also because it deprives the individual of the human right to die alone—privacy at its mini-mum—and in so doing cuts the roots of individual creativity.

Faulkner plunged into this work right after the Japanese attack on Pearl Harbor and on and off for a decade wrote the latter half always under the threat of possible nuclear war between the US and the USSR. During the Cold War, widespread areas of land and sea suffered from repeated nuclear testing by both sides. Since the end of the Cold War, nuclear power has become widespread, and wars and disputes verging on wars have become localized in increasing numbers. The Gulf War was watched like a show of new weapons in living rooms all over the world, with war casualties shown only as numbers. What would the author of *A Fable* say of those scenes enacted at the end of his century?

It surprises the reader that the book called "a huge parable on peace" by its author was published in the McCarthy era. *A Fable* is more radical than Communism in that it puts the importance of individuals over that of nation. In this it verges on anarchism, the denial of the nation as a political entity. Faulkner thus transcends the Cold War through his intense individuality. This speaks well of America as a union of states with a uniting principle of democracy. Faulkner has said many times, including at the Nagano Seminar, that although democracy is a clumsy, inefficient method, a better system has yet to be found. This reader, who till this day carries the scar of bowing in the direction of the Imperial Palace, after the War, spent her childhood amid paeans to democracy. In her teens in the 50's, she was under the impression that peace, freedom, equality and justice had come from America with the new Constitution. So naïve she was.

The author of *A Fable* almost demands of his readers that they rid themselves of professionalism, a stance which can corrode the minds of literary critics, and become again creatures who stand on their hind legs, attending to their share of daily cares and problems. The author, who argues against war in his literature, demands of his readers "deliberate will power, concentration"[21] as well. *A Fable* is Faulkner's and the twentieth century's "magnum o[pus],"[22] offering new discoveries at every reading. The chronicler of the Yoknapatawpha saga has proved himself a son of those proud settlers who crossed the ocean in search of spiritual freedom. Half a century ago, those Americans brought Japan a Constitution which carried the dreams of America and of humankind. This reader of *A Fable* wishes to be one of those who carry the dream of an everlasting peace pledged in Article 9 of the Japanese Constitution, and "not to let it drop, falter, pause for even a second" (84). "He shall judge between many peoples and impose terms on strong and distant nations; They shall beat their swords into plowshares, and their spears into pruning hooks; One nation shall not raise the sword against another, nor shall they train for war again" (Micah: 4, 3).

11. Sound and Silence
Bellow's *Herzog, Mr. Sammler's Planet,* and *Humboldt's Gift*

> If you wanted to talk about a glass of water, you had to start
> back with God creating the heavens and earth; the apple;
> Abraham; Moses and Jesus; Rome; the Middle Ages; gun-
> powder; the Revolution; back to Newton; up to Einstein; then
> war and Lenin and Hitler. After reviewing this and getting it
> all straight again you could proceed to talk about a glass of
> water. "I'm fainting, please get me a little water."
>
> Saul Bellow, S*eize the Day,* 83.

I

Words originated as a means of communication: to pray, to express feeling, to love, to unite separate beings. Do words still function as they once did? Are the words we are accustomed to use real, communicative? Saul Bellow tries to cope with these questions in his *Herzog, Mr. Sammler's Planet,* and *Humboldt's Gift.* What has gone wrong with words, and how can we make our language rich and creative in the flood of words in the modern world? Communication is not achieved by the mere collection of words, but in action through words—that is, by deeds.

The title character Herzog suffers the agony of knowing too many words. Knowing too many words and keeping everything under verbal control leaves him crippled in communication. He cannot respond to reality, which consists of concrete particulars, without counterpoising it against the general ideas he has read of in books. Amid floods of words, this killing abstraction causes personal particulars to lose touch with reality. He keeps writing letters, which are never mailed, to just anyone: the president of the U.S., Nietzsche, Spinoza, God—those whom Bellow calls his "little deads." In the act of writing down and explaining his ideas or opinions, he asserts that he really exists. He fears that if he stops writing these letters he will disintegrate. He fears even to slow down the pace of writing, as the speed of his writing has to catch up with the speed of his imagined disintegration. He writes mental letters even to persons in his presence instead of committing an actual, responsive act. However, this letter writing, which is supposed to be a means of communication, only serves to alienate him from other people.

For Herzog, words are also a means to soften the fear of death. He has tried to shield himself from the fear of death, which is a constant reality to him, through his verbal intellectuality, through abstraction by words. When he was young and his mother was dying, he read *The Decline of the West*, preferring to think about the decline of culture rather than to face the reality of personal death. Herzog goes "after reality with language. Perhaps [he would] like to change it all into language."[1] By pinning everything down in language, real incidents are neutralized into ideas. Static ideas keep him always behind immediate incidents, causing him to lose touch with reality.

At the same time, his yearning for love, which can be provided only in communal life, is intense. Alienated from his community, his heart is attached to the memory of his childhood, where there "was a wider range of human feelings than he had ever again been able to find. . . . All he ever wanted [communal life, love, words which communicate] was there" (140). What has gone wrong with Herzog, with the Western culture by which he has educated himself? He feels he has to do something while he, "a poor soldier of culture," has not yet lost all of his human faculties.

He ponders how the real life, real communication has been lost in the course of the intellectual history of Western man. Democracy stressed the importance of the self, of the individual. Man has become self-aware. However: *"in man, self-awareness has been accompanied at this stage with a sense of the loss of more general natural powers, of a price paid by instinct, by sacrifices of freedom, impulse . . ."* (163).

When man began to suffer the painfulness of consciousness he welcomed the rise of Romanticism, which taught him to glorify self. To be individual, to be unique, "to sustain [his] own version of existence," man has begun to think he has to keep explaining himself since explanation is a necessity for survival (307). Thus, intellectuals like Herzog have fallen into the habit of explaining and categorizing every phenomenon. Man has begun to live in words. Words as deeds of communication are lost in the flood of ideas. To recover words as deeds, man has to overturn: "the last of the Romantic errors about the uniqueness of the Self; revising the old Western, Faustian ideology; investigating the social meaning of Nothingness" (39). Man's strength should be measured by his actions in daily life, not by his ideas.

Herzog wonders if he will die when his thinking stops. His thought keeps being dispersed in all directions, leaving him a separate, self-conscious being, one who is unable to act or to communicate with others. He will not die when his thinking stops, though; instead, he will die of loneliness. He realizes that man does not communicate by the head, but by the heart and that man has to follow the "law of Heart." Each has to examine his heart in silence. He feels the urge to "do something, something practical and useful, and must do it at once," leaving a life which consists mostly of verbal activities (207):

> I really believe that brotherhood is what makes a man human. If I owe God a human life, this is where I fall down. . . . The real and essential question is one of our employment by other human beings and their employment by us. (272)

Only through such mutual "employment" can one keep one's identity from drowning into nothingness and into death. To secure his identity and to live, Herzog tries to "move away from selfhood toward brotherhood, to community" (Clayton, 223).

Words should be tools for this mutual employment. When Herzog picks some flowers on his way to meet Ramona, he knows he will stop writing letters.

"At this time he had no messages for anyone. Nothing. Not a single word" (341). He feels the strength of his quietness for the first time. "For the first time also he is enjoying the exhilaration of being free from the intellectual compulsion to explain his life, to synthesize the complexities of experience with theoretical, systematic philosophies" (Porter, 157). Man can be a vessel of real communication by absorbing his crying individuality into something larger than personality and by preparing to meet the activity of other souls in the silence of vigilance. This something may be referred to as God. Herzog confesses he cannot explain his conduct and his life if God's existence is not taken for granted: "Evidently I continue to believe in God. Though never admitting it" (231). Yet the realm of non-words he has finally found is not clearly equated to God in his consciousness.

Bellow, in his effort to get free of Aristotelian causality, tries to catch the spontaneity of Herzog's feeling of being alive. As Irving Howe says, analytical refinement is sacrificed to sensuous vigor, and careful psychological notation, to the flowing of energy. Bellow aims to communicate the sensation of immediacy and intensity, to communicate the sense that men are still alive in spite of all abstract-ions.

II

Mr.Sammler in *Mr.Sammler's Planet* is an extension of Herzog. Nearing his eightieth year and a survivor of the Holocaust, Mr. Sammler is an accumulation of Post-Renaissance Western attitudes and wisdom. In Mr. Sammler, who is forced to be disinterested because of his age and his experience with death, Bellow finds an ideal commentator on present-day America, a commentator with a civil heart. Looking at the people around him, Mr. Sammler feels that compassionate utterance is a mortal necessity. While before the war he was a "high-principled intellectual" who was engaged in changing reality into abstraction, Mr. Sammler come to have more power to communicate than anyone around him. Unlike the case with Herzog, people come to talk to him as a mysterious source of comfort. He has been changed, his transformation brought about by his experience with death and by his coming back from the world of death. The pregnant silence of *Herzog* is supplanted by the death experience in *Mr. Sammler's Planet*. Though feeble in his attempt, Mr. Sammler tries to utter words of comfort.

Like Herzog, Mr. Sammler is tired of explanations; he repeats that an intellectual man has become an explaining machine who is constantly urged to explain how he is right. However, being right or wrong has little relevance to his being. "The soul wanted what it wanted. It had its own natural knowledge,"[2] which lies beyond explanation. That which matters is to distinguish and not to explain, to distinguish love that creates bonds among human beings, from that which is not love. What man needs is "the short view," not intellectual eloquence. Words should be employed not to explain but to act toward others. It is a shame to substitute words for actions.

Like Herzog, Mr. Sammler comments on the modern world. Liberated into individuality and claiming the privilege of being a separate person, man is urged by "a strange desire for originality, distinction, *interest*—yes, *interest!*" (184). Words are employed to assert oneself: "And by way of summary, perhaps, each accented more strongly his own subjective style and the practices by which he was known" (223). This is what Mr. Sammler calls the condensed view. By either condensation or contraction, one becomes uncommunicative because he becomes insensitive to the needs of other souls.

In high-powered American life, people are constantly on the run, always urged "to have a piece of the action" (98). At the point of anarchy and breakdown, everyone goes to a psychiatrist, who only gives labels to their trouble. Tortured under the burden of being individuals, people begin to long for non-being. As they try to escape from consciousness, it becomes almost conventional for people to turn to primitivism. The flight to the primitive cure results in an obsession with sex. The life force in a person has come to be measured by his sexual ability. In this novel, a black pickpocket symbolically exhibits his huge organ as a "metaphysical warrant." Mr. Sammler judges that a sexual madness is over-whelming the Western world and that the primitive cure will bring forth only more destruction.

It is urgent to ask what can be done. The best one can do is to examine one's heart in silence, to stop being afraid of ambiguity, and to utter words which affirm human bonds. Mr. Sammler tries, for example, to find some words of comfort for his dying nephew, Gruner. He is sorry because Gruner's own daughter cannot put aside, for once, her own demands to be a special individual, and go to her father to say something, to make some sign of love. Later, Mr. Sammler's silent prayer for the dead Gruner affirms that "He was aware that he must meet, and he did meet . . . the terms of his contract" by doing what was required of him daily and promptly (252). These terms, which in his inmost heart each man knows, are to make this planet a home for himself and for others by signs, by outer forms which define him, by actions, by words which communicate.

Bellow has confessed in an interview that *Mr. Sammler's Planet* is his "thoroughly non-apologetic venture into ideas." Bellow's dilemma is that he has to explain why he is tired of explanations. In every situation he offers a didactic interpretation, "Instead of offering short views as he continually promises to do . . . making it virtually impossible for anyone to get a word in edgewise" (Cohen, 207). The contradiction is that Bellow is courting silence in literature, which is itself built up of utterances.

III

How about literature, then, which is supposedly the highest form of communication? Bellow, a prophet, again meditates on this question in *Humboldt's Gift* in the person of a writer, Citrine: "There's the most extraordinary, unheard-of poetry buried in America, but none of the conventional means known to culture can even begin to extract it."[3] Humboldt, a poet whom Citrine had long admired and attached himself to, could not find words for his poems and died frustrated with many poems unwritten. He wanted to possess words that had definite meaning, words uttered out of real thought. When Humboldt escaped from his habitual depression and, in a spasm of inspiration, wrote irresistible poems, he taught Citrine a new way of looking at things. However, his creative imagination was soon exhausted, and he was driven to madness; Humboldt died a failure. A sort of genius, he was stuffed with bookish knowledge: "He believed in victorious analysis, he preferred 'ideas' to poetry, he was prepared to give up the universe itself for the subworld of higher cultural values" (263). Yet imaginative power is not born of high consciousness or knowledge. Nor does the state of madness, which alternates with the state of being blessed with spasmodic inspiration, produce poetry.

Citrine, who also feels the danger of losing his creative power as a writer, is not interested in associating with anyone on his own mental level. Having decided "to follow the threads of spirit he had found within himself to see where they might lead," he feels a peculiar stimulus in people who live "here" in the physical world, not "there" in ideas or thought (249). The people he is attached to, or is forced to associate with, are non-intellectuals: a small villain who is one thousand percent "here," always in action; an old friend who is obsessed with everybody's physical well-being; a beautiful crook; a childhood sweetheart who is "a completely non-alien person;" a quiet woman whose deep feelings are unknowable, and so on.

Also engaged in some sort of anthroposophic meditation,[4] he ponders how literature that really talks to people can be created. "In ancient times poetry was a force, the poet had real strength in the material world." Now, when "many souls [hope] for the strength and sweetness of visionary words to purge consciousness of its stale dirt," a poet, Citrine thinks, has to possess words which are as cosmically expressive and articulate as Humboldt wished (332). To possess those words, a poet should first nurture and strengthen his own soul. To attain that strength, he has to get rid of his fear of death. Believing in the immortality of the soul, Citrine goes as far as to try to communicate with dead souls. Citrine defines the fear of death for modern man as a fear of tedium and states that the sources of tedium are "the lack of a personal connection with the external world" and "the self-conscious ego." The poet does not have creative imagination when he thinks of his own self as being separated from the outer world which surrounds him.

"Mankind must recover its imaginative power" by listening "in secret to the sound of the truth that God puts into us" (465). To listen to that voice, which talks "about the essence of things" though, a poet must have an unusual strength of soul. That voice should sound in his soul with a power equal to the power of society. A writer should be an "empty vessel," one who listens in complete silence before he begins to write. To let the deepest elements disclose their deepest information, he must get out of himself, out of his self-consciousness, which separates him from the outer world: "Everything possible must be done to restore the credit and authority of art, the seriousness of thought, the integrity of culture, the dignity of style" (244). The story ends with the re-burial of Humboldt, with a eulogy to the dead poet and his poems. Bellow thus buries the poems of the past as dead.

Bellow, in his attempt to create communicative language, here adopts a conversational tone, as if talking to persons in front of him, except for occasional lapses into "speech." In place of the didactic discourse of *Mr. Sammler's Planet*, in *Humboldt's Gift* there is a flood of supposedly "real" incidents. It goes on and on, with no climax. Like Joyce, Bellow tries to charge literature with "music and meaning." The attempt might have been a success, were it not so lengthy. Bellow has thus proved that the communicative style does not necessarily create communicative language. It is ironical that, in his attempt to create more and more communicative language from *Herzog* through *Mr. Sammler's Planet* to *Humboldt's Gift*, Bellow's own language in literature has become less and less rich—more uncommunicative, so to speak. In spite of Bellow's aversion to being a man of ideas, as a novelist he has become more and more ideological rather than artistic.

Bellow's skepticism is directed against the usage or effectiveness of words in human life, but not against the words themselves. In this, Bellow's concern over the problem of language can be said to be more moralistic than artistic, when compared with other modern writers. He does not experiment with language by breaking or inventing it. His main concern is with its function, with how to make language alive and communicative. Bellow argues that communication is in danger of being lost in contemporary culture, while real, live feeling is being changed into static thought and ideas.

IV

We live immersed in words. According to Bellow, this is especially true of Jews. "The most ordinary Yiddish conversation is full of the grandest historical, mythological, and religious allusions." This tendency of being forced to have recourse to words is seen not only in Jews, but also in intellectuals in general in the modern world. Yet the Jew, as Bellow mentions several times, is an Oriental:

> He was driven out of his land and dispersed throughout the lands of the Occident; he was forced to dwell under a sky he did not know, and on a soil he did not till; he has suffered martyrdom and, worse than martyrdom, a life of degradation; the ways of the nations among which he has lived have affected him, and he has spoken their languages; yet, despite all this, he has remained an Oriental. (Buber, *On Judaism* 75)

He is an Oriental in the sense that his thinking does not necessarily follow the inductive method; he is also enormously sensitive to the corruption and corrosion of words, to the loss of a spirit of immediacy in language. He is not a Greek who simplifies the world image by classifying its phenomena according to universal categories. Bellow himself, part Oriental, copes with the problem of words through his struggle to find a remedy in the area of non-words, in silence.

He concludes in *Herzog* that the secret of possessing creative language is found not in words but in the strength of quietness. However, the method of gaining this strength is not expounded in *Herzog*. Hezog's pregnant silence may be misunderstood as a sign of exhaustion. The title character in *Mr. Sammler's Planet* is a disinterested commentator who has come back virtually from the world of death. He feebly tries to utter words of comfort for the people around him. The experience of nearing death has brought about his change and his subsequent strength of soul. The experience of death also belongs to the realm of non-words. In *Humboldt's Gift*, Bellow deals with the problem of creating literature as the highest means of communication. Citrine asserts that in order to possess rich, expressive words the writer should be an empty vessel who listens in silence to the sound of truth God puts into him. In *Humboldt's Gift*, Bellow finally and inevitably touches upon the practice of meditation as a means of withdrawing into one's own self.

Meister Eckhart, a thirteenth century mystic whose book is the only one Mr. Sammler comes to read other than the Bible, tried to approach God by a vertical path, withdrawing into himself in meditation, as contrasted with the horizontal approach through a medium like words. He stressed communication with God, who is "present now" without any medium; that is, he advised opening oneself to the richness that is contained within the self:

> The affirmations about God are incoherent, but the negations are true. In brief, God is known (that is, best known) by negation, for He is incomprehensible. Any attribute applied to Him is misleading, and to that extent untrue. If we use of Him the epithets applied to men, such as 'good', 'just', 'wise', 'merciful', they drag Him down to human stature, because our ideas of goodness, justice, wisdom and mercy are necessarily imperfect. (Eckhart, 27)

This communication with God is achieved in the spark of spirit, and the man comes back richer than when he went off from society.

Eckhart was examined by the Inquisition and condemned for heresy. His practice, if not exactly heresy, truly embodies danger not only for the Church as an institution, but also for the Christian doctrine itself, for Eckhart comes to the threshold of denying the very principle of Christianity: "In the beginning was the Word, and the Word was with God, and the Word was God." In this exposition, the words are the only medium by which to approach God as pure reason. On this reasoning Western culture is based.

Faulkner shares Bellow's concern over how words have come to become abstractions, though Faulkner approaches the question through a different channel. Faulkner examines how the balance of words and actions shapes human life in *As I Lay Dying*. Like Bellow, he views the phenomenon of the separation of words and actions in the contemporary world:

> I would think how words go straight up in a thin line, quick and harmless, and how terribly doing goes along the earth, clinging to it, so that after a while the two lines are too far apart for the same person to straddle from one to the other . . . . (*As I Lay Dying*, 117)

When he speaks of "the dark voicelessness in which the words are the deeds," Faulkner's "voicelessness," however, seems to be different from Bellow's silence or wordlessness (*As I Lay Dying*, 117). Voicelessness is the state in which words cease to be mere sound but instead become life. For Faulkner, the opening of John's Gospel embodies the idea of words incarnated; the words are incarnated into flesh and transformed into life. Faulkner yearns for the world of the Old Testament, where the words of God were always orders or covenants to be enacted by the people, never abstractions; thereby, human life cut sharp outlines. What is a silence devoid of words in Bellow is, in Faulkner, an incarnation of words into deeds, into life.

Martin Buber, a Jewish philosopher whose books were widely read on university campuses at the time Bellow wrote *Herzog*, expounds the problem of communication in *I and Thou*. Buber and Bellow have much in common and draw similar conclusions, yet Bellow seems to suffer something like a kinship-aversion to Buber (*Herzog* 64). Martin Buber distinguishes Ego from Person. "Egos appear by setting themselves apart from other egos," while "Persons appear by entering into relation to other persons" (Buber, *I and Thou*, 112). This Person can be resurrected only in pregnant silence, through forgetting words and withdrawing into one's self.

Genuine communication demands a commitment of one's whole being;

one's head alone, a mere part of his being, cannot achieve communication. Dialogue is achieved only in the immediacy of an encounter, and the essential element in establishing directness is not a word but feeling. Feeling is what is "in here;" when the act of abbreviation, categorization, occurs, its immediacy is lost. As Buber suggests, "—Speaker, you speak too late" (*I and Thou*, 97). The fleeting moment ought to be caught while the responding spirit is at work. It is an act of an instant. Time is fleeting; there is no time to recall memories or to build new ideas. Though language may be used, no verbal reasoning should dominate the whole scene. Dialogue is achieved only when each stands in a reciprocal relationship to another, creating a single, living center. This occurrence should not be forestalled by intellectual eloquence.

In the modern world, people's reliance upon words is immense. Everything must be explained to the fullest; otherwise, it seems to be non-existent. Silence is a void to be hastily filled with words. Yet, in truth, silence is the axis around which communication occurs. To have words which communicate, we should stop fearing silence. We should stop treating silence as an emptiness which must be constantly repaired or filled with words. For an encounter, which demands the commitment of one's whole being, we have to realize the importance of silence. This realm of non-words could be T. S. Eliot's "still point of the turning world," the silent point around which the world turns. Words constitute only the index through which we communicate. We must not let not words control the whole situation. Words are external, not at the heart. Yet—and here lies the paradox in Bellow—the heart can not be communicated apart from these external symbols.

12. Who is Carlos Fuentes's Artemio Cruz?

Carlos Fuentes once said in an interview with *The New York Times*:

> Roger Caillois, the French critic, used to say that the literature of
> the second half of the 19th century belonged to Russia, the
> literature of the first half of the 20th century to North America, and
> that the latter half would belong to Latin America. It has proved to
> be more or less correct.[1]

Octavio Paz, the philosopher-poet who followed Gabriel Garcia Marquez
in receiving the Nobel Prize for literature in 1990, answered questions at a press
interview in Tokyo, saying:

> In Latin America, every political attempt failed, in revolutions,
> coup d'etats, dictatorship, modernization and so on. It is quite
> interesting that writers and poets have created masterpieces writing
> about these failures.[2]

In other words, political chaos has occasioned high productivity in the field of

literature in the South American countries. Carlos Fuentes belongs to the generation of Mexican writers influenced by Octavio Paz.

More than any other study of Fuentes, Paz's *The Labyrinth of Solitude*
helps our reading of *The Death of Artemio Cruz*. Joseph Sommers points out:

> *The Labyrinth of Solitude* is a sweeping analysis of the Mexican
> psyche, taking into account the phases of national history, applying
> throughout a dialectical approach . . . Fuentes creates individuals
> out of Paz's Mexican types, weaves a story out of his own genera-
> tion's national preoccupations, builds dreams out of the tensions
> between Paz's dialectical opposites, solitude and communion.
> (Sommers, 133, 149)

Every modern Mexican, especially a member of the intelligentsia, faces
difficulties in his or her search for identity since he or she must first ask what the
national identity of Mexico is. In Mexico, mestizos (hybrids of the Creole descendants of Spanish conquerors and the conquered Mexican Indians) bear the
weight of the culture. Spanish, their official language, was brought with the
Catholic religion by the conquerors, who evangelized as they conquered the Aztec
and Mayan tribes. After obtaining independence from Spain, they were able to
find little common ground or common purpose along the path to becoming true
Mexicans. To deny their ties to Spanish culture would be to deny half of themselves; even if they felt nostalgia for their origins, they could not return merely to
being Indians. Of this Mexican situation, Paz writes:

> The Mexican condemns all his traditions at once, the whole set of
> gestures, attitudes and tendencies in which it is now difficult to
> distinguish the Spanish from the Indian. . . . The Mexican does not
> want to be either an Indian or a Spaniard. Nor does he want to be
> descended from them. He denies them. And he does not affirm
> himself as a mixture, but rather as an abstraction: he is a man. He
> becomes the son of Nothingness. His beginnings are in his own
> self. (*The Labyrinth of Solitude*, 87)

Fuentes does, however, "affirm himself as a mixture," a hybrid, such as all
modern humans are more or less—not only Mexicans. *The Death of Artemio Cruz*

can be approached in various ways, but first of all it must be seen as a brilliantly developed study of identity. Fuentes, born in Mexico City in 1928, "spent most of his childhood and early youth on the move between various American capitals— Santiago de Chile, Rio de Janeiro, Buenos Aires, Montevideo, Quito, Washington —to which duty assigned his father." He then received his education at some of the best schools on the Continent, finishing law school in Geneva.[3] This reader, living in what is usually considered to be a homogeneous society of the Far East, yet not quite at ease within it, is stunned by the difficulty Fuentes must have faced in defining his affiliation. It is no wonder that he deals with the theme of identity in all his major works.

To cope with this theme of the hybridity of modern man, Fuentes counterpoints three different ways of looking at time, those of Dos Passos, William Faulkner, and D. H. Lawrence:

> I was interested in time play, and their different ways of looking at time were helpful to me. Apart from whatever tendency a first novel may have to be a showcase of literary parentage, I was reading Dos Passos a lot, looking for a way to build dead time into a novel. In Dos Passos everything is in the past tense. Even when he places his action in the present, we know it is past. In Faulkner everything is in the chronic present. Even the remotest past is present. And in D. H. Lawrence what you find is a tone of prophetic imminence. He is always on the brink of the future; it is always there, latent. So I very consciously drew on those three influences, three aspects of time I wanted to counterpoint and overlap in *La Región Más Tranparente*. (Harss and Dohmann, 294-95)

In *The Death of Artemio Cruz*, Fuentes tells the life story of the title character, in three different modes of narration and in three different verb tenses. There is no one narrator who speaks from a definite point of view, confined in one particular tense. Rather, Cruz narrates his tale in the three voices of I, he, and you. The "I" voice, in the major character's last twelve hours, speaks in the present tense for twelve sections; "He", the third person, tells of twelve important choices Cruz made in the past tense; "You", the second person, voices Cruz's subconscious in the future tense.

This fragmentation of narration naturally results in an absence of moral judgement since only an integrated narrator can judge. Therefore, the reader, deprived of the passive pleasure of enjoying a well-made story told from a well focused point of view, is expected to construct the story on his or her own, drawing his or her conclusions. This absence of the authorial point of view, carried nearly to the point of the total erosion of the author, is double edged. Designed to imply the apparent absence of the author, this narrative involves the reader from beginning to the end; at the same time, the narrative lacks climactic scenes and endings, aspects of the narrative that require the author's presence.

Therefore, Fuentes has to explain:

> there is a third element, the subconscious, a kind of Virgil that guides [Cruz] through the twelve circles of his hell, and that is the other face of his mirror, the other face of Artemio Cruz: the You that speaks in the future tense. It is the subconscious that clings to a future that the I—the dying old man—will never know. The old I is the present while the He digs up the past of Artemio Cruz. It's a question of a dialogue of mirrors between the three people, the three times that constitute the life of this hard and alienated character. In his agony, Artemio tries to regain through memory his twelve definitive days, days which are really twelve options. (Faris, 61)

Cruz, as the "I" of his last hours, struggles to flee from pain. That is, what he is as he grapples to regain himself through his memory of the past. Yet memory belongs to the irrevocable past, to what happened and cannot be retrieved; therefore, the subconscious voice begins to speak in the future tense, as if destined to live forever. This voice is then suppressed, becoming independent of the first person, cut off from it, and flows into the second person narration. This "You" tries to reverse the crucial decisions which Cruz had made, the decisions that have formed the present Cruz; the future is a past reconstructed on the basis of not-yet-chosen possibilities, as if the choices are still open.

Artemio Cruz, "a dialogue of mirrors between three people, and the three times," meets still other mirrors all through the book. For example, the dying Cruz with his limited view, sees a woman's purse encrusted with silvered glass, each piece reflecting one of his own numberless distorted faces: "I am this, this am I: old man with his face reflected in pieces by different-sized squares of glass."[4] The author shows in the opening section that the life of a man is to be told from divided point of views, with an apparent disregard for the flow of time.

Wherever he goes, he finds mirrors reflecting his divided self. For example, the fifty-two-year-old Cruz, entering a building with a total disregard of the encircling beggars, is momentarily disoriented when he sees his own reflection in a glass door; Cruz, seventy-one, seeing the image of his sick twin reflected in the glass top of his desk, falls unconscious, whereupon the twin joins the dying man. Only water mirrors, instantly ruffled and fleeting, reflect love and communion: two young faces, his own and Regina's. The water mirror is invented by her to beautify their encounter begun by rape. In another water mirror, father and son on horseback are reflected in the seawater.

This divided person's field of choices is enfolded by the Mexican revolution, a period well-known to his Mexican readers:

1910   Beginning of the Mexican revolution; Porfirio Díaz is overthrown and goes into exile.

1911   Madero elected president; the Revolution has apparently won its objectives with little bloodshed.

1913   Madero assassinated as the result of a military coup engineered by Victoriano de la Huerta. Venustiano Carranza, joined by Alvaro Obregón, Plutarco Elías Calles, Adolfo de la Huerta and Pancho Villa, organizes the Constitutionalist forces against de la Huerta and his "Federal" Government. The war phase of the Revolution begins.

1915   Pancho Villa quarrels with Carranza and is defeated by General Alvaro Obregón.

1917   Military victory of the Constitutional forces under Carranza; the end of the war phase of the Revolution.

1919   Emiliano Zapata ambushed and assassinated.

1920   Assassination of Carranza, after his resignation had been forced by Obregón. Obregón elected president.

1924   Plutarco Elías Calles elected president.

1928   Obregón elected again, but assassinated before taking office.

1934   Lázaro Cárdenas elected president; he exiles Calles.

1938   Expropriation of the oil industry by Cárdenas (deGuzman, chronology extracted).

Cruz, born to a Spaniard hacienda owner and a mixed-blood Indian girl, has green eyes, dark hair, and olive skin. When his pastoral living by a river with his mulatto uncle is suddenly ended, the boy in fury learns that life involves having enemies and that separation is about to occur. Fallen from a paradise where split selves and choices were unknown, the boy Cruz, high on the mountain, now looks down on multiple crossroads with his uncertain future spreading before his eyes:

> from this day on—this night—an unknown adventure begins, the world opens to you and offers you its time. . . . You are going to live. You are going to be the point of encounters, and the reason for the universal order of things. Your body has its reasons. Your life has its reasons. You are, you will be, you have been the universe incarnate. . . . You, standing, Cruz, thirteen years old, on the edge of life. (303-04)

With his instinct for survival, the boy begins "to fill up time, to execute the steps and poses of the macabre dance . . . a mad dance in which time devours itself and no one can hold back" (303). This life is defined by choices:

> you will tell yourself that one cannot choose, that one does not need to choose, that on that day you didn't choose: you merely let it happen, you were not responsible, you created neither of the two possibilities that called to you for choice . . . . (115-16)

Yet, in spite of everything, it is he who has chosen to become one thing rather than another, and whenever he has chosen to become one thing, he has abandoned the possibility of becoming another:

> you will choose, in order to survive you will make choices, you will choose from the infinite array of mirrors only one, the one that will reflect you irrevocably and will throw a black shadow over all other mirrors: you will destroy them before they offer you, once again, that infinity of possible paths to be chosen from . . . . (200)

Let us look at the paths Cruz chose to follow and at those he did not choose. The youth, when asked by his maestro, takes up arms and fights to liberate Mexicans, to do what the old man can no longer do. However, as a captain in the battle, he deserts the front line so that he can return to his lover, an Indian girl. After her death, he decides to go on living, to keep her alive by remembering her. Running to the South, where Regina has promised to wait for him, he abandons a wounded soldier with green eyes, a young man devoted to the cause of revolution who could be his twin. On his way south, on the pretext of saving his own life as a vessel for the memory of Regina, Cruz betrays and abandons Gonzalo Bernal, the brother of Catalina whom he will marry to promote himself, and Indian Tobias.

Denied communion, or liberated from love, he comes to choose in the Mexican vein; that is, he chooses masculinity. He abandons the possibility of love with his wife because he cannot ask her to accept him with his guilt, as a man with needs. About this "masculinity" that chooses to violate rather than to be violated, Paz spoke in poetic detail in "The Sons of La Malinche" chapter in *The Labyrinth of Solitude*. By devoting one whole chapter to elaborating on the word "chingar (fuck)" Fuentes was accused of pedantic deviation made in imitation of Paz. Yet, he needed to do this to follow faithfully the vein along which Cruz had shaped himself.

Constantly siding with the rising and not the descending, he makes himself into Don Artemio, a man to be feared and hated:

> you sacrifice by choosing, you will cease to be the man you might have been, and you will want other men—one other—to fulfill for you the life you mutilated by choosing, by saying yes and when you said no, when you decided it was not your desire, which is one with your freedom, that would be infinitely ramified, but rather your self-interest, your fear, your pride . . . . (201)

Cruz wants his son to fulfill the life he himself mutilated by choices; he wants Lorenzo to learn to love the land of Mexico and to believe in God—the land and God that Cruz betrayed. Cruz obliges his son to carry out his own unchosen choice, to live out his other destiny, by continuing in the fight for the cause of revolution. After Lorenzo dies in the Spanish Civil War, Cruz heads straight for material success, the only choice left open to him.

Cruz comes to be most attached to things and regrets he is not one of those inanimate objects which exist in their own absolute identity. His love of material possessions extends to the sensual acquisition of a woman, bought for his convenience. Similarly, his collection of national antiques substitutes for his love of the Mexican earth. He invites guests to his mansion filled with these antiques; this collection of guests enable him to retreat into the identity by which they know him.

Yet Cruz, on his deathbed, is bored by his taped voice—authoritative, insinuating, playing the role he has himself chosen. Nothing but physical pain now tells him that he exists. He recognizes that he has been reduced to a body, a body that is now mastering and conquering him: "I am a body." After his lifetime of choosing, he meets his dying body, which moves toward death beyond his choice.

He owes his choices, his life, to the pride that made him choose to be hated and feared rather than to be pitied. Loves poisoned, friendships broken, tender feelings hardened, himself divided and destroyed, he becomes the victim of his own pride—his "last enemy in the depopulated land of the victims of [his] pride . . ." (86).

His time split between "the reconstruction of isolated memory and the flight of isolated desire," desire gives direction to his life. He must desire to bind his scattering selves into a recognizable person, to make his "will and fate decide." And in order to desire, he must oppose everyone, all obstacles standing between him and his desire, until no enemies are left. Only by desiring, by always reaching out his hands ahead, can he be recognized as Artemio Cruz. He desires, at every moment of his life, to establish a recognizable, integrated self in the eyes of others: "desiring that your desire and its object may be one and the same; dreaming of instant fulfillment, of the identification without hiatus of the wish and the wished for . . ." (200).

He secretly seeks the "intermediate zone of ambiguity between light and shadow, that zone where [he] can find forgiveness" (29). This aspiration for God, for the absolute who can forgive and change his time into one eternal present, finds its expression only in blasphemy. He cannot pray, because prayer would involve permitting himself to be pitied. The humility required in these last hours has, a long time before, been irretrievably thrown away.

He has lived to betray God because every act that has affirmed his life has required the violation of God's commandments, written without his participation. Unable to pray to God, he has made himself into a god in his own small universe, his world that would not have been built if he had been virtuous and humble:

> And the heaven that is power over uncounted men with hidden faces and forgotten names, named by the thousand on the payrolls of my mines, my factories, my newspaper . . . . Heaven that indeed exists and belongs to me. (155)

Cruz is a man no longer able to desire, except that he wants to forget himself. The man he now finds himself to be can only curse. However, by his very rebellion he admits that God exists since he would not need to blaspheme against Him if He did not. To deny himself, he has but to reverse all the choices he has made, to undo the choices that have made him. Who is Artemio Cruz then, if he is the sum total of all the not-chosen, unrealized possibilities? Cruz is someone absolutely and endlessly someone who is not Cruz.

In *The Death of Artemio Cruz*, we find some common Western ideas; man's life consists of a series of choices, and in the end desire and destiny becomes one and the same. Along with these ideas, we also find the motif of "sacrifice." This is, however, not quite the same as the Christian concept rendered by the same word, for here it is not only Cruz's unfulfilled possibilities, but also other people's lives that are demanded as sacrifices for his survival:

> you will bequeath the futile dead names, the names of so many who fell that your name might stand: men despoiled of their names that you might possess yours: names forgotten that yours might be remembered . . . . (269)

Regina, Bernal, Tobias, Lorenzo—these remembered names do indeed cause pain and regret in Cruz, as does the idea of an unknown soldier. Still, when he repeats "I survived," there also enters an element other than pain; these names transfer to him the possibility of their interrupted existences. Cruz wishes those faces, now only dimly seen and having little force to cause him pain, to die again so he might live again. As for the faces he can see around his bed, he resents the fact that he may die as a substitute for them.

Cruz, a modern man in existential agony, is also an ancient Aztec god who voraciously demands sacrifices. In Christianity, every fall and salvation is taken to be made in terms of individual sacrifice; Jesus, the Lamb of God, offered his individual self to give life to all other individuals, separately and individually. In the culture of old Mexico, though, the collective cycle of life is manifested in an individual, one who, in his transformation, demands sacrifices. This transformation manifests itself in a way quite different from the Buddhist idea of the passive transmigration of life. The philosophy of transformation, so brilliantly developed further in *Terra Nostra,* has in *The Death of Artemio Cruz* not yet matured into a principle of hope. In this latter book, the transformation of an individual in his life's cycle and his existential quest of identity co-exist, contradicting one another.

Death, as it is connected with this transformation, is understood here as a binding force. At his death, Cruz, previously divided into "I", "he", and "you" fuses with the universe, becoming one with his time for the first and last time: "The three, we . . . will die. You . . . die, have died . . . I will die" (306). His death, as his life, does not belong to him exclusively, as it does in the Christian thinking; rather we see in the death of Artemio Cruz no sharp break between life and death. Consciously or unconsciously, Fuentes brings into his work the ancient Mexican concept of death. As Paz wrote in "The Day of Dead" chapter in *The Labyrinth of Solitude*:

> The opposition between life and death was not so absolute to the ancient Mexicans as it is to us. Life extended into death, and vice versa. Death was not the natural end of life but one phase of an infinite cycle. Life, death and resurrection were stages of a cosmic process which repeated itself continuously. Life had no higher function than to flow into death, its opposite and complement; and death, in turn, was not an end in itself: man fed the insatiable hunger of life with his death. Sacrifices had a double purpose: on the one hand man participated in the creative process, at the same time paying back to the gods the debt contracted by his species; on the other hand he nourished cosmic life and also social life, which was nurtured by the former. (*The Labylinth of Solitude*, 54-5)

This theme also runs through the work of Fuentes.

Like Cruz, with his many points of view and multiple voices, Fuentes is many-faceted: a boy departing onto a world of choices, sung in epic grandeur; his son, Lorenzo, and his death in the Spanish Civil War, written with lyrical realism; an old man in the present tense, smelling of feces and urine, full of hate and curses (both other forms of human excrement). Of the multiple Fuenteses, which is the "true" author, which his "true" style? The answer is, "All."

When *Where the Air is Clear* was first published, some critics wondered if it had been translated from English. That remark was occasioned by the literary parentage of this bi-(or rather multi-)lingual author, and the sensitive reader can clearly see traces of Anglo American writers. About his literary parentage, Fuentes once declared in an interview:

> I think culture, and especially literature, lives through communication; isolation doesn't breed anything worthwhile . . . I think in the same way that the American writers drew from Dostoyevsky, Tolstoy and Chekhov, we drew from Faulkner, Hemingway and, yes, Dashiell Hammett. And if now the circle is coming around, well, this means that we will go on enriching ourselves, and enriching our literatures. So I am glad it is that way. It has to be that way. As I repeat, literature perishes in isolation.[5]

He came on Faulkner as a thirsty man comes on a fountain of fresh water. "When I first read Faulkner," he recalls, "I thought: 'I must become a writer'" (Harss and Dohmann, 322).

Faulkner, on this same topic, said in one of his question-and-answer sessions, with a Nobel Prize winner's composure:

> I think the writer, as I said before, is completely amoral. He takes whatever he needs, wherever he needs, and he does that openly and honestly because he himself hopes that what he does will be good enough so that after him people will take from him, and they are welcome to take from him as he feels that he would be welcome by the best of his predecessors to take what they've done. (Gwynn and Blotner, 20-21)

Of Fuentes' Mexican parentage, Daniel deGuzman says that he is not essentially a Mexican writer:

> The very fact that a writer such as Fuentes can turn his back on his place while constantly using it as the locale of his books is most intriguing in itself . . . he *uses* it as a sort of exotic milieu, to give color and fascination to his work, uses it as a foreign writer might . . . not ever being part of it or allowing it to be part of him, not showing any identification with or even acceptance of that part which is ineluctably his. (deGuzman, 50-51)

I do not hesitate to see Fuentes as both a true Mexican and, at the same time, a fellow traveler of every reader, an everyman in the vale of tears we all share. Faulkner, who lived and died in the American South, defined himself as a vagabond and a tramp by temperament. Who is not? Living in Mexico in the 1980's, Fuentes, a Mexican, criticized the Latin-American policy of the Reagan administration, and he now lives in Paris as a literary celebrity. (Since I took it for granted that he lived in Mexico, his unexpected presence at the Faulkner Centennial in Paris filled me with great joy and happiness.)

Fuentes follows Faulkner more than any other North American writer in the exploration of universal human destiny. He offers us, in his exploration of his Latin America, the width and depth of his view, along with a unity of theme and structure. Squarely accepting his hybrid origin and freely "stealing from" predecessors both in and out of Mexico, he has created literature of his own. By asking "Who is Artemio Cruz?" in *The Death of Artemio Cruz*, a work cosmopolitan yet tribal, universal yet local, Fuentes pursues the universal in the individual and the individual in the universal. This Mexican heir to Faulkner has his main character in *Where the Air is Clear* say:

> it will be known that there has been no suffering, no upheaval, no treason, comparable to that which Mexicans have experienced. And it will be known that if Mexicans do not save themselves, not a single man in all creation will save himself. (*Where the Air is Clear*, 300)

Fuentes says he feels "so close to Faulkner's works" because:

only Faulkner, in the literature of the United States, only Faulkner, in the closed world of optimism and success, offers an image that is common to both the United States and Latin America: the image of defeat, of separation, of doubt: the image of tragedy. (Tao, 62)

The moralist Fuentes, not distinctly present in the fragmented narratives of *The Death of Artemio Cruz*, once said in an interview:

> man is responsible for his history, including the past. He's also responsible for his past. It was not made by God, it was made by him. He must understand it. And I think that you can only have a present and a future if you have a past, if you remember your past, if you understand your past. Historical amnesia, I think, leads society to the greatest blunders of not understanding itself and not understanding others. (Brody and Rossman, 15)

Driven by desire and roaming about with no standard for judgement, any of us, not only Mexicans, can be like Artemio Cruz, wanderers each carrying his or her own cross. Born on our assigned patch of ground in time and space, we must fill that short period of time between birth and inevitable death; nevertheless, we are unable to escape from taking responsibility for our own destiny.

Notes

Notes to Chapter 1.

1. The number of Christians in Japan today, all sects included, amounts to less than one percent of the total population—far less than four hundred thousand out of about twenty million.

2. Shusaku Endo, *Silence*, trans. William Johnston (Tokyo: Kodansha International, 1982), 61. Subsequent page references to the novel will be based on this edition and will be given in parentheses.

3. William Johnston in his Translator's Preface says; "Yet Christianity's roots had gone too deep to be eradicated . . . They are still there in their thousands, in Nagasaki and the offshore islands, clinging tenaciously to a faith that centuries of ruthless vigilance could not stamp out. Some of them are united with the world-wide Church; others are not."

Notes to Chapter 2.

1. In translation by Alfred H. Marks, Chapter 32 of *Kinshoku* (*Forbidden Colors*) was omitted and the closing chapter, "Grand Finale," was numbered 32. No explanation was given. This omission, it seems, comes not from the negligence of the translator, but from the fact that this chapter contains an especially extraordinary number of Mishima's untranslatable, forced arguments. The English language expects logical consistency and makes less allowance for contradiction than does Japanese. Mishima maneuvers his arguments into sounding convincing by the use of his ornate style. The translator's decision to omit this chapter seems to be inspired by a desire not to embarrass Mishima in English.

2. Of all Mishima's major works *Kyoko no Ie* is not yet translated into English since the novel is widely considered to be his failure. In truth, revealing Mishima's inner world that has lead him to his death, to write his own epitaph, tetralogy *The Sea of Fertility*, *Kyoko no Ie is* one of his most intrieguing novels.

3. Faulkner was as keenly aware of "the corrosive function of words" as Mishima, but Faulkner never gave up his aspiration to fuse words and actions into deeds; he always tried to use words which could "uplift" his own heart and, in the process, those of his readers as well.

Notes to Chapter 3.

1. "*The Great God Brown* requires explanation, and this the author himself furnished in a letter to the papers. I reprint all of it here, as printed in the New York *Evening Post*, Feb. 13, 1926. 4." (Clark, 104 -6).

2. Eugene O'Neill, *The Great God Brown* (London: Jonathan Cape, 1960), 19. Subsequent page references to the play will be based on this edition and will be given in parentheses.

3. Eugene O'Neill, *The Iceman Cometh* (London: Jonathan Cape, 1954), 15-16. Subsequent page references to the play will be based on this edition and will be given in parentheses.

Notes to Chapter 4.

1. Gwynn and Blotner, 36.

2. Gwynn and Blotner, 36.

3. " . . . your correspondent has been reading and admiring *Pylon* by Mr. William Faulkner" (Blotner, *A Biography*, 889).

4. "I like to help all these earnest magazines, but I have too goddamn many demands on me requiring and necessitating orthodox prostitution to have time to give it away save it can be taken from me while I sleep, you might say" (*Selected Letters*, 85).

5. William Faulkner, *Pylon* (New York: The Modern Library, 1967), 51. Subsequent page references to the novel will be based on this edition and will be given in parentheses.

6. ". . . he knows he has a short span of life, that the day will come when he must pass through the wall of oblivion, and he wants to leave a scratch on that wall—Kilroy was here—that somebody a hundred, a thousand years later will see" (Gwynn and Blotner, 61).

7. ". . . the Christian legend is part of any Christian's background, especially the background of a country boy, a Southern country boy . . . I grew up with that. I assimilated that, took that in without even knowing it. It's just there." (Gwynn and Blaotner, 86).

8. Meriwether and Millgate, 246.

9. ". . . every time I see anything tameless and passionate with motion, speed, life,being alive, I see a young passionate beautiful living shape" (*Selected Letters*, 372).

10. Blotner, *Faulkner: A Biography*, 898

Notes to Chapter 5.

1. Hoffman and Vickery, 305-322.

2. Kiyoko Tôyama, "Futatsu no Ai no Katachi (Two Types of Love)," *Faulkner to*

Gendai no Guwa: Kotoba to Inochi 2 (Faulkner and Fables of Modern Times: Words and Deeds 2), 35-45. When I wrote the original paper in 1981, whole-heartedly following Faulkner's lead, I treated Wilbourne as the man worthy enough to choose grief "between grief and nothing."

3. William Faulkner, *The Wild Palms* (London: Chatto & Windus), 51. Subsequent page references to the novel will be based on this edition and will be given in parentheses.

Notes to Chapter 6.

1. Meriwether and Millgate, 253.

2. William Faulkner, *As I Lay Dying* (New York: Random House, 1957). Subsequent page references to the novel will be based on this edition and will be given in parentheses.

3. Mishima's views of personality are most clearly expressed in *Kyoko no Ie*.

Notes to Chapter 7.

1. William Shakespeare, *Macbeth: The Works of William Shakespeare*, vol.7, 255-378. Subsequent page references to the play will be based on this edition and will be given in parentheses.

2. Gwynn and Blotner, 86.

3. Meriwether and Millgate, 246.

4. William Faulkner, *The Sound and the Fury* (New York: The Modern Library, 1956), 222. Subsequent page references to the novel will be based on this edition and will be given in parentheses.

5. Hoffman and Vickery, 225-32. While I was an undergraduate on early 60th at Waseda University, Jean-Paul Sartre was so enthusiastically accepted among students that many of my friends in French Department chose Sartre as the subject for their B.A thesis. Even I in English Department enjoyed several of his plays, novels and essays in translation.

6. Meriwether and Millgate, 245.

7. Mishima also tried to have his apotheosis, his identity, and his peace only at the moment of death. The difference between Mishima and Quentin is; the one is aggressive, the other passive.

Notes to Chapter 8.

1. Meriwether and Millgate, 56, 119, 217 & 238.

2. Norman Holmes Pearson, "Lena Grove," 3-7. Faulkner wrote this article in 1925, three years after he did an anonymous article, "American Drama: Eugene O'Neill" while he was briefly attending the University of Mississippi.

3. William Faulkner, *Light in August* (New York: Random House, 1959). Subsequent

page references to the novel will be based on this edition and will be given in parentheses.

Notes to Chapter 9.

1. Kiyoko Nozaki Tôyama, *"Absalom, Absalom!,"* *Eibungaku*, No.51, Tokyo: Waseda University Eibungakkai, 1979. Acting upon Faulkner's advice, I have concentrated on Sutpen. Sutpen, determined to found his dynasty in the South "tomorrow," destroys his "today," loses everything, and meets his destiny; Sutpen is killed by Wash John with a scythe that Sutpen loaned to Wash.

2. William Faulkner, *Absalom, Absalom!* (New York: Random House, 1936), 9. Subsequent page references to the novel will be based on this edition and will be given in parentheses.

3. In *The Sound and the Fury*, Quentin wishes to purify and eternalize the unstable love between man and woman by going through the hell-fire of punishment. Quentin, though, unable to commit actual incest, has to support himself only by verbalizing it; by telling to his father that he has committed incest with Caddy.

Notes to Chapter 10.

1. Blotner, *A Biography*, 1152.

2. William Faulkner, *A Fable* (New York: Random House, 1954), 344. Subsequent page references to the novel will be based on this edition and will be given in parentheses.

3. Hoffman and Vickery, 349-72.

4. Inge, *The Contemporary Reviews*, 401-10.

5. Abner Keen Butterworth, Jr., *A Critical and Textual Study of William Faulkner's "A Fable."* Although critical of his reading, I have to confess I was greatly indebted to his thesis in my first reading of *A Fable*.

6. *Faulkner after the Nobel Prize*, 110-26.

7. *Ibid.*, 45-60.

8. *Ibid.* 29-44.

9. *A Biography*, 1502-3

10. Joseph R. Urgo, *Faulkner's Apocrypha:* A Fable, *Snopes and the Spirit of Human Rebellion.* His book encouraged me to write this paper originally for Japanese audience using my reading of *A Fable* as played out on the Japanese scene, just as he critiqued *A Fable* as played out on the American scene.

11. *A Biography*, 1126.

12. Meriwether and Millgate, 68-73. This interview reveals Faulkner's view of God more than any other of all his interviews.

13. *Ibid.*, 192.

14. Albert Camus, *The Rebel: An Essay on Man in Revolt*, trans. Anthony Brewer (New York: Random House, 1956). The quotation is from Urgo. With Camus' "I rebel—therefore we exist" as epigraph, Joseph Urgo wrote "The Spirit of Apocrypha: *A Fable*" in his *Faulkner's Apocrypha*. On page 113 of this chapter, Urgo wrote, "through [the runner's] rebellion comes, in Camus' words, 'the sudden, dazzling perception that there is something in man with which he can identify himself, if only for a moment.'"

15. Gwynn and Blotner, 62.

16. *A Biography*, 1236.

17. Ohashi, *Faulkner Kenkyu vol.3*, 165-246. In chapter 5 of this book, Ohashi makes the point that Cleanth Brooks has made it more than a little difficult for Faulkner readers to evaluate *A Fable* correctly.

18. *A Biography*, 1241.

19. Cox, 369-93.

20. Meriwether and Millgate, 142.

21. *A Biography*, 1445.

22. Faulkner reported to Malcolm Cowley that he is "working at what seems now to [him] to be [his] 'magnum o.'"

Notes to Chapter 11.

1. Saul Bellow, *Herzog* (New York: Viking Press, 1975), 272. Subsequent page references to the novel will be based on this edition and will be given in parentheses.

2. Saul Bellow, *Mr. Sammler's Planet* (New York: Penguin Books, 1970), 5. Subsequent page references to the novel will be based on this edition and will be given in parentheses.

3. Saul Bellow, *Humbolt's Gift* (New York: Penguin Books, 1975), 464. Subsequent page references to the novel will be based on this edition and will be given in parentheses.

4. "Anthroposophy: system of religious philosophy developed by the German mystic and educationalist Rudolf Steiner. Designed to develop the whole human being, anthroposophy stresses the importance of awakening latent spiritual perception by training the mind to rise above material things. Anthroposophists believe that an appreciation of art is one of the keys to spiritual development and that music and colours have curative properties." (Santa Barbara: *ABC-CLIO, 1994*).

Notes to Chapter 12.

1. Shrady, *New York Times*, 1&26.

2. Yukiko Nakazato, *Asahi Shimbun*, trans. mine. Octavio Paz, the 1990 Nobel Prize winner talked at the press interview while he was visiting Japan in April, 1994.

3. Harss and Dohmann, 280.

4. Carlos Fuentes, *The Death of Artemio Cruz*, trans. Sam Hileman (New York: Farrar, Straus and Giroux, 1974), 4. Subsequent page references to the novel will be based on this edition and will be given in parentheses.

5. *New York Times*, 1&26.

Bibliography

Adams, Richard P. *Faulkner: Myth and Motion*. Princeton: Princeton
   University Press, 1968.

Backman, Melvin. *Faulkner: The Major Years: A Critical Study*.
   Bloomington: Indiana University Press, 1966.

Barth, Robert J. *Religious Perspectives in Faulkner's Fiction: Yoknapatawpha
   and Beyond*. Notre Dame, Ind.: University of Notre Dame Press, 1972.

Basett, John, ed. *William Faulkner: The Critical Heritage*. London: Routledge
   & Kegan Paul, 1975.

Beck, Warren. *Man in Motion: Faulkner's Trilogy*. Madison: University of
   Wisconsin Press, 1961.

Bedell, George C. *Kierkegaard and Faulkner: Modalities of Existence*. Baton
   Rouge: Louisiana State University Press, 1972.

Bellow, Saul. *The Actual*. New York: Viking Press, 1997.

-------. *The Adventures of Augie March*. New York: Penguin Books, 1976.

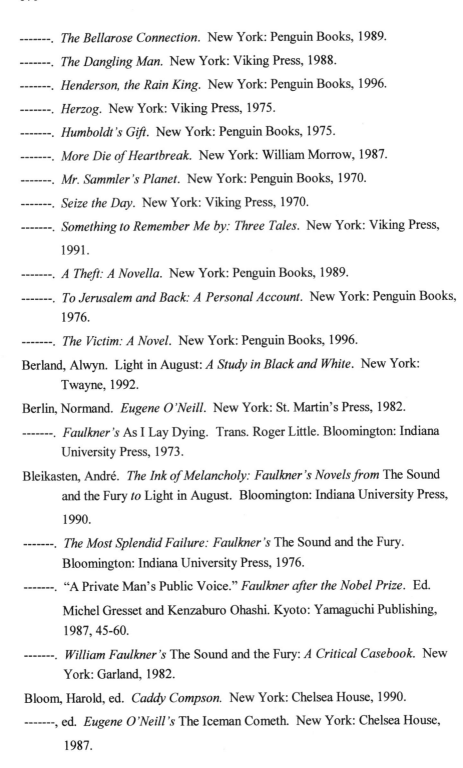

-------. *The Bellarose Connection*. New York: Penguin Books, 1989.

-------. *The Dangling Man*. New York: Viking Press, 1988.

-------. *Henderson, the Rain King*. New York: Penguin Books, 1996.

-------. *Herzog*. New York: Viking Press, 1975.

-------. *Humboldt's Gift*. New York: Penguin Books, 1975.

-------. *More Die of Heartbreak*. New York: William Morrow, 1987.

-------. *Mr. Sammler's Planet*. New York: Penguin Books, 1970.

-------. *Seize the Day*. New York: Viking Press, 1970.

-------. *Something to Remember Me by: Three Tales*. New York: Viking Press, 1991.

-------. *A Theft: A Novella*. New York: Penguin Books, 1989.

-------. *To Jerusalem and Back: A Personal Account*. New York: Penguin Books, 1976.

-------. *The Victim: A Novel*. New York: Penguin Books, 1996.

Berland, Alwyn. Light in August: *A Study in Black and White*. New York: Twayne, 1992.

Berlin, Normand. *Eugene O'Neill*. New York: St. Martin's Press, 1982.

-------. *Faulkner's* As I Lay Dying. Trans. Roger Little. Bloomington: Indiana University Press, 1973.

Bleikasten, André. *The Ink of Melancholy: Faulkner's Novels from* The Sound and the Fury *to* Light in August. Bloomington: Indiana University Press, 1990.

-------. *The Most Splendid Failure: Faulkner's* The Sound and the Fury. Bloomington: Indiana University Press, 1976.

-------. "A Private Man's Public Voice." *Faulkner after the Nobel Prize*. Ed. Michel Gresset and Kenzaburo Ohashi. Kyoto: Yamaguchi Publishing, 1987, 45-60.

-------. *William Faulkner's* The Sound and the Fury: *A Critical Casebook*. New York: Garland, 1982.

Bloom, Harold, ed. *Caddy Compson*. New York: Chelsea House, 1990.

-------, ed. *Eugene O'Neill's* The Iceman Cometh. New York: Chelsea House, 1987.

-------, ed. Macbeth: *Major Critical Characters*. New York: Chelsea House, 1991.

-------, ed. *William Faulkner's* Absalom, Absalom! New York: Chelsea House, 1987.

-------, ed. *William Faulkner's* Light in August. New York: Chelsea House, 1988.

-------, ed. *William Faulkner's* The Sound and the Fury. New York: Chelsea House, 1988.

-------, ed. *William Shakespeare's* Macbeth: *Modern Critical Interpretations*. New York: Chelsea House, 1987.

Blotner, Joseph. *Faulkner: A Biography*. 2 vols. New York: Random House, 1974.

-------, ed. *Selected Letters of William Faulkner*. New York: Random House, 1977.

Bockting, Ineke. *Character and Personality in the Novels of William Faulkner: A Study in Psychostylistics*. Lanham, Md.: University Press of America, 1995.

Bogard, Travis. *Contour in Time: The Plays of Eugene O'Neill*. New York: Oxford University Press. 1988.

Bogard, Travis and Jackson R. Bryer, ed. *Selected Letters of Eugene O'Neill*. New Haven: Yale University Press, 1988.

Bolton, W. F. *Shakespeare's English: Language in the History Plays*. Cambridge: Basil Blackwell, 1992.

Boulton, Agnes. *Part of a Long Story: Eugene O'Neill as a Young Man in Love*. New York: Doubleday, 1958.

Bouvard, Loïc. "Interview with William Faulkner (1952)." *Lion in the Garden*. Ed. James B. Meriwether and Michael Millgate. Lincoln and London: University of Nebraska Press, 1980, 68-78.

Brodsky, Louis D. and Robert W. Hamblin, ed. *Faulkner: A Comprehensive Guide to the Brodsky Collection*. 5 vols. Jackson: University Press of Mississippi, 1982-1988.

Brody, Robert and Charles Rossman, ed. *Carlos Fuentes: A Critical View*. Austin: University of Texas Press, 1982.

Brooks, Cleanth. *On the Prejudices, Predilections and Firm Beliefs of William Faulkner*. Baton Rouge: Louisiana State University Press, 1987.

-------. *Toward Yoknapatawpha and Beyond*. New Haven: Yale University Press, 1978.

-------. *William Faulkner: First Encounters*. New Haven: Yale University Press, 1983.

-------. *The Yoknapatawpha Country*. New Haven: Yale University Press, 1963.

Brooks, Peter. *Reading for the Plot: Design and Intention in Narrative*. New York: Alfred A. Knopf, 1984.

Broughton, Panthea Reid. *William Faulkner: The Abstract and the Actual*. Baton Rouge: Louisiana State University Press, 1974.

Brunstein, Robert. *The Theater of Revolt: An Approach to the Modern Drama*. Boston: Atlantic Monthly Press, 1962.

Bryer, Jackson R., ed. *The Theatre We Worked for: The Letters of Eugene O'Neill to Kenneth Macgowan*. New Haven and London: Yale University Press, 1982.

Brylowski, Walter. *Faulkner's Olympian Laugh: Myth in the Novels*. Detroit: Wayne State University Press, 1968.

Buber, Martin. *I and Thou*. Trans. Walter Kaufman. New York: Charles Scribner's Sons, 1970.

-------. *On Judaism*. Trans. Walter Kaufman. New York: Schocken Books, 1967.

Budd, Lois T. and Edwin H. Cady, ed. *On Faulkner: The Best from American Literature*. Durham: Duke University Press, 1989.

Bulman, James C. *The Heroic Idiom of Shakespearean Tragedy*. Newark: University of Delaware Press, 1985.

Butterworth, Abner Keen Jr. *A Critical and Textual Study of William Faulkner's* "A Fable" (Ph.D. thesis, University of South Carolina, 1970: Anne Arbor: Michigan University Microfilm, 1971).

Butterworth, Nancy. *Annotations to William Faulkner's* A Fable. New York: Garland, 1989.

Campbell, Harry Modean and Ruel E. Foster. *William Faulkner: A Critical Appraisal*. New York: Cooper Square, 1970.

Carey, Glenn O. *Faulkner: The Unappeased Imagination*. New York: The Whitson, 1980.

Cargill, Oscar N., Bryllion Fagin and William J. Fisher. *O'Neill and his Plays*. New York: New York University Press, 1961.

Carothers, James B. *William Faulkner's Short Stories*. Ann Arbor, Mich.: UMI Research Press, 1985.

Carpenter, Frederick. *Eugene O'Neill*. New York: Twayne, 1979.

Chabrowe, Leonard. *Ritual and Pathos: The Theater of O'Neill*. London: Associated University Press, 1976.

Chappell, Charles. *Detective Dupin Reads William Faulkner: Solutions to Six Yoknapatawpha Mysteries*. San Francisco: International Scholars Publications, 1997.

Clark, Barret H. *Eugene O'Neill: The Man and his Plays*. New York: Dover Publications, 1947.

Clark, Deborah. *The Robbing Mother: Women in Faulkner*. Jackson: University Press of Mississippi, 1994.

Clayton, John Jacob. *Saul Bellow: In Defense of Man*. Bloomington: Indiana University Press, 1971.

Cohen, Blacher S. *Saul Bellow's Enigmatic Laughter*. Urbana, Chicago: University of Illinois Press, 1974.

Collins, Carvel, comp. *Faulkner's University Pieces*. Tokyo: Kenkyusha, 1962.

Coughlan, Robert. *The Private World of William Faulkner*. New York: Cooper Square, 1972.

Cowley, Malcolm. *The Faulkner-Cowley File: Letters and Memories, 1944-1962*. New York: Viking Press, 1966.

Cox, Leland H., ed. *William Faulkner: Critical Collection*. Detroit, Mich.: Gale Research, 1982.

Cronin, Gloria L. and L. H. Goldman, ed. *Saul Bellow in the 1980's: A Collection of Critical Essays*. East Lansing: Michigan State University Press, 1989.

deGuzman, Daniel. *Carlos Fuentes*. New York: Twayne, 1972.

Delden, Maarten van. *Carlos Fuentes, Mexico, and Modernit*. Nashville, Tenn.:

Vanderbilt University Press, 1998.

Dowling, David. *William Faulkner*. New York: St. Martin's Press, 1989.

Dubost, Thierry. *Struggle, Defeat, or Rebirth: Eugene O'Neill's Vision of Humanity*. Jefferson, North Carolina: McFarland, 1996.

Duran, Gloria B. *The Archetype of Carlos Fuentes: From Witch to Androgyne*. Hamden, Conn.: Archon, 1980.

Duran, Victor Manuel. *A Marxist Reading of Fuentes, Vargas Llosa and Puig*. Lanham, Md.: University Press of America, 1994.

Dutton, Robert. *Saul Bellow*. New York: Twayne, 1982.

Duval, John N. *Faulkner's Marginal Couple*. Austin: University of Texas Press, 1990.

Eckhart. Select., annotat. and trans. James M. Clark. *Meister Eckhart: An Introduction to the Study of his Works with an Anthology of his Sermons*. London: Thomas Nelson and Sons, 1957.

Endo, Shusaku. *The Deep River*. Trans. Van C. Gessel. New York: New Directions, 1994.

-------. *The Final Martyrs*. Trans. Van C. Gessel. New York: New Directions, 1994.

-------. *Foreign Studies*. Trans. Mark Williams. New York: Linden/Simon & Schuster, 1990.

-------. *The Girl I Left Behind*. Trans. Mark Williams. New York: New Directions, 1995.

-------. *The Golden Country: A Play*. Trans. Francis Mathy. Chester Springs, Pa.: P. Owen, 1990.

-------. "Japanese Catholic Novelist." *Thought*, Winter 1967. Trans. F. Mathy. Tokyo: Sophia University Press, 1967.

-------. *Kirishitan Jidai: Jyunkyo to Kikyo no Rekishi*. Tokyo: Shogakkan, 1992.

-------. *Kirishitan no Sato*. Tokyo: Chukobunko, 1974.

-------. *A Life of Jesus*. Trans. Richard Schuchert. New York: Paulist Press, 1978.

-------. *The Samurai*. Trans. Van C. Gessel. New York: New Directions, 1997.

-------. *Scandal*. Trans. Van C. Gessel. New York: Vintage Books, 1989.

-------. *The Sea and Poison.* Trans. Michael Gallagher. New York: New Directions, 1992.

-------. *Shukyo to Bungaku.* Tokyo: Nanbokusha, 1963.

-------. *Silence.* Trans. William Johnston. Tokyo: Kodansha International, 1982.

-------. *Stained Glass Elegies.* Trans. Van C. Gessel. New York: New Directions, 1990.

------. *Volcano.* Trans. Richard A. Schuchert. Tokyo: Charles. E. Tuttle, 1979.

-------. *When I Whistle: A Novel.* Trans. Van C. Gessel. New York: Taplinger, 1980.

-------. *Wonderful Fool.* Trans. Francis Mathy. Chester Springs: P. Owen, 1995.

Engel, Edwin. *The Haunted Heroes of Eugene O'Neill.* Cambridge, Mass.: Harvard University Press, 1953.

Falk, Doris. *Eugene O'Neill and the Tragic Tension: An Interpretive Study of the Plays.* New Brunswick, N. J.: Rutgers University Press, 1958.

Faris, Wendy B. *Carlos Fuentes.* New York: Frederick Ungar, 1983.

Faulkner Concordance Advisory Board, The, comp. *The Faulkner Concordance.* 35 vols. Ann Arbor, Mich.: UMI Research Press, 1977-1991.

Faulkner, William. *Absalom, Absalom!* New York: Random House, 1936.

-------. "American Drama: Eugene O'Neill." *The Mississippian*, February 3, 1922, 5. Reprint. in *Faulkner's University Pieces.* Comp. Carvel Collins. Tokyo: Kenkyusha, 1962, 82-85.

-------. *As I Lay Dying.* New York: Random House, 1957.

-------. *Big Woods.* New York: Random House, 1955.

-------. *Collected Stories.* New York: Random House, 1950.

-------. *Essays, Speeches and Public Letters.* Ed. James B. Meriwether. New York: Random House, 1965.

-------. *A Fable.* New York: Random House, 1954.

-------. *Go Down, Moses and Other Stories.* New York: Random House, 1942.

-------. *The Hamlet.* New York: Random House, 1964.

-------. *Intruder in the Dust.* New York: Random House, 1948.

-------. *Knight's Gambit.* New York: Random House, 1949.

-------. *Light in August.* New York: Random House, 1959.

-------. *The Mansion.* New York: Random House, 1959.

-------. *The Marionettes: Play in One Act.* Ed. Noel Polk. Charlottesville: University Press of Virginia, 1977.

-------. *Mosquitoes.* New York: Liveright, 1955.

-------. *New Orleans Sketches.* New Brunswick: Rutgers University Press, 1958.

-------. "On Privacy. The American Dream: What Happened to It." *William Faulkner: Critical Collection.* Ed. Leland H. Cox. Detroit, Mich.: Gale Research, 1982, 61-72.

-------. *Pylon.* New York: The Modern Library, 1967.

-------. *The Reivers: A Reminiscence.* New York: Random House, 1962.

-------. *Requiem for a Nun.* New York: Random House, 1951.

-------. *Sanctuary.* New York: Random House, 1958.

-------. *Sartoris.* London: Chatto & Windus, 1954.

-------. *Selected Short Stories.* New York: Modern Library /Random House, 1962.

-------. *Soldiers' Pay.* New York: Liveright, 1954.

-------. *The Sound and the Fury.* New York: Random House, 1956.

-------. *The Sound and the Fury.* New York: Modern Library College Editions, 1956.

-------. *The Town.* New York: Random House, 1957.

-------. *Uncollected Stories of William Faulkner.* Ed. Joseph L. Blotner. London: Chatto & Windus, 1980.

-------. *The Unvanquished.* New York: Random House, 1938.

-------. *The Wild Palms.* London: Chatto and Windus, 1962.

Fayen, Tonya T. *In Search of the Latin American Faulkner.* Lanham, Md.: University Press of America, 1995.

Floyd, Virginia. *The Plays of Eugene O'Neill: A New Assessment.* New York: Ungar, 1985.

-------, ed. *Eugene O'Neill: A World View.* New York: Ungar, 1979.

-------, ed. and annotat. *Eugene O'Neill at Work.* New York: Frederick Ungar, 1981.

Foster, Kevin. *Fighting Fictions: War, Narrative and National Identity*. London, Virginia: Pluto Press, 1999.

Fowler, Doreen. *Faulkner: The Return of the Repressed*. Charlottesville and London: University Press of Virginia, 1997.

Fowler, Doreen and Ann J. Abadie, ed. *"A Cosmos of My Own": Faulkner and Yoknapatawpha, 1980*. Jackson: University Press of Mississippi, 1981.

-------. *Faulkner and Humor: Faulkner and Yoknapatawpha, 1984*. Jackson: University Press of Mississippi, 1986.

-------. *Faulkner and Religion: Faulkner and Yoknapatawpha, 1989*. Jackson: University Press of Mississippi, 1991.

-------. *Faulkner and the Southern Renaissance: Faulkner and Yoknapatawpha, 1981*. Jackson: University Press of Mississippi, 1982.

-------. *Faulkner: International Perspectives: Faulkner and Yoknapatawpha, 1982*. Jackson: University Press of Mississippi, 1984.

-------. *Fifty Years of Yoknapatawpha: Faulkner and Yoknapatawpha, 1979*. Jackson: University Press of Mississippi, 1980.

-------. *New Directions in Faulkner Studies: Faulkner and Yoknapatawpha, 1983*. Jackson: University Press of Mississippi, 1984.

Frazer, Winifred L. *E.G. and E.G.O. Emma Goldman and* The Iceman Cometh. Gainesville: The University Press of Florida, 1974.

-------. *Love as Death in* The Iceman Cometh: *A Modern Treatment of an Ancient Theme*. Gainesville: The University Press of Florida, 1974.

Frenz, Horst. *Eugene O'Neill*. New York: Frederick Ungar, 1971.

Frenz, Horst and Susan Tuck, ed. *Eugene O'Neill's Critics: Voices from Abroad*. Carbondale: Southern Illinois University Press, 1984.

Fuchs, Daniel. *Saul Bellow: Vision and Revision*. Duke University Press, 1984.

Fuentes, Carlos. *Aura*. Trans. Lysander Kemp. New York: Farrar, Straus and Giroux, 1975.

-------. *The Buried Mirror: Reflections on Spain and the New World*. Boston: Houghton Mifflin, 1992.

-------. *Burned Water*. Trans. Margaret Sayers Peden. New York: Farrar, Straus

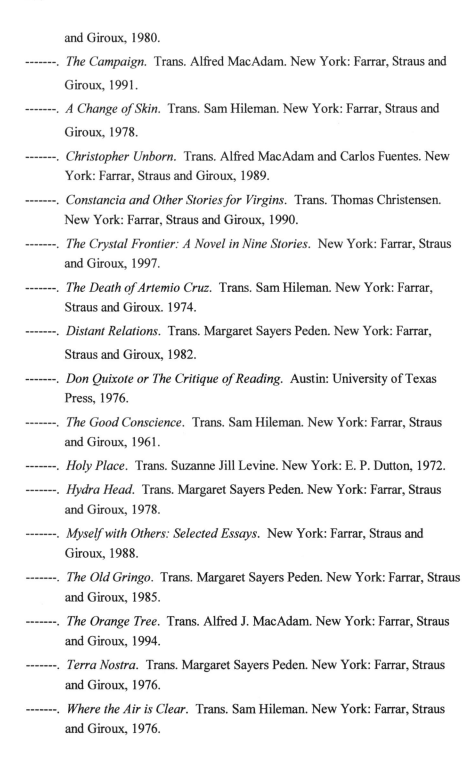

and Giroux, 1980.

-------. *The Campaign.* Trans. Alfred MacAdam. New York: Farrar, Straus and Giroux, 1991.

-------. *A Change of Skin.* Trans. Sam Hileman. New York: Farrar, Straus and Giroux, 1978.

-------. *Christopher Unborn.* Trans. Alfred MacAdam and Carlos Fuentes. New York: Farrar, Straus and Giroux, 1989.

-------. *Constancia and Other Stories for Virgins.* Trans. Thomas Christensen. New York: Farrar, Straus and Giroux, 1990.

-------. *The Crystal Frontier: A Novel in Nine Stories.* New York: Farrar, Straus and Giroux, 1997.

-------. *The Death of Artemio Cruz.* Trans. Sam Hileman. New York: Farrar, Straus and Giroux. 1974.

-------. *Distant Relations.* Trans. Margaret Sayers Peden. New York: Farrar, Straus and Giroux, 1982.

-------. *Don Quixote or The Critique of Reading.* Austin: University of Texas Press, 1976.

-------. *The Good Conscience.* Trans. Sam Hileman. New York: Farrar, Straus and Giroux, 1961.

-------. *Holy Place.* Trans. Suzanne Jill Levine. New York: E. P. Dutton, 1972.

-------. *Hydra Head.* Trans. Margaret Sayers Peden. New York: Farrar, Straus and Giroux, 1978.

-------. *Myself with Others: Selected Essays.* New York: Farrar, Straus and Giroux, 1988.

-------. *The Old Gringo.* Trans. Margaret Sayers Peden. New York: Farrar, Straus and Giroux, 1985.

-------. *The Orange Tree.* Trans. Alfred J. MacAdam. New York: Farrar, Straus and Giroux, 1994.

-------. *Terra Nostra.* Trans. Margaret Sayers Peden. New York: Farrar, Straus and Giroux, 1976.

-------. *Where the Air is Clear.* Trans. Sam Hileman. New York: Farrar, Straus and Giroux, 1976.

Gallup, Donald C. *Eugene O'Neill and His Eleven-Play Cycle*. New Haven: Yale University Press, 1998.

Gassner, John, ed. *O'Neill: A Collection of Critical Essays*. Englewood Cliffs, N.J.: Prentice-Hall, 1964.

Gelb, Arthur, and Barbara Gelb. *O'Neill*. New York: Harper and Row, 1962.

Glendy, Michael K. *Saul Bellow and the Decline of Humanism*. New York: St. Martin's Press, 1990.

Glynn, Paul. *A Song for Nagasaki*. Grand Rapids, Mich.: Eerdmans, 1990.

Gold, Joseph. *William Faulkner: A Study in Humanism: From Metaphor to Discourse*. Norman: Oklahoma University Press, 1966.

Goldman, Arnold, ed. *Twentieth Century Interpretations of* Absalom, Absalom! Englewood Cliffs, N. J.: Prentice-Hall, 1971.

Gray, Richard J. *The Life of William Faulkner: A Critical Biography*. Oxford: Blackwell, 1994.

Grene, Nicholas. *Shakespeare's Tragic Imagination*. Hampshire and London: Macmillan, 1992.

Gresset, Michel and Kenzaburo Ohashi, ed. *Faulkner after the Nobel Prize*. Kyoto: Yamaguchi Publishing, 1987.

Gresset, Michel and Noel Polk, ed. *Intertextuality in Faulkner*. Jackson: University Press of Mississippi, 1985.

Gresset, Michel, and Patrick Samway, eds., *Faulkner and Idealism*: *Perspective from Paris*. Jackson: University Press of Mississippi, 1983.

Griffin, Ernest G., ed. *Eugene O'Neill: A Collection of Criticism*. New York: McGraw-Hill, 1976.

Grimwood, Michael. *Heart in Conflict: Faulkner's Struggle with Vocation*. Athens and London: The University of Georgia Press, 1987.

Guerard, Albert J. *The Triumph of the Novel: Dickens, Dostoevsky, Faulkner*. Chicago: The University of Chicago Press, 1976.

Gwynn, Frederick L. and Joseph L. Blotner, ed. *Faulkner in the University: Class Conferences at the University of Virginia, 1957-1958*. Charlottesville: University Press of Virginia, 1977.

Hamblin, Robert W. and Charles A. Peek, ed. *William Faulkner Encyclopedia.* Westport, Conn.: Greenwood Press, 1999.

Harrington, Evans and Ann J. Abadie, ed. *Modernism and Film: Faulkner and Yoknapatawpha, 1978.* Jackson: University Press of Mississippi, 1979.

-------. *The South and Faulkner's Yoknapatawpha: The Actual and the Apocryphal: Faulkner and Yoknapatawpha, 1976.* Jackson: University Press of Mississippi, 1977.

Harrington, Gray. *Faulkner's Fables of Creativity: The Non-Yoknapatawpha Novels.* Athens: University of Georgia Press, 1990.

Harss, Luis and Barbara Dohmann, ed. *Into the Mainstream: Conversations with Latin-American Writers.* New York: Harper and Row, 1967.

Hassan, Ihab. *Radical Innocence.* Princeton: Princeton University Press, 1973.

Hlavsa, Virginia V. James. *Faulkner and the Thoroughly Modern Novel.* Charlottesville: University Press of Virginia, 1991.

Hoffman, Daniel. *Faulkner's Country Matters: Folklore and Fable in Yoknapatawpha.* Baton Rouge: Louisiana State University Press, 1989.

Hoffman, Frederick J. *William Faulkner.* New York: Twayne, 1966.

Hoffman, Frederick J. and Olga W. Vickery, ed. *William Faulkner: Three Decades of Criticism.* East Lansing: Michigan State University Press, 1960.

Holmes, Edward M. *Faulkner's Twice-Told Tales: His Re-use of Materials.* The Hague: Mouton, 1966.

Honnighausen, Lothar. *Faulkner: Masks and Metaphors.* Jackson: University Press of Mississippi, 1997.

-------, ed. *Faulkner's Discourse: An International Symposium.* Tubingen: Max Niemeyer, 1989. Jackson: University Press of Mississippi, 1997.

Horton, Merril. *Annotations to William Faulkner's* The Town. New York: Garland, 1996.

Houchin, John H, ed. *The Critical Response to Eugene O'Neill.* Westport, Conn.: Greenwood Press, 1993.

Houston, John Porter. *Shakespearean Sentences: A Study in Style and Syntax.* Baton Rouge: Louisiana University Press, 1988.

Howe, Irving. *William Faulkner: A Critical Study*. New York: Vintage Books, 1962.

Hunt, John W. *William Faulkner: Art in Theological Tension*. New York: Haskel House, 1973.

Hussey, S.S. *The Literary Language of Shakespeare*. London/New York: Longman. 1982.

Ienaga, Saburo. *Nihon Bunkashi*. Tokyo: Iwanami Shoten, 1968.

Inge, M. Thomas, ed. *Conversations with William Faulkner*. Jackson: University Press of Mississippi, 1999.

-------. ed. *William Faulkner: The Contemporary Reviews*. Cambridge: Cambridge University Press, 1995.

Jelliffe, Robert A, ed. *Faulkner at Nagano*. Tokyo: Kenkyusha, 1959.

Johnson, Susie Paul. *Annotations to William Faulkner's* Pylon. New York: Garland, 1989.

Kartiganer, Donald M. *The Fragile Thread: The Meaning of Form in Faulkner's Novels*. Amherst: University of Massachusetts Press, 1979.

Kartiganer, Donald M. and Ann J. Abadie, ed. *Faulkner and the Artist: Faulkner and Yoknapatawpha, 1993*. Jackson: University Press of Mississippi,1996.

-------. *Faulkner and the Natural World: Faulkner and Yoknapatawpha, 1998*. Jackson: University Press of Mississippi, 1999.

Kato, Shuichi. *Nihon Bungakushi Josetsu*. Tokyo: Chikuma Shobo, 1975.

Kegan, Robert. *The Sweeter Welcome: Voices for a Vision of Affirmation: Bellow, Malamud, and Martin Buber*. Needham Heights, Mass: Humanities Press, 1976.

Kellogg, Jean. *Dark Prophets of Hope: Faulkner, Camus, Sartre, Dostoevsky*. Chicago: Loyola University Press, 1975.

Kerr, Elizabeth M. *William Faulkner's Yoknapatawpha: A Kind of Keystone in the Universe*. New York: Fordham University Press, 1983.

Kinney, Arthur F. *Faulkner's Narrative Poetics: Style as Vision*. Amherst: University of Massachusetts Press, 1978.

-------, ed. *Critical Essays on William Faulkner: The Compson Family*. Boston: G. K. Hall, 1982.

-------, ed. *Critical Essays on William Faulkner: The Sartoris Family*. Boston: G.
    K. Hall, 1985.

-------, ed. *Critical Essays on William Faulkner: The Sutpen Family*. Boston: G.
    K. Hall, 1996.

Kitagawa, Joseph M. *Religion in Japanese History*. New York: Columbia
    University Press, 1966.

Leal, Luis. "History and Myth in the Narrative of Carlos Fuentes." *Carlos
    Fuentes: A Critical View*. Ed. Robert Brody and Charles Rossman.
    Austin: University of Texas Press, 1982, 3-17.

Liu, Haiping and Lowell Swortzell, ed. *Eugene O'Neill in China: An
    International Centenary Celebration*. Westport, Conn.: Greenwood Press,
    1992.

Lockyer, Judith. *Ordered by Words: Language and Narration in the Novels of
    William Faulkner*. Carbondale: Southern Illinois University Press, 1991.

Long, Michael. Macbeth: *Harvester New Critical Introduction to Shakespeare*.
    New York: Harvester Wheatsheaf, 1989.

Longley, John L., Jr. *The Tragic Mask: A Study of Faulkner's Heroes*. Chapel
    Hill: North Carolina University Press, 1963.

Malin, Irving. *William Faulkner: An Interpretation*. Stanford: Stanford
    University Press, 1982.

Manheim, Michael. *Eugene O'Neill's New Language of Kinship*. Syracuse, New
    York: Syracuse University Press, 1982.

-------, ed. *The Cambridge Companion to Eugene O'Neill*. New York:
    Cambridge University Press, 1998.

Matthews, John T. *The Play of Faulkner's Language*. Ithaca and London Cornel
    University Press, 1982.

-------. The Sound and the Fury: *Faulkner and the Lost Cause*. New York:
    Twayne, 1990.

McHaney, Thomas L. *William Faulkner's* The Wild Palms: *A Study*. Jackson:
    University Press of Mississippi, 1975.

Meriwether, James B., ed. *A Faulkner Miscellany*. Jackson: University Press of
    Mississippi, 1974.

Meriwether, James B. and Michael Millgate, ed. *Lion in the Garden: Interviews with William Faulkner, 1926-1962*. Lincoln and London: University of Nebraska Press, 1980.

Miller, Henry. *Reflections on the Death of Mishima*. Santa Barbara: Capra Press, 1972.

Millgate, Michael. *The Achievement of William Faulkner*. Lincoln: University of Nebraska Press, 1978.

-------. *Faulkner: Writers and Critics*. New York: Capricorn, 1971.

-------. *Faulkner's Place*. Athens and London: Georgia Press, 1997.

-------, ed. *New Essays on* Light in August. Cambridge: Cambridge University Press, 1987.

Minc, Rose S., ed. *Latin American Fiction Today*. Takoma Park, Maryland: Montclair State College, 1980.

Minter, David L. *William Faulkner: His Life and Work*. Baltimore: Johns Hopkins University Press, 1980.

Mishima, Yukio. *Acts of Worship: Seven Stories*. Trans. John Bester. New York: Kodansha International, 1989.

-------. *After the Banquet*. Trans. Donald Keene. Tokyo: Charles E. Tuttle, 1987.

-------. *Confessions of a Mask*. Trans. Meredith Weatherby. Tokyo: Charles E. Tuttle, 1992.

-------. *Death in Midsummer and Other Stories*. Trans. Edward G. Seidensticker. Tokyo: Charles E. Tuttle, 1990.

-------. *The Decay of the Angel*. Trans. Edward G. Seidensticker. Tokyo: Charles E. Tuttle, 1991. [Part Four of *The Sea of Fertility: A Cycle of Four Novels*]

-------. *Five Modern No Plays*. Trans. Donald Keene. Tokyo: Charles. E. Tuttle, 1991.

-------. *Forbidden Colors*. Trans. Alfred H. Marks. Tokyo: Charles E. Tuttle, 1991.

-------. *Kinshoku: Mishima Yukio Zenshu*. vol.5. Tokyo: Shinchosha, 1974

-------. *Kyoko no Ie: Mishima Yukio Zenshu*. vol.11. Tokyo: Shinchosha, 1970.

-------. *Madam de Sade*. Trans. Donald Keene. Tokyo: Charles. E. Tuttle, 1971.

-------. *Patriotism*. Trans. Geoffrey W. Sargent. New York: New Directions, 1995.

-------. *Runaway Horses*. Trans. Michael Gallagher. Tokyo: Charles E. Tuttle, 1987. [Part Two of *The Sea of Fertility: A Cycle of Four Novels*]

-------. *The Sailor who Fell from Grace with the Sea*. Trans. John Nathan. Tokyo: Charles E. Tuttle, 1990.

-------. *The Sound of Waves*. Trans. Meredith Weatherby. Tokyo: Charles E Tuttle, 1992.

-------. *Spring Snow*. Trans. Michael Gallagher. Tokyo: Charles E. Tuttle, 1990. [Part One of *The Sea of Fertility: A Cycle of Four Novels*]

-------. *Sun and Steel*. Trans. John Bester. Tokyo: Kodansha International, 1990.

-------. *The Temple of Dawn*. Trans. E. Dale Saunders and Cecilia Segawa Seigle. Tokyo: Charles E. Tuttle, 1990. [Part Three of *The Sea of Fertility: A Cycle of Four Novels*]

-------. *The Temple of the Golden Pavilion*. Trans. Ivan Morris. Tokyo: Charles E. Tuttle, 1992.

-------. *Thirst for Love*. Trans. Alfred H. Marks. Tokyo: Charles E. Tuttle, 1991.

-------. "*Watashi no Henreki Jidai*." *Mishima Yukio Zenshu*. vol.30. Tokyo: Shinchosha, 1975.

-------. *The Way of the Samurai: Yukio Mishima on* Hagakure *in Modern Life*. Trans. Kathryn N. Sparling. New York: Vintage Books, 1994.

Moorton, Richard F. Jr., ed. *Eugene O'Neill's Century: Centennial Views on America's Foremost Tragic Dramatist*. Westport, Conn.: Greenwood Press, 1991.

Mortimer, Gail L. *Faulkner's Rhetoric of Loss: A Study in Perception and Meaning*. Austin: University of Texas Press, 1983.

Nakamura, Hajime. *Toyojin no Shiihoho* vol.3. Tokyo: Shunjusha, 1962.

Nakazato, Yukiko. "Questions to Octavio Paz." Asahi Shimbun, April 19, 1994. Trans mine.

Napier, Susan J. *Escape from the Wasteland: Romanticism and Realism in the Fiction of Mishima Yukio and Oe Kenzaburo*. Cambridge, Mass.: distr. by Harvard University Press, 1991.

Nathan, John. *Mishima: A Biography*. Boston: Little, Brown, 1974.

Nietzsche, Friedrich. *The Birth of Tragedy*. Trans. Francis Golffing. New York:

Doubleday, 1956.

Nihon Bunka Kaigi, ed. *Nihonbi ha Kanoka*. Tokyo: Kenkyusha, 1971.

Nordanberg, Thomas. *Cataclysm as Catalyst: The Theme of War in William Faulkner's Fiction*. Uppsala: Almqvist, 1983.

O'Connor, William Van. *The Tangled Fire of William Faulkner*. New York: Gordian Press, 1968.

Ohashi, Kenzaburo. *Faulkner Kenkyu (Faulkner Studies)*. vol.1. Tokyo: Nan'undo, 1977.

-------. *Faulkner Kenkyu (Faulkner Studies)*. vol.2. Tokyo: Nan'undo, 1979.

-------. *Faulkner Kenkyu (Faulkner Studies)*. vol.3. Tokyo: Nan'undo, 1982.

-------. "Behind the "Trinity of Conscience": Individuality, "Regimentation, and Nature in Between," *Faulkner after the Nobel Prize*. Ed. Michel Gresset & Kenzaburo Ohashi. Kyoto: Yamaguchi Publishing House, 1987, 29-43.

Ohashi, Kenzaburo and Kiyoyuki Ono, comp. *Faulkner Studies in Japan*. Ed. Thomas L. McHaney. Athens: University of Georgia Press, 1985.

O'Neill, Eugene. *Ah, Wilderness!* and *Days without End*. London: Jonathan Cape, 1955.

-------. *All God's Chillun Got Wings, Desire under the Elms* and *Welded*. London: Jonathan Cape, 1955.

-------. *Beyond the Horizon*. New York: Dover Publications, 1996.

-------. *The Emperor Jones, The Straw* and *The Diff'rent*. London: Jonathan Cape, 1955.

-------. *The Great God Brown* and *The Fountain, The Dreamy Kid, Before Breakfast*, together with *Lazarus Laughed* and *Dynamo*. London: Jonathan Cape, 1960.

-------. *The Hairy Ape, Anna Christie* and *The First Man*. London: Jonathan Cape, 1958.

-------. *Hughie*. London: Jonathan Cape, 1959.

-------. *The Iceman Cometh*. London: Jonathan Cape, 1954.

-------. "A Letter to the Press." *New York Evening Post*, Feb. 13, 1926. Reprint. in Barret H. Clark. *Eugene O'Neill: The Man and His Plays*. New York: Dover publications, 1947, 104-106.

-------. *Long Day's Journey into Night.* London: Jonathan Cape, 1956.

-------. *'Marco's* Millions.' New York: Boni and Liveright, 1927.

-------. "Memoranda on Masks." *American Spectator*, Nov. 2, 1932, 3.

-------. *A Moon for the Misbegotten.* London: Jonathan Cape, 1953.

-------. *The Moon of the Caribees and Six Other Plays of the Sea.* London: Jonathan Cape, 1955.

-------. *More Stately Mansions.* London: Jonathan Cape, 1965.

-------. *Mourning Becomes Electra.* London: Jonathan Cape, 1956.

-------. *Strange Interlude.* London: Jonathan Cape, 1953.

-------. *Ten 'Lost' Plays.* London: Jonathan Cape, 1964.

-------. *A Touch of the Poet.* London: Jonathan Cape, 1957.

Opdhl, Keith Michael. *The Novels of Saul Bellow: An Introduction.* University Park: Pennsylvania State University Press, 1972.

Page, Sally. *Faulkner's Women: Characterization and Meaning.* Deland, Fla.: Everett/Edward, 1972.

Parker, Robert Dale. Absalom, Absalom!: *The Questioning of Fictions.* Boston: Twayne, 1991.

-------. *Faulkner and the Novelistic Imagination.* Urbana: University of Illinois Press, 1985.

Paz, Octavio. *The Labyrinth of Solitude: Life and Thought in Mexico.* Trans. Lysander Kemp. New York: Grove Press, 1981.

Pearson, Norman Holmes. "Lena Grove." *Shenandoah* III, Spring, 1952, 3-7.

Pifer, Ellen. *Saul Bellow: Against the Grain.* Philadelphia: University of Pennsylvania Press, 1990.

Pitavy, François. *Faulkner's* Light in August. New York: Garland, 1982.

Polk, Noel *Children of the Dark House: Text and Context in Faulkner.* Jackson: University Press of Mississippi, 1996.

-------. *Faulkner's* Requiem for a Nun: *A Critical Study.* Bloomington: Indiana University Press, 1981.

-------. "Enduring *A Fable* and Prevailing." *Faulkner After the Nobel Prize.* Ed. Michel Gresset and Kenzaburo Ohashi. Kyoto: Yamaguchi Publishing

House, 1987, 110-126.

-------. "The Nature of Sacrifice: *Requiem for A Nun* and *A Fable.*" *William Faulkner: Critical Collection.* Ed. Leland H. Cox. Detroit Michigan: Gale Research, 1982, 369-393.

-------, ed. *New Essays on* The Sound and the Fury. Cambridge: Cambridge University Press, 1993.

Porter, Carolyn. *Seeing and Being.* New York: Harper and Row, 1986.

Porter, John Houston. *Shakespearean Sentences: A Study in Style and Syntax.* Baton Rouge: Louisiana University Press, 1988

Porter, M. Gilbert. *Whence the Power?: The Artistry and Humanity of Saul Bellow.* Columbia: University of Missouri Press, 1974.

Putzell, Max. *Genius of Place: William Faulkner's Triumphant Beginnings.* Baton Rouge: Louisiana State University Press, 1985.

Ragan, David Paul, ed. *William Faulkner's* Absalom, Absalom!: *A Critical Study.* Ann Arbor, Mich.: UMI Research Press, 1987.

Railey, Kevin. *Natural Aristocracy.* Tuscaloosa and London: The University of Alabama Press, 1999.

Raleigh, John Henry. *The Plays of Eugene O'Neill.* Carbondale: Southern Illinois University Press, 1972.

-------, ed. *Twentieth Century Interpretations of* The Iceman Cometh. Englewood Cliffs, N.J.: Prentice-Hall, 1968.

Ranald, Margaret Loftus. *The Eugene O'Neill Companion.* Westport: Greenwood Press, 1984.

Richardson, Kenneth E. *Force and Faith in the Novels of William Faulkner.* The Hague: Mouton, 1967.

Rodrigues, Eusebio L. *Quest for the Humans: An Exploration of Saul Bellow's Fiction.* Lewisburg: Bucknell University Press, 1967.

Ross, Stephen M. *Fiction's Inexhaustible Voice: Speech and Writing in Faulkner.* Athens: University of Georgia Press, 1983.

Ross, Stephen M. and Noel E. Polk, ed. *Reading Faulkner:* The Sound and the Fury. Jackson: University Press of Mississippi, 1996.

Rovit, Earl H. *Saul Bellow.* Minneapolis: University of Minnesota Press, 1967.

Ruppersburg, Hugh M. *Reading Faulkner*: Light in August. Jackson: University Press of Mississippi, 1994.

Scheer-Schazler, Brigitte. *Saul Bellow*: Modern Literature Monographs. New York: Ungar, 1972.

Schoenbaum, Samuel, ed. Macbeth: *Critical Essays*. New York: Garland, 1992.

Schoenberg, Estella. *Old Tales and Talking: Quentin Compson in William Faulkner's* Absalom, Absalom! *and Related Works*. Jackson: University Press of Mississippi, 1977.

Scholes, Robert. *Fabulation and Metafiction*. Urbana/Chicago/London: University of Illinois Press, 1980.

Scott-Stokes, Henry. *The Life and Death of Yukio Mishima*. New York: Noonday Press, 1995.

Sensibar, Judith L. *The Origins of Faulkner's Art*. Austin: University of Texas Press, 1984.

Shakespeare, William. *Macbeth: The Works of William Shakespeare* vol.7, 255-378. Ed. William Aldis Wright. London: Macmillan, 1923

Shaughnessy, Edward Lawrence. *Down the Nights and Down the Days: Eugene O'Neill's Catholic Sensibility*. Notre Dame, Ind.: University of Notre Dame Press, 1996.

Shrady, Nicholas. "Carlos Fuentes: Life and Language." *New York Times Book Review*, August 19, 1984, 1 & 26.

Sinfield, Alan, ed. Macbeth: *Contemporary Critical Essays*. London: Macmillan Education, 1992.

Singal, Daniel J. *William Faulkner: The Making of a Modernist*. Chapel Hill: The University of North Carolina Press, 1997.

Slatoff, Walter J. *Quest for Failure: A Study of William Faulkner*. Ithaca: Cornell University Press, 1960.

Sommers, Joseph. *After the Storm: Landmarks of the Modern Mexican Novel*. Albuquerque: University of New Mexico Press, 1968.

Spae, Joseph J. *Japanese Religiosity*. Tokyo: Oriens Institute for Religious Research, 1971.

Stein, Jean vanden Heuvel. "Interview with William Faulkner (1956)." *Lion in the Garden*. Ed. James B. Meriwether and Michael Millgate. Lincoln and London: University of Nebraska Press, 1980, 237-256.

Sundquist, Eric. *Faulkner: The House Divided*. Baltimore: John Hopkins University Press, 1983.

Swiggart, Peter. *The Art of Faulkner's Novels*. Austin: University of Texas Press, 1970.

Tao, Jie, ed. *Faulkner: Achievement and Endurance: Peking International Conference on William Faulkner, 1997*. Beijing: Peking University Press, 1998.

Thompson, Lawrence. *William Faulkner*. New York: Barnes and Noble, 1963.

Tiusanen, Timo. *O'Neill's Scenic Images*. Princeton: Princeton University Press, 1968.

Tornqvist, Egil. *A Drama of Souls: Studies in O'Neill's Super-naturalistic Technique*. New Haven: Yale University Press, 1969.

Tôyama, Kiyoko M. *Ikyo de Yomu Nihon no Bungaku: Kotoba to Inochi 1*. 2nd ed. Tokyo: Libel Press, 1999.

-------. *Faulkner to Gendai no Guwa: Kotoba to Inochi 2*. Tokyo: Yushodo, 1995.

-------. "A Huge Parable on Peace — Faulkner's War and Peace," *Faulkner: Achievement and Endurance:Peking International Conference on William Faulkner, 1997*. Ed. Jie Tao. Beijing: Peking University Press, 1998, 208-229.

Tôyama, Nozaki, Kiyoko. "*Absalom, Absalom!*" *Eibungaku* No.51. Tokyo: Waseda University Eibungakkai, 1979.

Turner, Dixie M. *A Jungian Psychoanalytic Interpretation of William Faulkner's As I Lay Dying*. Washington, D.C.: University Press of America, 1981.

Umehara, Takeshi. *Bi to Shukyo no Hakken*. Tokyo: Chikuma Shobo, 1967.

Urgo, Joseph R. *Faulkner's Apocrypha: A Fable, Snopes, and the Spirit of Human Rebellion*. Jackson: University Press of Mississippi, 1989.

van Delden, Maarten. *Carlos Fuentes: Mexico and Modernity*. Nashville Tenn.: Vanderbilt University Press, 1998.

Vanderwerken, David L. *Faulkner's Literary Children: Patterns of Development*. New York: P. Lang, 1997.

Vena, Gary. *O'Neill's* The Iceman Cometh: *Reconstructing the Premiere.* Ann Arbor: UMI Research Press, 1987.

Vickery, Olga W. *The Novels of William Faulkner: A Critical Interpretation.* revis. ed. Baton Rouge: Louisiana State University Press, 1964.

Visser, Irene. *Compassion in Faulkner's Fiction.* Lewiston, N.Y.: Edwin Mellen, 1996.

Volpe, Edmond L. *A Reader's Guide to William Faulkner.* New York: Noonday, 1964.

Wadlington, Warwick. As I Lay Dying: *Stories out of Stories.* New York: Twayne, 1992.

Waggoner, Hyatt H. *William Faulkner: From Jefferson to the World.* Lexington: University of Kentucky Press, 1966.

Warren, Robert Penn, ed. *Faulkner: A Collection of Critical Essays.* Englewood Cliffs, N. J.: Prentice-Hall, 1966.

Waswo, Richard. *Language and Meaning in the Renaissance.* Princeton: Princeton University Press, 1987.

Watson, James G. *William Faulkner: Letters & Fiction.* Austin: University of Texas Press, 1987.

Watson, James G., ed. *Thinking of Home: William Faulkner's Letters to His Mother and Father, 1918-1925.* New York: Norton, 1992.

Weinstein, Philip. *Faulkner's Subject: A Cosmos No One Owns.* New York: Cambridge University Press, 1992.

-------, ed. *The Cambridge Companion to William Faulkner.* New York: Cambridge University Press, 1995.

-------, ed. *William Faulkner's* The Sound and the Fury: *A Critical Casebook.* New York: Garland, 1982.

Weisgerher, Jean. *Faulkner and Dostoevsky: Influence and Confluence.* Trans. Dean McWilliams. Athens, Ohio: Ohio University Press, 1974.

Williams, Mark B. *Endo Shusaku: A Literature of Reconciliation.* New York: Routledge, 1999.

Williams, Raymond Leslie. *The Writing of Carlos Fuentes.* Austin: University of Texas Press, 1996.

Williamson, Joel. *William Faulkner and Southern History*. New York: Oxford University Press, 1993.

Wilson, Jonathan. Herzog: *The Limit of Ideas*. Boston: Twayne, 1990.

Wolfe, Peter. *Yukio Mishima*. New York: Continuum, 1989.

Wright, George T. *Shakespeare's Metrical Art*. Berkeley: University of California Press, 1988.

Yourcenar, Marguerite. *Mishima: A Vision of the Void*. Trans. Alberto Manquel and Marguerite Yourcenar. New York: Farrar, Straus and Giroux, 1986.

Zender, Karl F. *The Crossing of the Ways: William Faulkner, the South, and the Modern World*. New Brunswick: Rutgers University Press, 1989.

Index